The Baby Connection
Dawn Atkins

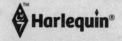
Harlequin®

TORONTO NEW YORK LONDON
AMSTERDAM PARIS SYDNEY HAMBURG
STOCKHOLM ATHENS TOKYO MILAN MADRID
PRAGUE WARSAW BUDAPEST AUCKLAND

Recycling programs
for this product may
not exist in your area.

ISBN-13: 978-0-373-71729-3

THE BABY CONNECTION

www.Harlequin.com

Printed in U.S.A.

ABOUT THE AUTHOR

Award-winning author Dawn Atkins has written more than twenty novels for Harlequin Books. Known for her funny, poignant romance stories, she's won a Golden Quill Award and has been a several-times *RT Book Reviews* Reviewers' Choice Award finalist. Dawn lives in Arizona with her husband and son.

Books by Dawn Atkins

HARLEQUIN SUPERROMANCE

HARLEQUIN BLAZE

Don't miss any of our special offers. Write to us at the following address for information on our newest releases.

Harlequin Reader Service
U.S.: 3010 Walden Ave., P.O. Box 1325, Buffalo, NY 14269
Canadian: P.O. Box 609, Fort Erie, Ont. L2A 5X3

In memory of Maria Irene Dominguez,
con todo cariño, forever in my heart

Acknowledgments

Heartfelt gratitude to Iraq veteran U.S. Army
Sgt. Christopher Dodge, Scout Sniper,
1st Battalion, 8th Infantry, who made the Iraq
sequences come alive. (All errors are mine.)
Thanks to investigative journalists Eric Miller
and Susan Leonard—gracious friends—and the
Iraq war correspondents who contributed to
Embedded: The Media at War in Iraq,
by Bill Katovsky and Timothy Carlson.
Mil gracias to Julia Martinez,
who shared her life with me so I could more
clearly see Mel's; to Sonya Morillon,
who loved my little boy as her own; and to my
dear friend Irene Dominguez, who inspired me to
create Mel in the first place.

CHAPTER ONE

HIP-CHECKING A PERSISTENT blonde, Mel Ramirez broke through the clot of people to reach the star journalist who had packed half the Arizona State University student body into the auditorium. "Ready to head to the hotel?" she said to him.

"With you?" Noah Stone gave her a friendly once-over. "Oh, I'm down." He was clearly teasing, but sparklers went off in Mel's stomach all the same.

The blonde gave her the evil eye. *Who the hell are you?*

"I'm your driver," Mel clarified, her cheeks a bit hot. She'd jumped at the chance to escort the J-school graduation speaker to his hotel, but didn't want anyone to think she was propositioning the guy.

Cálmate, chica. Keep your dignity. She was no silly fan girl. She'd just graduated with highest honors and had a job at a prestigious newspaper, starting Monday. She and Noah Stone were now *colleagues.* The short drive ahead gave her precious minutes to glean secrets from a journalist at the top of his game.

Noah's reporting was incisive, searing, brilliant. She knew that. What she hadn't known was how flat-out *hot* he was.

Ay, Dios.

His publicity photos didn't convey the knowing gleam in his caramel eyes, the friendly tweak of his mouth that let you in on a private joke, how he pulled you close with his voice, and that small dimple that peeked out when he truly smiled. The guy was mid-thirties, but looked more her age, twenty-five, and—

"Happy to meet you, uh…?" He paused, waiting for her name.

"Mel. Mel Ramirez."

"A pleasure." He offered a firm grip, warm and solid. "So you're going to tuck me in?"

Tuck him in. Oh. Wow. She sucked in a breath. He'd read her as okay with a friendly come-on. Good. "More or less," she said, determined to match him, flirt for flirt.

"I vote *more.* You?"

The question stalled her thoughts, so she was relieved when Paul Stockton, one of her professors, approached, buying time for a comeback to occur to her.

"Torturing one of our top graduates?" Professor Stockton shook his head in mock disapproval. The two men had been J students at ASU ten years before. Professor Stockton told stories about Noah Stone in his classes. Even as a student, Noah had been known for risk-taking and relentlessness.

"I hope not." Noah shot his gaze to her, concerned. "Was I out of line, Mel?"

"Not at all." She smiled.

"This whole show has thrown me off my game. My good friend here asks me to be his fill-in speaker, then introduces me like I'm some celebrity."

"You don't think a Pulitzer means star status?" Paul asked.

"I do my job, that's all. I got lucky with a few stories."

"It was great you could fit us in before Iraq," Mel said. On Monday, Noah would start his embed with the last of the troops in Iraq. Professor Stockton had convinced him to detour to Phoenix to speak to the graduates of the Walter Cronkite School of Communications as a personal favor.

Noah turned to her, as if surprised she knew his plans, so she continued, "And what you said about self-censorship being more dangerous to investigative journalism than shrinking news staff was important for us to hear."

"I was quoting Carl Bernstein, not me." He smiled.

"Congratulations on the job, by the way," Paul said to her. "You'll like it at *Arizona News Day.* The pay's modest, but the circulation's huge and some pretty big names cut their teeth there."

"You, for instance," Noah said. "You won, what, two Virg Hills?" The Virg Hill was the top journalism prize in the state. "Which was why *National Record* was hot to hire him."

"You got me that job, Noah. Don't be modest." *National Record* was the magazine Noah worked for.

"And then—poof—you torpedoed your career."

"He means, I got married and started a family," Paul said.

"Not that there's anything wrong with that," Noah added.

"Man plans, God laughs." Paul shrugged, clearly not bothered by his friend's jabs. "And now I get to spend time with remarkable students like Mel."

"I'm jerkin' his chain," Noah said. "Paul's wife and daughter are great. They put me up last night. Or, I mean, put up with me."

ASU had paid him an honorarium and hosted two nights at a hotel, she knew. He'd evidently come earlier to spend time with Paul.

"You made Cindi laugh, which she needs these days. The guesthouse is yours anytime the in-laws aren't using it."

He nodded, then homed in on Mel. "So you nailed a job already?"

"Yep. I start Monday. I'm a photographer." The award-winning alternative weekly had a rare opening in the art department. "It was your recommendation that got me there," she said to Professor Stockton. "Thank you again."

"I only got you the interview. Your portfolio got you the offer."

Noah's gaze seemed to linger on her face, then he glanced at the dwindling crowd. "So, Paul, if you're okay with me cutting out, I'd like to take Mel up on her offer of a ride to the hotel."

"No problem." Paul paused. "Good luck over there, Noah."

"Thanks." The two locked eyes for a quiet moment, then hugged farewell.

Noah watched Professor Stockton walk away. "They don't come more solid than that guy."

"He's a great teacher. Everyone loves him."

"No doubt." He drew his attention to her again. "So where were we? Waiting for you to vote on tucking me in, I believe."

Her long-neglected libido voted *yes, oh, yes,* but the rest of her had some discretion.

Noah stood close and looked even closer, so clearly interested that if he were interviewing her, she'd want to spill her guts…or take off her clothes. *Settle down, muchacha. You're his driver. Nothing more.*

Yet. Oh, she was tempted. Mel had put herself through school by working full-time at a department store photo studio, which left little time to date. Sex was a misty memory.

Picking up her hesitation, Noah's dark eyes went gentle. "I'm being obnoxious. Your job is to drive me to my hotel. If you'd do that, I'd be grateful, Mel."

Damn.

"Do you have bags?"

"Right here." He reached under a table for a scuffed black leather backpack covered in stickers from different countries. When he placed a friendly hand on her back, the touch burned through her blouse like a brand.

You melt from one touch now? she chided herself. Clearly, her sex drought had gone on too long.

"You coming to the bar?" a girl from her internet journalism class called to her from a group, eyeing Noah as though he'd be dessert.

Mel glanced at Noah, gauging his interest.

"If you want to go with your friends, I can get a cab," he said.

"No. I'm fine," she said to him. "Not tonight," she called to the girl.

"Where are they headed? We used to hit the Chuckbox. Older than dirt and grimy as hell, but the burgers were cheap and they didn't hassle you for tying up a table for hours."

"They go to Four Peaks Brewery now. Great food, good prices."

"*They* go? What about you?"

"I join them when I can. I've been working full-time, too."

"So you're a real journalist, not one of those 'mass communications majors.'"

"You mean, *I reeeeally want to do news, I mean, to-*

tally, be on TV, helping people to understand, like, the world." She flipped her hair.

He laughed. "You've got that impression down solid."

"I've had many class hours to study it. I shouldn't make fun. They're young."

"And you're, what, all of twenty-two?"

"Twenty-five, thank you very much."

"Not that old. The difference is that you seem to know what you want." He looked her over again, holding the exit door so that she passed close enough to catch the dark spice and deep woods scent of his cologne.

She led him to her Jetta and unlocked the doors. The car was stuffy from the day's heat. It was only May, but the broil hit early in Arizona. Noah sat, then lifted something from the floorboard, which he held out. "Your portfolio?"

"Yeah. Thanks." She put it in the back. He followed it with his eyes, which she thought was cool. He seemed curious about her work.

"I liked your description of the nitty-gritty of an investigation," she said, making the most of the short drive to the hotel. "Combing through boxes of legal files, Dumpster diving for phone bills, waiting hours in a parking lot to ambush a bad guy trying to slip away."

"Yeah, it's a glamorous life, all right," he said, chuckling. "I've got the scars." He shoved up his sleeve to show her a bite mark. "Drug dealer's pit bull."

"Was that for the *Life of a Banger* series?"

"You read that?"

"I've read all your pieces." She hoped that didn't come out too breathless. Why wouldn't she study the best in the business? He said he'd just been doing his job and she intended to follow his lead. She couldn't wait to get started.

"Some of that early stuff was pretty rough." He shifted in his seat.

"Not that I could tell. And you got a Pulitzer for the pain-med racket series that came out before that."

"The team got the prize, Mel. And the magazine."

She liked his modesty. "How did you get that guy to give up the doctors' names to start with?"

"I found out his sister died of an OD, and when I mentioned her, he folded. It was pretty heavy. Sometimes you get deeper than you intend."

"But it was so worth it. Those stories led to new regulations."

"They were a factor, sure, but lots of people were in that fight."

She let a second pass, then said, "My favorite was your story on that national guard soldier who missed his child's birth due to redeployment."

"Yeah? That one was tough. I knew he'd get flack from his superiors for breaking rank and talking to me. Afterward, though, he told me he was glad. That's not always the case. A hell of a lot of people regret talking to me."

"But it's your job to get the truth, even when it hurts."

He shot her a look, then stared out the windshield. She could tell he liked what she'd said. The conversation felt so natural. It had to be their shared passion for journalism, but it felt good to her. Damn good.

She'd been thirsty for this kind of talk, dreamed of it from the first day of her first class, but rarely experienced it, because she never had time to hang with classmates or professors. And now she was doing it with *Noah Stone,* the best of the best.

The hotel sign appeared, signaling the end of the trip. Damn. She pulled in and stopped. "The reservation's prepaid for two nights, so you shouldn't have any charges or—"

"Have a drink with me, Mel," he said. "In a couple of days, I'll be lost to the assignment and I won't come up for air until it's over. This feels good, talking with you. How about it?"

Yes, oh, yes, please. But she made herself look at her watch. "I guess I've got time for one drink...."

"Great." He reached around for her portfolio. "All right if I look at your stuff?"

"If you want to. Sure." She felt like pinching herself with excitement.

They headed straight to the bar, where they sat knee-to-knee at a small table, leaning in to hear each other over the soft piano someone played.

"This feels like a martini night to me," he said. "We're both about to take off—me to Iraq, you to your new job. Sound okay?"

"Sounds great." She was celebrating her graduation, after all. The launch of her career. At last, she'd achieved what she'd worked so hard for. And she was doing it with Noah Stone, no less. This called for more than an ordinary glass of red wine for sure.

"Two martinis, up, two olives," he told the waiter. "With gin, as God intended."

As soon as the waiter left, Noah opened her book, shifted to the side so they could both look at the pages. They were so close she could see the crinkles around his eyes, the streaks of darker color in his light brown hair, which curled, untamed, to his collar. He had a beauty mark above one ear, and his cologne filled her head.

Their arms touched and they breathed in sync as he

flipped the pages, commenting on the subtlest detail of shot after shot. His praise thrilled her, but she kept getting distracted by how *close* he was, how *sexy,* how *mmm.*

"I like these street graffiti ones a lot," he said.

"The gang-squad cop told me they signified a turf war. I thought the way the styles clashed told that story."

"Only because you got the right angles and depth of field. Your composition is, hell, poetry."

"Thanks." He really got what she'd been trying to do. And he knew what he was talking about, so it was high praise indeed. Meanwhile, his nearness electrified her. It was as though her skin was vibrating. Sparks flew so hot and fast she swore she could see blue flashes.

The drinks came and Noah tapped his to hers. "To good gin, remarkable art and great company."

"To all that," she said, and they both drank, watching each other over their glasses. The icy cocktail burned all the way to her toes.

"Good?" Noah asked, his chocolate-brown eyes twinkling.

"Mmm." She smiled. "Perfect."

He nodded, satisfied, then flipped to the next page. "This guy has a great face." He tapped the shot of a Hispanic man with a leathery tan and sad eyes beneath a white straw hat. "How'd you get so close?"

"It wasn't easy. He waved me off at first. People tend to stiffen, preen or shy away from a camera, but I hung around long enough to become scenery."

"Smart. Are Latino issues of particular focus to you?"

"I'm passionate about my heritage, but I won't let that limit me. There's a knee-jerk tendency to slot Latino reporters into any story that involves brown skin or speaking Spanish. I intend to resist that."

"Good for you." He closed the book. "This is great stuff, Mel. No wonder *News Day* snapped you up." He searched her face. "So why photojournalism? Why not art or commercial photography?"

"How can you ask that?" she demanded. "You know why. Journalism matters. And with people barely reading these days, photos are crucial. A picture stops you cold, makes you see what you'd rather ignore. Think of the photo of the Viet Cong soldier being shot in the head, the leash shot at Abu Ghraib. The starving children in Darfur. News photos galvanize people. They can change the world." She realized she'd gotten louder. "Sorry. I get carried away."

"Don't apologize. You need that kind of passion or this work will kick you in the teeth." He hesitated. An emotion she couldn't identify flickered in his eyes. Fatigue? Sadness? "Keep your fire, Mel. No matter what."

"What else is crucial in an investigative reporter? Personality traits, I mean." She was eager for his answer.

"You interviewing me, Ramirez?"

"Taking notes." She tapped her skull.

He smiled. "Curiosity is bedrock. For me, anyway. It's like an itch, a craving to know. I hate secrets. I have to get to the bottom of things. You're that way, too. I can see it in your work. You drill to the core, the essence."

"That's what I go for, yeah."

He nodded. "You also have persistence, which is vital. You have to be unstoppable. I think Bobby Kennedy said *truth is ruthless.* Sometimes that's all that gets you through the black nights of doubt."

"You have doubts?"

"Always. Am I asking the right questions? Talking to the right people? Am I being fair? Is every fact checked and double-checked? Have I gone too far or not far enough?"

"That's a lot of pressure."

"Part of the package. It's our job to speak up for the underdog. The powers that be will steamroller the little guy every time. We have to shine a light on that." He took a sip of his drink. "For investigative work, you have to ask *why*. Humans never act without motivation, usually selfish, so you have to dig for who would gain, how and why."

One drink turned into two and the words flew, both of them full of the same fire for their work. She was so attracted to the man that she was afraid if he touched her, she might combust on the spot.

"You have to follow the story wherever it leads for however long it takes," Noah said. "It helps to be single."

"Lots of reporters have families."

"If you're good, the job has to be number one. The hours are unpredictable and always long. I've watched my married colleagues struggle. They're always on the phone apologizing to their kids, their wives, their boyfriends. Apologizing or fighting. Paul hated leaving *National Record*, but Cindi got pregnant and that was that."

"He seems happy to me."

"People adjust." He slid his martini glass forward and back. "Maybe it's just me. I was an Army brat, so we moved a lot when I was a kid. I learned how to make friends easily and let them go when I had to."

He took the last sip, clearly thinking about what he'd

said. Then he smiled. "That's me, though. What about you? You have a family?"

"It's just me and my mom."

"What about…a boyfriend?" He spoke slowly, tracking her reaction.

She shook her head.

"That's hard to believe."

"Not really. I've been busy."

"School and work, sure. I get that. But for certain things, you make time…" He was looking at her like *that* and she returned the look, full throttle. The gin, the talk, the fact she was sharing her graduation night with a man whose work she so admired made her bold. She wanted him to touch her, to kiss her. She wanted to touch and kiss him. She *wanted,* period. The roar of a vacuum cleaner startled her and she jumped.

Noah smiled. "We should let these folks close up." He'd long ago paid the tab, but he laid a twenty on the table and nodded at the bartender.

When they stood, Mel swayed, surprised by how unsteady she felt.

Noah caught her elbow. "You okay?"

"Martinis are not for sissies," she said, embarrassed to be such a lightweight. She'd been so excited she hadn't felt the effects of the gin. "I'd better not drive. I'll get a cab."

"I have a better idea," he said with a slow smile. "Stay with me, Mel. Tuck me in."

Dios mio. That was the sexiest thing a man had ever said to her. He clasped her hand, pulled her closer and kissed her.

Pure power roared through her—like lightning or a nuclear blast, something spinning off a supercollider maybe. Her knees turned to water and her body shook so hard that her teeth bumped Noah's.

Noah broke off the kiss, looking equally blown away. "What the hell was that?"

"I'm not sure, but I vote for more," she managed to say.

He laughed, deep and easy. "Then it's unanimous. Come on." He took her arm and they headed out of the bar.

The elevator ride was a forever of agony while Mel's body burned with desire—pure, raw, uncut—the best rush of all. When they had to stop at the door for Noah to find his key card, frustration made her groan.

"Hang on, let me get us to a bed," he said, kissing her temple tenderly, as if to sustain her through the wait for the lock to whir and flash green.

Inside the room, they kissed in the dark. Mel held on tightly to Noah, afraid if she didn't she'd melt to the floor. She felt the ridge of his erection against her stomach while his hands kneaded her backside. *Wow. Just wow.*

With a groan, he broke off. "Hang on…I need to make sure…" He bent for his backpack and unzipped a compartment, from which he tossed a toothbrush, comb, other stuff, then held up a strip of three condoms. "Let's hope these haven't passed their use-by date."

She started to tell him they didn't need condoms—pregnancy was virtually impossible for her, plus she was on birth control for irregular periods—but by then Noah had her on the bed and nothing else mattered. They tore off their clothes as though they were each other's most-longed-for Christmas gift, tossing items left and right like so much shredded wrapping paper.

Once they were naked, though, everything slowed

way, way down. Noah lay on top of her, taking her in. "You are so beautiful."

And he was so handsome. His tousled hair framed his face, looking soft, but masculine. His eyes, a mesmerizing brown with swirls of gold, seemed to study her forever. His dimple was a hint of a dent, like a secret he shared only with people who really pleased him. And he seemed really, really pleased with her.

"I can't believe I'm actually here." She'd been thrilled about a ten-minute car ride with the man. Now she was in bed with him.

"If you're not, then this is a damn fine dream." He cupped her face with warm palms. "I hope it lasts all night."

She lifted her hips against him, bending her knees, letting him know where she wanted him to be.

"I need more of this," he said, casting a hungry eye over her body.

Inwardly, she groaned with impatience. Then his fingers traced her nipples and she shuddered with pleasure. *Maybe he had a point. Slow could be very good....*

He explored her with careful fingers—her breasts and stomach, her hips and thighs. When he finally touched her where she most burned for him, she bucked against his hand, white-hot need coursing through her.

"Be...inside...before I...come." She could barely form the words.

He applied the condom and did what she'd been waiting for with one sweet stroke. It felt so good she nearly yelped.

He stilled there, inside her, letting the desire between them build, while their hearts pounded, their breaths came in harsh gasps, their bodies pumped out heat. Finally, they began to move together, sliding forward and back in glorious unison, like a dance they knew to their bones.

Mel's climax came fast.

Noah watched, holding her. "Yeah…that's it… So nice," he said while she quivered and quaked against him, saying "Oh" over and over again.

When she stilled, he murmured, "Beautiful," and sped his thrusts and soon pulsed inside her.

Afterward, she lay across him, recovering little by little, amazed by what had happened. She'd had sex with a man she hardly knew, except through his work, and it had been easy and natural, with none of the usual first-time awkwardness or adjustments.

This felt like a dream. It looked like one, too, with the lamplight washing them in gold, the same glowing shade that colored her best dreams—all of the sex ones, where she awoke rocking her hips against the sheets.

Noah rose on an elbow to study her, tracing her jaw with the tips of his fingers, then her cheek. "You have a great face. Like a model. The cheekbones and shape. Beautiful skin, too."

"That's the Indian in me. The bone structure and skin color. Some Latinos think the whiter you are, the more class you have, but my mother taught me to be proud to be *mestizo*—a mix of Spanish and Indian."

"Were you born in the U.S.?"

"Just barely. When my mother fled Salvador, she was pregnant. The trauma of the crossing put her into labor."

"She fled?"

"She'd been speaking out against the death squads, even though her family begged her not to. Others who'd protested had been killed or disappeared. The guerrillas helped her escape. Sympathetic clergy connected her with American college students who got her over the border, but the desert trek was brutal."

"She must have been very brave."

"She was. She was only twenty. She had a mission, too. A journalist named Xavier Sosa had taken pictures of a village massacre he wanted the rest of the world to see. She brought the film to the U.S."

"And…?"

"And the photos did shift public opinion, but not enough to change U.S. policy, which supported the re-gime at the time. Her request for asylum failed as a re-sult." She paused. "Eventually, she applied for amnesty and got her papers."

"I'm glad to hear that."

"The tragedy was that Xavier Sosa 'disappeared.' Killed, like other brave reporters and dissidents, even clergy. I think about him a lot. He laid down his life for the truth."

Noah didn't speak, simply held her tighter.

She didn't usually get so fervent, but this night was special.

"Did what happen to him influence your career choice?" he asked.

She returned his gaze. "Yes. He's a good part of why I wanted to become a news photographer. I never told anyone before." In a way, that was more intimate than the sex they'd shared. She knew he would respect her secret.

"It's a powerful story, Mel." He paused. "I'm curi-ous. What about your father? Where was he during all this?"

"Chasing an earthquake probably. He was with the Red Cross and left her village before my mother even knew she was pregnant. She wrote to him. He visited when I was little. It was…strange." She shrugged, her feelings so mixed she kept them shut away. "He had a different life in mind for himself."

"You were still his child."

"By accident. Not his decision."

He let her words hang for a few seconds. "When my mother got pregnant, my father married her. He was nineteen, he'd just joined the Army, and the last thing he wanted was to be tied down. He loved the nomad life. If he was stationed somewhere too long, he got irritable and antsy. He should never have married."

"That's harsh, don't you think? He was young."

"Some people aren't cut out for families. They're too restless, too tied up in their work, too selfish maybe. I'm like him that way, but at least I figured it out before I did any real damage."

"So, no broken hearts in your wake?"

"We parted by mutual agreement." He gave her a rueful smile. She could see he'd be easy to fall for. He was warm and sexy and so interested in whatever she said. But he was restless and his career came first.

She felt the same way, though when the time was right she wanted a family and a man to share it with, of course. "How do you get along with him now? Your dad?" she asked him.

"He's gone—killed in a truck crash on the base when I was in college. I hope to hell he never knew what hit him. He would have hated dying so stupidly."

"Was that hard on you, losing him?"

"I didn't really know him." He shrugged.

She understood the feeling well enough. Her father wasn't dead, but he hadn't wanted Mel any more than Noah's father had wanted him. "What about your mom?"

"After he died, Eleanor *found her wings,* she told me. Started traveling. She has a condo in Florida, but she's rarely there."

"Are you close with her?"

"We're different people. She wasn't that happy about having a kid, I don't think, though she did her best and I turned out okay. How about you and your mother?" He clearly didn't want to talk about this.

"We're close. She's my best friend. I'm lucky that way." She yawned, her body sinking into the mattress, feeling drowsy. She should probably head home before she drifted to sleep.

"You have plans this weekend?" he asked softly.

"Laundry, groceries, sleeping in." She'd quit the studio job and the free weekend was her graduation gift to herself. "What about you?"

"Background reading and research calls. I fly to Fort Bragg Sunday afternoon, then leave for Iraq two days later." He ran his fingers lightly along her arm. "What I'd rather do is order room service and enjoy you." He traced her side, then moved to her thigh. "Stay with me, Mel."

"Mmm." She breathed, waking to his touch. Stay? Should she? It was such a non-Mel thing to do, but how could she pass up more time with this glorious man, talking about the work they both loved and having great sex? "I vote yes."

"That's settled then." He shifted so they faced each other, lying on their sides. "So what's Mel short for? Melanie? Melissa?"

"Melody. Actually, *Melodía,* but I prefer Mel."

"*Melody* is pretty. *Melodía* even prettier."

"Exactly. Pretty like a song, la-la-la. No, thanks. I

want people to take my work seriously. Plus *Mel* is gender neutral."

"One of the toughest reporters I know goes by Chrissie, so I don't know that that makes much difference. Your work will speak for you, *Melodía*."

Her name on his lips didn't sound weak or frivolous. It sounded like a beautiful, powerful song. He lay back and pulled her on top of him, looking up at her with so much heat it took her breath away.

Noah made love the way he worked, with persistence, curiosity and a hunger to get at her core, her essence, her truth. What better way to launch her new life?

CHAPTER TWO

"MY PLANE LEAVES SOON," Noah murmured near Mel's ear, hating the fact that he would have to get out of this bed they'd rarely left all weekend.

Mel snuggled into him with a little moan of pleasure—a fainter version of the sound she made when she climaxed. In response, he went hard as a rock.

Damn, he didn't want to go yet. He studied her golden skin, the way her dark hair shone in the gray light leaking through the hotel curtains.

She had the best smell—reminding him of that old-school tropical drink, the Zombie—sweet with a peppery stinger. The cocktail was red, too, which felt like Mel's color. Intense and fire-bright.

He would have to hustle once he got to Fort Bragg to get his advance work done before he flew out with officers headed to Iraq, where U.S. troops remained to advise and train Iraqi soldiers.

Not the way he usually approached a big assignment, but he wasn't sorry he'd spent his last free days with Melodía Ramirez. She was one of a kind. A straight shooter and passionate as hell, with a laugh like liquid silver.

She reminded him of himself after J school—hard-driving, totally on fire for the work. Which was how she was in bed, too, he'd been happy to discover.

She lifted her head to shove her thick hair out of her

face. He helped her with the rest, running his knuckle along her cheek, enjoying the buttery firmness of her skin—strong and soft like her personality and her name. She had the best mouth. What she could do with that sweet tongue of hers…

She noticed the tent he'd raised and smiled, taking hold of him. "How much time do we have?"

"Enough for what you've got in mind." He rolled her onto her back, she shifted her hips and he entered her, easy as breathing.

All weekend long, when they weren't having sex, they were talking nonstop and they kept at it all the way to the airport. Mel had a million questions and more ideas than that. At the terminal curb, she bounded out of the car. "I had a great time," she said, clearly trying to sound cheerful despite the wistful mood that had descended on them both.

"Me, too, Mel." He pulled her against him, holding tight. *I'll miss you.* He had the urge to say it. She was a smart, sexy woman who knew who she was and what she wanted. In life and in bed. It didn't get much better than that.

"I wish I could go with you," she said, quickly adding, "to take pictures." As if he might think she was being clingy. Not Mel.

She stood on her own two feet. He liked that about her.

"Me, too," he said. "Sadly, I'm taking my own shots, since they won't spring for a photographer. I'm no Mel Ramirez." But he wanted her along for more than her camera.

Predictable, he supposed. The result of that postcoital glow, when it all seemed perfect. That was where he'd gone wrong with Pat, his girlfriend for almost a year. Because she was a reporter, he'd figured she would roll with the punches, but he would return from weeks on the road to stony silence and slammed doors, then tears and bitterness when she finally did speak. It was a mistake he hadn't made since. He knew better than to let anyone or any place sink its hooks in him.

"You're my hero, you know," she said.

"God, don't say that. I'm just a news monkey. I'm all about the byline."

"We both know better than that."

He'd told her how hard it had been to convince his editor there were still important stories in Iraq. "If I don't hit this one out of the park, I'm dead."

"I have no doubt you will."

"Talking with you has been good. You remind me why I'm in this crazy business. I owe you for that." To lighten the moment, he added, "And for the sex. Man, do I owe you for that." He wrapped both arms around her and she tucked in tight. Damn, she felt good in his arms.

Don't drag this out. He released her for the crucial reality check. "I'm not good about staying in touch," he said. "Once I get deep into an assignment, I'm lost. The bases have good internet and cell reception, but away from there, there's next to nothing, so I—"

"We had a great weekend, Noah," she said. "That's what matters."

She was making it easy for him. He leaned in and kissed her goodbye. "You're something else." He couldn't get enough of her eyes, which crackled with intelligence, humor and fire. They stayed with him on the plane.

Her mother's story stuck with him, too. She'd risked her life in Salvador to speak out for the truth. And

Xavier Sosa, who had died trying to force the world to see a reality it refused to admit.

Mel would carry Sosa's mission forward, with her eye and her art, exposing truths, large and small, beautiful and surprising, hard to look at, but crucial to see. She was strong-willed, idealistic, but practical, too, with her head on square and her heart as big as hearts got.

Noah had had a weekend he wouldn't soon forget with a woman he doubted he ever would. Her scent lingered on his clothes all the way to Fort Bragg—one last pleasure to hang on to before the hard work ahead.

Two months later
Phoenix, Arizona

"BE RIGHT BACK." MEL tossed her camera bag over her shoulder, and hightailed it to the gas station restroom. It was big and shiny and very clean, *gracias a Dios*.

Since she'd been working for *Arizona News Day* she'd become a pro at identifying good restrooms from the outside. Lately, she'd spent more time in them than usual. She'd assumed it was some weird stomach flu, since her mother had complained, too. In fact, Irena had gone to the doctor that morning to find out what was causing her cramps and nausea.

Lately, though, Mel had had another idea about her own stomach upset and it had nothing to do with a virus.

She and Dave Roberts, the reporter she was working with, were about to leave for the housing development where police believed human smugglers were using foreclosure homes as drop houses, but she had enough time to test her theory about her health. She slipped into the bathroom and locked the door.

Five minutes later, she stared at the plus sign on the

stick she held with shaking fingers. For some reason, it made her think of the X's over the eyes of a cartoon character who'd been knocked unconscious. She could relate. She felt as though someone had kicked the wind right out of her.

She was *pregnant?* How was that possible? She'd been on birth control—well, transitioning from pills to a patch. But that shouldn't have mattered, considering the condition of her fallopian tubes. Endometriosis had so scarred them the doctor had told her she would need in vitro fertilization to get pregnant.

Someone tapped on the door. "We gotta roll, Mel."

"Right, Dave. Coming." She tossed the stick and the box in the trash. Her stomach surged, so she bolted back to the stall to lose what was left of lunch.

"You okay?" Dave asked when she emerged. He'd clearly heard her puke.

"The enchiladas were too spicy," she mumbled, though Dave would never buy that—the two of them had regular contests over who could mouth-surf the hottest peppers in town.

Pushing back her panic, she hitched her camera bag higher on her shoulder and focused on the job ahead.

Their timing was ideal, as it turned out. Dave scored interviews with the smugglers' neighbors and a family of immigrants who were held hostage in the drop house while the coyotes extorted more money from their people back home.

Mel got great shots, including one of a mournful immigrant couple sitting against the post of a *for sale* sign in the yard. It would make a perfect cover. So far, she'd scored three covers. Not bad for two months at a new job.

Her job was exactly as great as she'd dreamed it

would be. *Arizona News Day* wasn't afraid of the tough stories, allowed its journalists to take risks and gave tons of editorial space to photos.

She'd picked up shortcuts and tips from veteran photographers, honed her instincts and was proud that her candid images often seemed lit and composed as well as a studio shot.

Her editor loved her initiative and the managing editor, Randall Cox, called her "magic behind the lens," though he seemed to dole out praise to distract them all from their less-than-fabulous salaries. Her highest compliment was that Dave, their top reporter, often asked for her to accompany him.

As the weeks passed, she'd loaded her print clips and photos into her portfolio so that it was always current and kept her eye on openings at bigger papers in other cities.

She would miss her mother, but when a spot opened up, she was ready to go. She longed to take the kind of world-changing photos she'd carried on about to Noah—whom, after a mere three emails, she hadn't heard from in a month. Noah who, it turned out, had gotten her pregnant.

It was her fault. When they'd run out of condoms, they could have simply hit the gift shop, but, oh, no, she'd told Noah she had it *handled.*

Evidently not.

On the way home, she dropped into a Planned Parenthood clinic to learn how the impossible had happened. It turned out she'd missed the warning about elevated pregnancy risk while switching methods. As to her fallopian tubes, "The body is amazingly resilient, Mel," the nurse practitioner told her sympathetically, then went through her options, giving her pamphlets for each. "Are there questions I can answer right now?"

"Yes. How could I have been so stupid?"

"No contraceptive is flawless. And we're all human. We make mistakes. Think this through, talk about it with people you trust. Family. Clergy. A counselor. Are you in contact with the father?"

"No. He's not in the country." When Noah heard about this...

She cringed. She was already embarrassed by how often she replayed their time together—the sex and the conversation. She'd made too much of it, she knew. He'd warned her that he disappeared, so she had no right to feel hurt, yet she did. She'd thought they had a connection.

They did now, all right. A baby—the last thing either of them wanted.

"Do you feel faint?" the nurse asked, reaching toward her.

She shook herself back to the moment. "No. I'm just shocked. You've been very helpful." She left the clinic, desperate to go home to think, but she'd promised she'd stop by Bright Blossoms, her mother's day-care business, to take photos of the Fourth of July party.

Mel parked in front of the strip mall where her mother's business nestled. An American flag proudly jutted from its eaves, waving in the light breeze. It was muggy, with monsoon clouds heavy on the horizon and the muted sunlight looked nearly golden. The magical smell of creosote filled the air from last night's warm drizzle.

Bright Blossoms stood out among the bland shops in the mall. The bricks were painted canary-yellow and covered with tropical flowers and birds matching what

Irena remembered of how her father had painted their small home not far from San Vicente in Salvador.

The place was so much like Mel's mother—bright and colorful and cheerful. Though, behind Irena's constant smile, Mel knew she missed her family terribly. Irena's father had died a year after she left, and her mother, brother and two sisters never forgave her for leaving. Irena had visited three times, bringing Mel when she was five, but Irena found the trips almost more painful than missing her people from half a continent away.

Inside the building, Mel's ears were hit with a Sousa march and a confusion of percussion. Through the glass wall, she saw the preschoolers marching around the refreshment table, wearing patriotic paper hats, beating toy drums, shaking maracas, banging cymbals or clacking castanets. A few parents sat in the tiny chairs, clapping along.

In the hallway, her mother crouched beside a sobbing toddler. Irena wiped his tears with a flag-decorated napkin. "Where does it hurt, *mi'jo?*" she murmured, her voice rich as music.

"My finger," he said, holding it out, clearly not in pain. He wanted the little ritual that came next. Her mother gently rubbed the boy's finger while reciting the Spanish rhyme that translated as: *"Get well, get well, little tadpole. If you don't get well today, you'll get well tomorrow."* All through Mel's own childhood, Irena had soothed her with the incantation that magically took away all hurts, big and small.

Her mother had filled Mel's life with poems and songs and sayings. Spanish was so beautiful, sensual and full of rhymes. Whenever Mel heard it, she remembered the comfort of childhood in the tiny apartment they'd lived in until Mel had graduated high school.

"Next time, keep your fingers away from drumsticks that are playing, eh, *muchacho?*" her mother said, giving the boy a hug. He nodded solemnly and ran into the parade room.

"Mamá," Mel said.

"Melodía, you're here." Her mother smiled, but her eyes stayed serious.

"Is everything okay?"

"Of course. Come take the pictures." She motioned Mel into the room. Her mother was in her element, surrounded by children. She'd never made a big deal of it, but she'd clearly wished for more babies after Mel, though it wasn't possible. Bright Blossoms helped relieve that sorrow, Mel believed.

Mel nodded at Rachel and Marla, two of the caregivers who'd been here since they'd opened five years ago, then moved around the room taking shots of the kids marching and playing along with "God Bless America."

As always, the song put tears in her strong mother's eyes. The promise of America had sustained Irena through her terrible trip and the dark days and nights in a foreign land, where the warm welcome she'd hoped for had been denied over politics. She'd survived…and, in the end, thrived.

The final activity was decorating cupcakes and soon the small faces were smeared with bright frosting. As Mel took shot after shot, her mother's words played in her head: *You modern girls, you wait and wait for children. You will have gray hair and be chasing your niños with a cane if you're not careful.*

And that was without knowing about Mel's fertility

problem. Against all odds, a miracle had occurred. Mel was pregnant. What would her mother say?

"Estás bien, mi' ja?" her mother asked, her eyes lingering on Mel's face.

Mel forced a smile. "Will you be home soon?"

"Soon. Yes. And we will talk." Her mother started to walk away, then came abruptly close and hugged Mel hard. *"Mi cariña."* My beloved.

"Mamá? What's up?" Her mother was an affectionate person, but this felt as though they were parting for years, not an hour or so.

"Hablámos en casa." We'll talk at home.

An hour later, Mel's mother shut the front door behind her and said, point-blank, "It is cancer," pronouncing it the Spanish way—*kahn-sare*. "In the ovaries. There is treatment, now, the doctor says to me, that is better than before. First a surgery, then chemotherapy and, perhaps, radiation."

"Oh, *Mamá*." She threw her arms around her mother, who was holding herself stiffly erect, fighting emotion, Mel was certain.

Cancer. Her mother had cancer. She might die.

And Mel was pregnant.

She felt as though the world was closing in on her.

"You're strong, *Mamá*. You'll beat this," she said, holding back the tears, keeping her voice steady. "We'll get you through this." The idea of losing her mother was almost more than she could bear. Her mother was so vibrant, so alive. She had so much to live for. She was Mel's best friend, her entire family. She fought a swirl of nausea.

"The doctor says that with my fibromyalgia, the treatment will be *difícil*. I will be more sick for longer times and some medicines will not work so well."

"We'll do what we have to do to get you better."

"Of course. I have to live to be an old woman if I am to finally be a grandmother." Her mother winked, making a joke she had no idea was no longer funny at all.

What if her mother died?

Ice froze Mel's heart in her chest.

She had to be strong for her mother. She had to hope for the best. It's what Irena would do. But Mel was too realistic to deny the terrible possibility. If the worst happened, if her mother's life was cut short, then Mel would make every day that remained as happy and joyful as possible.

The answer was obvious. Mel would keep the baby. It would turn her life upside down, ruin her plans, but *así es la vida. That's how life is.* She would make the most of it. *Man plans, God laughs.* Professor Stockton had foretold her future the night she'd met Noah.

Noah. What about him? Should she tell Noah about the baby?

Would he even want to know? He didn't want children, he'd told her that first night. She would raise the child on her own, so what was her obligation to him? Her head was already spinning with too many questions.

Noah Stone would have to wait.

Five months later, near Balad, Iraq

"So, NO BULLSHIT, YOU'RE seriously going to quote me about my girl in your article?" Sergeant Reggie "Horn Dog" Fuller turned from his shotgun seat in the Humvee to talk to Noah, sitting behind him.

"Of course. It's a great quote." Fuller was squad

leader and Noah had convinced him to allow Noah to jump onto the patrol from Forward Operating Base River Watch, east of Balad, along the Al-Dhiluya peninsula, promising the quote, which would appease Fuller's girl who was angry at him for reenlisting.

Fuller had discretion to patrol as he saw fit, but his commanding officer, Captain Gerald Carver—the officer Noah answered to—would not be pleased if he learned about it. Carver was totally by the book. Fully squared away, with combat experience in Afghanistan, he was primed for advancement, eventually to become a general, and would want no blot on his command.

Carver made it no secret he considered reporters deadweight best kept in the dark and tucked to the rear—the polar opposite of Noah's purpose. Noah liked the guy. He was smart, worked hard, stood up for his officers and the enlisted men trusted him. He wasn't afraid to get his hands dirty—he had once fixed an engine rather than wait for the mechanic to arrive.

Not clearing this reporter-carry with his CO would be a minor infraction for Fuller, who might get "smoked"—given some humiliating duty, such as filling sand bags in front of the chow hall—so Fuller wasn't that concerned.

The patrol consisted of three vehicles—two HMVs and a small troop carrier. Noah rode in the lead Hummer, keeping his eyes open for the turnoff he wanted. What he hadn't told Fuller was that he intended to be dropped off for an interview with the Iraqi captain, Sajad Fariq.

Regulations forbade embedded reporters from traveling on their own, but the elite Iraqi unit Noah wanted to meet with was being trained by Carver's men and the area was virtually secure.

There were rumblings of an insurgent assault being planned farther north, and Noah wanted to talk with Fariq, who spoke decent English. If he could manage it, Noah hoped to ride north with the Iraqis. He'd be off his embed and Carver would ream his ass later, but it was easier to get forgiveness than permission, in Noah's experience.

The deal was he needed a big story. His editor, Hank Walker, was demanding more blood, guts and glory and Noah was determined to get it. The stories he'd been writing were rich with characters and insights about U.S. troops here, Iraqi troops and the future of Iraq. They were some of his best work, important human stories, he believed, but if he wanted to keep writing them, he had to satisfy Hank's bloodlust.

"So why did you volunteer for patrol?" Noah asked the driver, Bo Dusfresne, a trucker from Georgia.

"'Cause I'm sick of sittin' on my ass," he said, scratching at his head beneath the ghutrah, the white Arab scarf he wore do-rag style. "I'd rather be making a goddamn motocross track for the Hajjis to practice RPG runs on than sit around the base, stewin' in my own tang."

Noah brushed his boonie back on his head. The canvas cap with a soft brim was far more comfortable than the helmet he'd had to wear on his first embed, early in the war. He shook out the ends of his ghutrah, which kept sun and mosquitoes off his neck, to generate a tiny breeze. Fuller had insisted Noah wear body armor, which made Noah feel like roast in a pot.

Over the Kevlar, he wore a khaki T-shirt, then his pocketed vest, stuffed with a mini tape recorder and his digital camera, along with spare media cards and batteries for both. He worked mostly old-school—pencil and small pad.

The Humvee stank of sweat and hot metal. The humidity was high this close to the Tigris. Flies were few, but mosquitoes buzzed at dawn and dusk. The dust wasn't bad here and haboobs—gigantic wind storms—were rare. The one he'd experienced had been strange. It was as if dust had instantly coated every nook and cranny, human or object, inside the CHU—Containerized Housing Unit—that served as barracks.

The road beside them was lined with short palm trees. They passed a small orchard of pomegranate trees.

"Somethin' at my eleven," Specialist Chuy Gomez barked from where he stood in the gunner position beside Noah. A sharpshooter, Gomez hailed from East L.A. and claimed he'd honed his skills in drive-bys. Half his blood-curdling stories were total bull, designed to distract the guys from their poker hands, but they were convincing as hell. *Shee-it. You crackers believe any evil thing a Mexican says.*

"Can't you tell goat herders from a hunter-killer RPG team?" Private First Class Emile Daggett growled. "You been in the sun too damn long, Spic."

"Be glad I have crystal clear vision, Hick. If I hadn't eyeballed that trip wire on that dud IED, you'd be missing the family jewels at *least, cholo.*"

"Who you calling *cholo?* There are no *cho-los* in the Upper Peninsula." Daggett talked nonstop about the bait shop he intended to buy and run when he returned to his small town in northern Michigan.

"There will be if I buy that worm shack you keep talkin' 'bout. Serious investment opportunity, *amigo.*

Get me one of those hot Upper Peninsula shorties. *Oye, cabrón,* that's the life."

"Shut the hell up," Daggett said. The two men, who'd named each other Spic and Hick, kept up running insults, but had each other's backs.

The goat farmers, now visible, wore the traditional *taloub*—a long tunic, loose pants and head wrap. They whistled and called to their animals, urging them across the narrow irrigation ditch at the side of the road. The pastoral sound of "baas" and bells seemed proof the country was striving for normalcy. If only the government could keep the uneasy peace.

Noah snapped a photo of an Iraqi on a horse, sagging in the saddle, looking as dispirited as the town council in Balad after mortar fire had destroyed the new police building.

He checked the image. Not bad, but not brilliant. Mel would have managed a far more striking shot, he was certain. She'd been in his thoughts a lot in the months since they'd slept together. Too much, really.

"So what's that picture for?" Fuller asked. "Some symbolic shit about tired old Iraq riding its broke-back nag into the sunset?"

Noah shrugged.

"You gotta be bored as shit watching us sweep sand into the sea."

Noah scribbled notes: *Soldiers pissed and bored and bitter. Missions seem pointless...sweeping sand into the sea, according to Fuller.*

The buildings and mosques of Balad rose in the distance. He picked up the tinny murmur of a prayer playing over loudspeakers.

"Hear the prayers?" Chuy said to Noah. "Five times a day, *hombre,* right? So we're driving down this street in Balad... Real narrow and twisty, sniper spots every-damn-where, and the prayer blares out. After, comes this eerie silence." He paused, milking the moment for drama.

"Yeah?" Noah said, unobtrusively clicking on his tape recorder.

"Yo, so, they all s'posed to be in their houses or mosques, prayin' like crazy. So anybody still runnin' the street is up to no good, right?"

"Right."

"I'm up in the gun, scalp pricklin', adrenaline so high I'm not even blinkin'—you can't blink when your blood's hitting that hard—watching for movement, any change, a clue to something coming down. So I see this kid at my three o'clock. He's holding something. A candy bar? An orange? Or maybe a detonator to an IED we're about to drive over."

"Sounds terrifying."

"Nah, man. 'S cool. Just a day in the neighborhood in East L.A." He laughed, but Noah could tell this situation had been bad.

"Then what?"

"The kid runs in front of us, across the road. Seconds later, boom. Direct hit on the troop carrier behind us. Driver got shrapnel, a first-class flight to the States, champagne all the way, and a Purple Heart. We all envied his ass."

Noah stayed silent, taking in the real story Chuy was telling. He'd had the lives of the men in his HMV and those in the vehicles behind in his hands. He could never have shot the kid because he *possibly* held a detonator, but that explosion could have killed a dozen of his comrades and it would be on Chuy—at least in his mind. That was a catch-22 that would be tough to endure, day after day, patrol after patrol. It was no wonder post-traumatic stress disorder rates were so high among Iraq vets. Friend and foe were impossible to tell apart, making civilian casualties common, but no less horrifying.

Bo hit a bump in the road and swore as the tobacco he constantly chewed missed the window and dribbled down the inside of his door.

They passed the low mud-brick wall with a chunk blasted away that Noah had been watching for. The turnoff was close. He leaned forward to talk to Fuller. "Half mile up, there's a road going west. I need you to drop me there. I want to walk up to talk with Captain Fariq."

"Say what?" Fuller shifted to glare at Noah. "This is not a bus line. You don't ring the bell at your stop. You go on patrol, you stay on patrol, Stone."

"It's Fariq. You know him. You work with his men. Drop me off and I'll meet you at the turnoff on your way back."

Fuller stared at him, unmoved.

"Look, I need this interview or my editor will yank me home. It's the dirt road up ahead. There's a sign pointing to Al-Talad. The area's secure."

Fuller turned and stared out the mud-spattered windshield. "No such thing as *secure* in this godforsaken land. Give a reporter an inch and he takes out a convoy," he muttered, but Noah picked up assent in his tone, so he kept his mouth shut.

When they reached the village sign, Fuller grumbled, "Halt." Yards back, spaced for safety, the other vehicles slowed, too.

Up the road, Noah could see corrugated-steel structures and smaller buildings, some military vehicles and a few Iraqi soldiers.

"Looks hinky to me," Chuy said.

"Everything's hinky to you," Noah said, opening his door. "I got this."

"Do not exit the vehicle, Stone!" Fuller barked. "Take us there, Dusfresne. You get twenty minutes, Stone, then we haul you into this truck. You got that?"

"Yes, sir," he said. "Got it." Damn. Depending on what Fariq said about him hitching a ride, he'd have some fast talking to do with Fuller, for sure.

Bo turned onto the dirt road.

As they drew nearer to the buildings, the Iraqis seemed to stiffen, weapons half raised, as if expecting a confrontation. Noah's scalp prickled. Chuy was right. This did feel hinky. The soldiers around him in the truck tensed, shifted positions, readying their weapons.

There was a sudden thud, as if a boulder had slammed into the driver's side of the vehicle, followed by pops and pings from bullets hitting the front grill. The windshield cracked.

Then an explosion rocked them. Noah's eardrums felt as if they'd burst. Smoke and dust filled the air. Around him, men were shouting, but it sounded like he was underwater in mud.

Noah fumbled with the door handle, but it wouldn't give. He was moving through a nightmare's quicksand, stunned and slow.

The door flew open and Daggett yanked him to the ground. A few feet out, Fuller was giving hand signals to the other men. He turned back to Daggett and yelled, "Get Stone under cover. Go, go—"

Abruptly, Fuller froze. A hole appeared in his forehead, his jaw sagged and he dropped to the ground. Before Noah or Emile could react, another blast struck—a direct hit on the HMV, now empty, behind them. A wave of heat and sound plowed him down. Hot knives seemed to slice his shoulders, belly and legs. He heard an ungodly scream. Just before everything went black, he realized the scream had come from him.

WHEN NOAH CAME TO, HIS body burned with pain and every breath was a stab of agony. He lay on his side, tasting dirt and swallowing blood. His ears rang and his mind kept flickering like a lightbulb about to blow. He tested his body for mobility. His right leg and left arm seemed to be broken. Any movement made him nearly pass out. His ribs were at least cracked and every breath was torture.

He was being shouted at, but with his ears ringing, he couldn't detect the language. A rifle jabbed him in the chest. An Iraqi soldier above him wanted Noah up.

Adrenaline was all that got Noah to his knees, despite his injuries. He saw Emile Daggett, also kneeling, bleeding from the head and mouth, one eye swollen shut, a rifle trained at his temple.

The two Iraqis arranged themselves in front of Noah and Emile, clearly readying to execute them. Dully, Noah wondered why his life wasn't passing before his eyes. Instead, he thought, *This is a great story, but you'll be too dead to write it.*

Suddenly, shots chinked nearby, zinging off metal, pocking the dirt. Another Iraqi ran up to the two guarding Noah and Emile and yelled something. Agitated, the soldiers dragged Emile and Noah to their feet and shoved them forward. Noah's leg gave out, so he got dragged along the ground into a machine shop, then to a small room filled with tarp-covered crates and what looked like engine parts. The space stank of wet earth, motor oil, blood and something foul.

Emile turned to speak and got slugged by a rifle butt. He dropped to the ground, unconscious, possibly dead. When Noah looked up, he saw the stock of a machine gun coming for his head. Once more, he dropped into blackness.

THE NEXT TIME NOAH WAS conscious, the dimness of the light leaking through the seams in the steel walls told him hours had passed. His mouth was coated with dust and he was desperate for water. His pain had localized to his injured parts, including his skull, where he fingered a baseball-size lump. Emile was out, but breathing.

Going under with a concussion was bad news, so he fought to stay awake, but failed. When he came to again, he heard machine-gun and rifle fire and an occasional mortar landing nearby. He wet Emile's lips from a bucket of foul-smelling water that had appeared while Noah was unconscious. Emile groaned.

Hours passed. Noah faded in and out. At one point, he heard men talking overhead. He thought he recognized Fariq and tried to say his name, but his mouth was too dry, his voice too faint.

He tried to find a way out. There was something about the crates he needed to check. He felt for his camera, thinking he should take pictures, if he could stay awake long enough and clear his vision....

He woke in different parts of the cramped room, forgetting what he'd been trying to do. At one point, a guard came in and caught him writing in his note-pad. This time, when the blow struck and the blackness came, Noah expected never to see light again.

CHAPTER THREE

Phoenix, Arizona

AT 3:00 A.M., MEL woke to wet sheets and a sharp pain. Instantly, she *knew.* Her baby was coming. Her water had broken and she was having contractions. Game on. A few weeks early, but safe, *gracias a Dios.* Endometriosis could lead to premature birth, but at her last appointment, the doctor had told her the baby was developed enough to be born anytime and likely not need neonatal care.

Okay. This is it. Here we go. Excitement poured through her. Adrenaline, too, waking her up, putting every cell of her being on alert. She was a little scared, her heart pounding, but she stayed in charge, her tasks scrolling through her mind: *Call the doctor. Wake* Mamá. *Dress. Pack a quick bag. Drive to the hospital.* She pushed to her feet and got started.

The doctor told her to meet him at the hospital, so she went to wake her mother. She hated to rob Irena of vital sleep, but her mother would have her head if Mel left without her. "*Mamá,* it's time."

Irena threw back the covers. *"Lista!"* she said, bounding out of bed. *Ready.* Mel's heart ached at how hard her mother tried to hide her pain from Mel.

Irena was still weak from a second surgery, required because her fibromyalgia flare-ups had delayed chemo-

therapy. Mel had moved home to be more useful to her
and had been helping out more at Bright Blossoms.

Mel carried her mother's condition constantly with
her—a drumbeat in her head, a throb in her heart. What
if she didn't recover? What if she got worse? What if
she died?

At least Irena would see her grandchild. Mel knew
that and it filled her with relief. No matter what happened, she'd have given her mother this gift.

"Are you excited, *mi' ja?*" her mother said, a happy
light overriding the gray exhaustion that ruled her features. Just the sight of Mel's growing belly had seemed
to cheer her and daily Mel had been grateful for that.

"Very," she said, going close to hug her mother, taking in the comfort, the warmth, the love that meant so
much to her.

"*Gracias a Dios* I am here to see this day," Irena
whispered, her voice urgent, her eyes gleaming with
tears. It was rare for her to admit this possibility and it
hit Mel hard.

She bit her lip and swallowed against the lump in her
throat. "Of course you are here. You'll be here for years
and years." She pressed her cheek against her mother's,
praying that what she'd said would prove true.

"Get dressed while I pack."

Then, in her room, throwing toiletries into a bag,
it hit: *What about Noah?* She'd put off calling him,
not wanting to deal with his shock and possible outrage over her carelessness with birth control. Plus, she
hadn't heard from him since that first month. He'd
clearly moved on. She should, too.

Oh, Noah. Her heart surged with longing for him,
as it had over and over again during her pregnancy. It
was weak and stupid, but at night, she'd often fantasized

him with her, spooning in bed, his warm hand cupping her swollen belly, cozy in their cocoon.

Pregnancy hormones, no doubt, but embarrassing as hell.

And now? Now that the baby was here? She had to tell him. The man hated secrets. She owed him this truth.

She reached for her cell phone, where she had his number, but a contraction gripped her. Pain ripped through her insides, twisting her organs, taking over her brain and body, making her gasp. She grabbed the bureau, panting, fighting to remember the Lamaze technique. *"Ow, ow, ow,"* was the best she could manage. How many minutes had gone by since the last contraction?

She didn't remember. There was no time for a phone chat, that was certain, so she settled for a text: Got pregnant that weekend. Baby coming. No need for anything. This is what I want. No regrets.

She took a deep breath and hit Send. For better or worse, Noah would know. Putting her phone in her bag, Mel set off to have her baby.

Two days after the attack
Landstuhl, Germany

NOAH OPENED HIS EYES and jolted upward. Pain stabbed his chest and his hand hit a metal bar. He saw he was in a hospital bed. Alive. Safe. At least that. He checked himself out, moving as little as he could to minimize the pain.

His chest was taped, he had casts on his left arm and right leg and stitches pulled at the skin at his shoulders and his thigh. He touched a thick bandage around his head. *Okay. Got it.* That was all the activity he could stand, so he closed his eyes and drifted off.

After that, he slipped in and out of awareness for a while, hearing voices, beeps, clicks, the whisk of curtains, feeling his body being shifted, getting jolts of pain, the stab of injections, hearing groans, seeing lights go bright, then dim.

Eventually, he was alert enough to understand that he was in the medical center at the Ramstein Air Force Base in Germany, where military personnel and some civilians were cared for when injured overseas.

The neurologist explained that Noah had suffered a traumatic brain injury. His language center had been damaged, so speech and attention span would be compromised, but they were hopeful he would recover.

They were *hopeful.* Okay. He'd hold on to *hopeful.* He was so foggy he could barely form a thought, let alone ask many questions.

Not long after that, he awoke to find an officer in a dress uniform at the end of his bed, hands crossed at his crotch, chest loaded with medals.

"I'm Brigadier General Wade Nelson," the man said, "here to extend the Army's best wishes for your recovery. What happened over there was regrettable."

"What about...the men?" Noah croaked out, fighting the gaps in his brain for words. "Daggett was...hurt. Others...?" Every thought was a battle.

"Private Daggett is recovering in this facility," Nelson said. "Sergeant Fuller, killed in action, yourself and PFC Daggett were the only casualties incurred during the incident in question."

Noah nodded, relieved no more men had been hurt.

Nelson then rattled off a military description of what had occurred. Noah concentrated as best he could, fighting to understand, though words kept dropping through holes in the sieve his brain had become.

In essence, Nelson told him that Fuller had acted against orders by allowing a civilian to join the patrol, that Noah had forced a detour to an unsecured area, where Fuller's men initiated unprovoked combat resulting in Fuller's death and the capture of Noah and Emile by the Iraqi soldiers who believed themselves under attack by U.S. troops.

Noah and Daggett had been "secured" some time later. There would be an investigation...disciplinary actions taken...and serious consequences.

"It was...me..." he managed to say. "I'm at fault."

"We are well aware of that fact," the brigadier general said, his mouth a grim line. He moved to the side of the bed and looked down at Noah, his eyes dark with anger. "Your irresponsible actions have jeopardized our status with the Iraqi military, its government and its people, Mr. Stone." The words hit like hammer blows, pounding straight through Noah's mental fog. He would remember each one, he knew.

"On behalf of the U.S. Army and the American people, I urge you, in any reporting you may do, to respect the men who risked their lives to save yours and be utterly clear about your culpability in what transpired on that ill-advised patrol."

My duty...is to...the truth. The words slowly lined up in his brain, but refused to become speech. The most he could manage was, "The men...were...brave." That was one truth he knew.

The remainder of Nelson's words became a meaningless jumble. After he was gone, Noah tried to recall the attack. All he got were flashing images: Chuy and Emile hassling each other...Bo spitting tobacco...goats in the road…spiderwebs of cracked glass in the HMV's windshield.…

Why couldn't he remember? He tried not to panic. The neurologist had warned him that he'd likely experience something called *retrograde amnesia* and be unable to recall anything around the time of the trauma, at least for a while, though it sometimes became a permanent loss.

Abruptly, a scene flashed into his mind—slowed down like a movie dream sequence. Pings…pops…a blast from behind…his body frozen…Daggett yanking him from the vehicle… Stumbling forward… Fuller: *Get Stone under cover*… The black spot between Fuller's eyes…Fuller on the ground.

Then the screen in Noah's brain went blank.

The horror of what he'd done rolled over him like a semi. Fuller had assigned Emile Daggett as Noah's bodyguard. Protocol said that reporters got babysat. Noah ignored that, believing it unnecessary in his case. But he'd been given a guard all the same and that fact led directly to Fuller's death and Daggett's capture.

Noah had caused this. It was on him. He gripped the sides of the bed, shaking with anger at himself and regret—so much regret.

Those soldiers. What they'd risked and lost.

All because Noah needed a hot story to impress his editor.

Sickness washed through him and he fumbled for the kidney-shaped dish on his tray to puke up bile. The spasm made his injured ribs seem to split wide-open, a punishment he welcomed.

A rattling sound made him notice his cell phone vibrating on his bed tray. Seemed someone had gathered the gear he'd left at FOB River Watch when he went on the fateful patrol. He scooped the phone close enough to see the call was from Hank.

His editor would want the story, of course, though Noah remembered little beyond what Nelson had told him. It didn't matter. He was a reporter. He had a job to do. Fighting pain, he answered the call.

It did not go well. Words failed him over and over. There were long gaps where he could only breathe and struggle for language. Finally, Hank said, "We'll get the basics and come back to you for a comment. You just get better." His tone was gentle, as if Noah were a child or a volatile mental patient..

"Yeah." He fought the helplessness, the frustration, the shame. He was a writer, but words were lost to him.

He still held the phone when a wave of terror washed over him. His heart pounded so hard he grabbed his chest, causing more pain. Was he having a heart attack? He was shaking and sweating and terrified. Of what? He was safe in a hospital bed. What the hell was going on?

Then he remembered the neurologist describing a panic attack, a common aftereffect of a trauma. *They hit out of the blue, scary as hell, mimicking a heart attack, but are essentially harmless.*

The terror and pain had barely released him when his phone buzzed again. He checked the display. A number he didn't recognize. He saw he had dozens of texts and voicemails, some from before the assault, he was sure.

People would want to know he'd survived. He couldn't deal with their sympathy or questions. He deleted all the voicemails, then highlighted batch after batch of texts to delete in groups. On the last set, as he clicked Delete, he saw *Mel Ramirez*.

Mel.

Her name sent warmth pouring through him. She'd been in his mind a lot in the months since they'd met— her face, her smile, her fire. He'd been thinking he would look her up when he got back. But that could never happen now. Not after this. Just as well that her message was gone, unread, like the rest.

He decided to write one general "I'm okay" message. It took forever, the words elusive, his spelling hopeless, but he managed the equivalent of, *Minor injuries. Be in touch.* He ticked "all contacts."

At the last second, he unchecked Mel, then hit Send. He owed her a personal note. She was probably doing great, living the life she'd been poised to launch that weekend. He mangled words and skipped letters in his communication, but the gist was: *Not sure where I'll end up. I know you'll do great. I wish you every happiness.*

Corny, but true. Thinking about her was a momentary escape from the hell of his thoughts. There was her number on his screen. He could hit Call and talk to her. Her voice would be like medicine. But he didn't deserve to feel better. Not for a long, long time. He pressed End until his phone went black.

He would answer the questions he had to for the *National Record* story, then get out a media statement expressing regret for his irresponsible actions and gratitude for the soldiers' bravery. The main thing he wanted right now was to get well enough to wheel down to Emile's room and say how sorry he was he'd put him in harm's way. If the soldier was well enough to punch his lights out, Noah would be happy to have him slug away.

Phoenix, Arizona

MEL STARED AT THE BABY she held, hardly able to believe they were home, in the room she'd prepared for him, painting and papering it in circus colors and accents.

Daniel Marco Ramirez, named for Irena's father and grandfather, had been born tiny, but healthy after twelve hours of labor the previous day. "Welcome to the world, *mi' jo,*" Mel whispered to him, her throat tight with joy.

She was so lucky and so happy.

Tired, too, of course. And worried. Now that the excitement had died down and reality set in, she was concerned. Would she be able to juggle caring for a new baby and her fragile mother? Irena had gone straight to bed when they got home from the hospital that afternoon. Mel had brought her soup on a tray for supper. There was a lot to handle now and it was all new.

Mel sighed. There was something else in her heart, too. She felt a little, well, sad. Her life had changed completely overnight. She already missed *News Day.* She would return to work after three weeks, but if her mother needed more help with Bright Blossoms, Mel would have to give up the job.

As for her goal of moving on to another paper in a bigger city? Out of the question for years, at least. In the ever-tightening market, news jobs would only grow scarcer.

She'd made the right choice, and she had no regrets, but she couldn't help missing the dream she'd worked so hard for and barely had a chance to taste the rewards of.

She hadn't heard from Noah yet.

She knew he was safe in a military hospital, recovering from his injuries. She'd been deep in labor when CNN on the TV in her hospital room scrolled the news of his rescue in Iraq. From what she could figure of the time differences, her text about the baby had reached him the day before the attack in Iraq.

Obviously, he had other things on his mind now. Her heart went out to him for what he'd been through. Eventually, he would respond to her.

Oh, Noah. Selfishly, foolishly, she wished he were here in the golden glow of the circus-seal night-light, sitting on the edge of the recliner, his arm around her, looking down at the brand-new person they'd created.

Daniel was so perfect, with ten tiny fingers and toes, two delicate shells for ears and his whole soul looking at her from huge, wise eyes.

It was ridiculous, of course, to even picture Noah in such a sappy, domestic scene. He would no more be here than sprout wings and fly. He never wanted kids. He'd been clear about that. He was too selfish, too restless, too career-focused. And she respected him for knowing what he wanted, for not playing games about it.

Still…

Maybe she would send a quick get-well text. She'd tried when she first saw the news, but hadn't been able to get through.

Shifting the baby slightly, she reached her purse, then her phone. She had to turn it on, since she'd had it off in the hospital. She was startled to see she'd received a text from Noah.

Hope soaring, she clicked it.

Nt sure whr I'll end up. I kno ull do great. I wish u evry happiness. N.

That was his response to the baby? *I'm in the wind. Good luck, be happy.*

She felt…abandoned…alone…lost…and so very *hurt*.

Get a grip, chica. What did she expect? She'd said she didn't want anything from him, so he'd only stated the obvious. They were both getting on with their lives. They wished each other well.

But how it hurt. Waves of lonely pain washed through her. She wanted him to care. She wanted him to come. She wanted him to wrap his arms around her and tell her it would be okay.

She scrunched up her face to keep from bursting into foolish tears. *Stupid, stupid, stupid.* Had to be a postpartum hormone dump, right? Mel was a sensible, sturdy and self-reliant woman, dammit. She and her mother and Daniel were plenty enough to make a wonderful family and an amazing life.

She looked at her sleeping boy to remind herself it was true. He had a mass of curly hair and a tiny dimple in his left cheek. Above one ear was a pale, but unmistakable beauty mark. Just like Noah. She had to laugh.

The bittersweet truth was that even if she never saw the man again, Noah would be with her every day of Daniel's life.

One year later
Albuquerque, New Mexico

"I'LL BE THERE AS SOON AS I can, Eleanor. Don't worry," Noah told his mother over the phone, running a towel across the battered bar of Jake's Hut. A patron entered, backlit, so Noah couldn't tell if it was a man or woman.

Either one would want a drink. "Got to work now. Enjoy your trip. I'll handle Grandma fine."

He hung up and sighed, shifting his weight to ease the strain on his bad leg. He'd told his mother he'd go to Phoenix to help his grandmother transition to an assisted-living place and empty out her home for the new buyers. His mother could have canceled her cruise and done it herself, but she and her mother fought like cats and dogs, so Noah's help was a good solution.

Nothing held him in New Mexico. Or anywhere else, for that matter.

He would get a job in Phoenix, since he was cash-strapped. He hoped to start reporting soon. He'd only recently been able to read an entire newspaper without losing focus. And he was still having nightmares and migraines.

"Noah? Jesus. What are you doing here?"

Instantly, Noah recognized the voice behind him. The backlit customer was none other than his friend Paul Stockton. Dread sank in him like a boulder in a lake. He figured he'd see the guy in Phoenix, but he'd have time to get his story nailed down. He forced a smile, then turned to face his friend. "Serving you a drink, looks like. What'll it be?"

"Draft… Whatever's on tap…" Paul sounded stunned.

"You got it." While he filled the glass, Noah steadied himself, so that when he pushed the beer forward, his smile was decent. "So what brings you to Jake's Hut?" The ancient bar was well off the beaten track.

"I'm speaking at a seminar at the college. Someone recommended this place. How did you end up here? You dropped off the map. I called *National Record* and they said you'd quit."

"They wouldn't run my story." Despite his brain's deficits, he'd pecked out an apology about his foolhardy quest for bloody headlines, damn the human cost. Hank called it self-indulgent moralizing and refused to print it.

He'd probably been right.

"Truth is, the head injury made it hard to think or write. I was deadweight." The first months his speech had been so faulty, he couldn't deal with the phone. Email gave him time to look up words, but wore him out. Mostly, he preferred to be alone.

"You're better now?"

"Getting there."

"You broke bones, too, right?"

"All healed up." His arm and leg were still stiff in the morning, coughing hurt his ribs and he would always limp. But he was alive and kicking, unlike Reggie Fuller.

"Well, you look good," Paul said, clearly lying.

"I look like shit. It's a hangover," he said, not wanting to get into the truth—he'd had a flashback the night before, waking up crouched beside the bed, trembling and sweating, the echoes of gunfire in his head, the smell of motor oil and blood in his nose. He'd numbed himself to sleep with tequila, so he was hungover on top of that.

The flashbacks weren't as bad as the nightmare—he remembered every detail of the nightmare. In it, he was carrying a wounded man to safety, while soldier after soldier got shot between the eyes, dropping dead so that he stumbled over their bodies, until he looked down and saw he held a machine gun, realizing to his horror, that he'd been the one mowing down the men.

Every time he had the nightmare, the horror hit just as hard.

The flashbacks happened less often. At first, he'd had them even in the daytime, triggered by sudden noises or quick movements—even smells. In crowds, he'd start sweating and shaking, his heart beating so fast he thought he might black out.

The doctor he'd seen when his leg flared had prescribed an anti-anxiety med, but Noah wasn't willing to fog his brain any more than it already was. He coped day-to-day. Small spaces and dark rooms still sent his pulse pounding, but he could fight it off better every day that passed.

"So you're bartending now?" Paul was clearly trying to hide his bafflement.

"Here, yeah. In Denver, I sold newspaper ads. I washed cars in Sacramento, parked them in Vegas. Whatever got me grocery money."

"But no reporting?"

"Soon, I hope." Besides, needing time for his brain to heal, he'd needed some soul-searching about the grievous harm his single-minded drive for copy-inches had caused. The thought sent a wash of shame through him. It always would. *Steady, man.* "How's the family?" He dispensed seltzer over ice from the gun to wet his dry throat.

"Great. Cindi's pregnant again. Surprise! Never take birth control for granted, bro." He gave a sheepish smile. "It's wild this time. She's had morning sickness from day one and Princess Emma, three-and-a-half going on fifteen, has started acting out big-time."

"Of course. Her kingdom's under siege." Jesus. Another kid to raise and worry about and send to college. "But you two were born to be parents."

"No one is, trust me. It's on-the-job training. Day one, they let you walk out of the hospital with this innocent being who depends on you for everything. You'll see."

"You know me better than that." He couldn't imagine a less-likely fate.

"One day, you'll get your gills caught in some poor girl's net and she won't have the sense to toss you back." He was joking like the old days, but his tone was faint. He was clearly disturbed by Noah's condition, which made Noah realize he maybe wasn't as improved as he'd imagined.

"You're catching me on a bad day. I'm in good shape. In fact, I'm headed to Phoenix to help my grandmother get moved. I need a job if you know of anything."

"Yeah? I bet I could get you on as an adjunct professor."

"I'm the last person you want teaching J school."

"It would be a coup to have you." Paul stopped as though sensing Noah's resistance, and because he was a good friend, letting it go. "Public affairs needs writers for the web, I think. I'll check the in-house postings. Where will you stay?"

"Camping at my grandmother's place out in Apache Junction until I get it emptied out, then renting somewhere, I guess."

"That's way the hell out there. Why don't you stay in our guesthouse?"

"Seriously?" They had a great location, which would help with whatever job he got. "That would be great."

"Absolutely. You'll be doing us a favor."

"How's that?" he said, taking a drink of the seltzer water he'd poured.

"Isn't it obvious? Emma needs a babysitter."

Noah choked on the water, but he was smiling. Smiling big.

"Oooh! Oooh! Can I have a Popsicle, Uncle Noah?" Emma asked from the backseat of his Jeep. He'd offered to drop her off at day care to save Cindi time, since he was headed to the downtown ASU office.

"You get *one* and *only* one. After school. Your mom said."

"*Pullleeeeze,* Uncle Noah?" Hanging out with the pint-size tornado two nights ago so that her parents could have a date, he'd unknowingly broken Cindi's one-Popsicle-a-day rule. Now the little terror figured him for an easy mark. She was correct.

He swung over to the ice cream truck she'd spotted. "What flavor?"

"Grape! Purply-purple! Yay! I love you, Uncle Noah!"

"Food does not equal love, little girl. That's half the reason we have an epidemic in childhood obesity. You'll have to bite it down, no licking, so it's all gone by the time we get there, or the other kids will feel left out."

She nodded, eager to please now that she'd wrapped him around her pinkie. He was a sucker for those big eyes of hers. When she smiled, they lit up like two blue flashlights in her elfin face. Had to be some biological wiring to make sure you didn't leave your offspring in the dust of the veldt when lions were on the prowl. Whatever it was, it worked like a charm.

He parked in the strip mall where the day-care center was and went to open Emma's door. "Good lord, look at you." Her mouth was purple and two rivulets of juice streaked her arm to her elbow. "We'll clean you up inside so they don't report your parents to Child Protective Services."

"What's *protector service?*"

"Sort of the police who look out for children in trouble."

"*I'm* not in trouble, Uncle Noah," she said, giving him a look of pure disdain. "*You* are if Mommy finds out."

"Then let's keep it our little secret."

She made a crisscross over her heart, then undid the belt on her car seat—she was better at it than he was. He set her on the sidewalk, then grabbed her glittery pink backpack, which weighed twenty pounds because she'd crammed half her toy chest into it before they left. You never knew when you might need a plastic pony or a comb the size of a toenail.

He pushed open the glass door of the place. No one stood at the reception desk and he spotted the restroom sign, so he headed that way, Emma clacking in the wooden shoes her mother had reluctantly let her wear.

The place was bright—painted yellow and purple with jungle flowers. One side of the hallway was a photo studio behind a glass wall. *Eyes of a Child* was lettered in gold on the door. He glanced inside. Huge framed prints of babies, toddlers and young children were everywhere. The photos were strikingly good.

The photographer, her back to him, was snapping a close-in shot of a little boy sitting on a giant ABC block in front of a bright blue backdrop. The woman rose and turned his way. He did a double take.

It was Mel Ramirez. Mel? He'd expected she'd be in Uganda by now, taking world-stopping photos for a wire service, but here she was snapping kiddie candids. How odd.

She looked startled to see him—her eyes wide, her lips parted.

They stood, staring at each other through the glass, neither moving for long seconds. Mel. Melodía. The fired-up angel he'd spent that last weekend with. He'd pictured her a million times, dreamed her twice that. He wasn't sure he wasn't dreaming her now.

"Uncle *Noooo-aaaah,* I want to *gooooo.*" Emma leaned back hard, struggling to escape his grip. He released her, his gaze still glued to Mel. He had to go in and talk to her. What the hell would he say?

CHAPTER FOUR

NOAH PUSHED THROUGH the door into the photo studio. "Mel."

"Noah." She smiled an uncertain smile.

He picked up her scent, that sweet peppery perfume, and was swamped by the memory of her from so long ago. They breathed at each other for a few seconds. "I didn't realize you were in Phoenix," she said finally.

"Just got here a week ago."

"How are you?" She glanced at his leg, so he knew she'd noticed his limp.

"Good." He straightened his shoulder. He tended to hunch to protect the weakened arm. "You?"

"I was sorry about what happened…what you went through over there." She tilted her head, ready to offer sympathy, which was the last thing he wanted or needed.

He shrugged it away. "Old news."

She blinked, as if unsure how to take that. "So… what brings you to Bright Blossoms?" She nodded at the backpack he still held.

"This? Oh, it's not mine." He laughed. "Neither is the little girl."

"Of course not." She went bright red, as if that embarrassed her.

"Emma is Paul Stockton's daughter," he said. "I'm

staying in their guesthouse and this place was on my way to work."

"I didn't realize we had Paul's daughter with us. I don't know all the kids. Bright Blossoms is my mother's business. So where do you work?" She glanced over at the little boy, who had left the block and was crawling across the room.

"ASU. I write for the alumni magazine right now. It's a paycheck while I'm getting my grandmother into assisted living and clearing out her house. What about you? Did you go part-time with *Arizona News Day?*"

"I had to quit. Life got in the way." She seemed to think that choice would make sense to him. Hardly. News photography had *been* her life. She turned to the kid, who had pushed himself upright and now teetered toward her like someone new to stilts.

She crouched down and held out her arms. "That's the way… You can make it." The kid made an excited sound and sped up, leaning perilously forward. Right before he took a header, Mel caught him. "Good boy!" she said, taking him into her arms, then standing to face Noah, almost as if showing him off.

"You're still taking pictures at least," he said, nodding at the wall shots.

"Mom had the space. I help her out here, too."

"Oh. Sure." She'd quit the paper to help her mother. What a shame, with her talent and ambition.

"This is Daniel," she said, very pink in the face all of a sudden.

"Cute kid," he said. He had curly brown hair and a big smile that showed a couple of tiny teeth, but his face was streaked with green paint, as were his clothes and hands. "You'd think his mother would clean him up for a portrait."

She looked startled. Then something seemed to dawn on her and she took a deep breath before speaking. "That would be me. I'm his mother."

"Oh. God. I didn't realize. Congratulations," he said, recovering from his shock. So that was what had gone wrong. She'd gotten pregnant, had a kid and quit her job. Her left hand, which braced the boy on her hip, had a bare ring finger, so she hadn't married the guy.

As these thoughts raced through his head, Mel studied him, looking nervous and embarrassed. Why? It was hardly his place to judge her.

Finally she spoke. "When I got your text, I assumed you'd gotten mine."

"Your text?" He flashed on the moment when, jumble-headed, barely past a panic attack, he'd deleted everything on his phone. "I wasn't up to much at the hospital."

"I should have verified, I guess…." She cleared her throat, looked away, then back. "See, the thing is—" She blew out a breath. "Okay, I'll just say it. I got pregnant that weekend."

"You what?" His brain glitched, shorting out his thoughts like so many bad fuses. "You got…? But you told me—"

"That I had birth control handled, yeah. I thought I did. It's a long story. I was between methods, but I wasn't supposed to be able to get pregnant in the first place. I'm not a careless person and I felt really stupid about it, so…" She paused. "Forget all that. The point is…Daniel is your son."

"My…son?" He felt as though someone had shoved him hard. He took a step back to stay upright. He looked at the kid in Mel's arms with the same round curls he had, its color halfway between Mel's black and his brown. The kid even had his dimple, he realized with a jolt.

As if on cue, the little boy reached out his arms, straining for Noah.

"You can hold him," Mel said, as if to reassure him.

Noah accepted the kid—small, but dense, a solid weight on his good arm. The little boy patted Noah's cheeks. "Da-da," he said. "Da-da."

Noah's jaw sagged. "He *knows?*"

Mel burst out laughing. "*D* is one of the first sounds babies make," she said. "He calls everything da-da— me, the dog, my mother. Cheerios even." Daniel leaned toward his mother, so Noah handed him back.

"Oh, okay. Good." Did he *mean* good? *Good* that Daniel didn't know Noah was his father? That sounded bad. Damn. He was in deep weeds here.

"You must have thought I was an asshole ignoring you like that."

"But you didn't. You wished me well and said I'd do great."

"I meant with your job, Mel, not…*that.* Christ, you were having a baby. That I…uh…*caused.*" He cleared his throat. "I should have been there." He seemed to be walking on ground that could disappear beneath his feet.

"No. That's the point. I didn't consult you about what you wanted. I didn't need you." She hesitated. "I mean, I didn't want you to feel obligated. I knew you never wanted kids. And I took full responsibility on my own."

"Okay. I get it. I just… Hell." He was stranded in a weird limbo. He always knew what to do. Here, he was stumped. "So, how old is he?"

"Almost a year. His birthday's the twenty-fifth. He's

small for his age—he came a little early—but he's very healthy."

"Hell, tall's not everything. So he can't play basketball. I ran track myself, so he'll probably... What am I saying?" He rubbed the back of his neck.

"This is a shock, I know." Daniel craned toward the floor, wanting down, and she placed him there. He crawled toward a scattering of toys beneath a computer desk on the other side of the room.

"I don't know what to say," Noah said.

"There's nothing *to* say. You didn't get my message, but there's no harm done. We're set, Daniel and I."

"Okay." He was completely at a loss.

She smiled at him. "It's good to see you again." She flushed with pleasure and her face softened.

"Yeah. It's good to see you, too." He felt the same pull of attraction he'd felt then. The urge swirled through him like a hot wind, as if no time had passed, no life-altering events had occurred.

"I still think about that weekend," she said.

"Me, too." He'd been mostly celibate since then. Overseas, he'd been too focused on work and since Iraq, he'd had a few hookups when the dreams were so bad he was afraid to try to sleep.

But at this moment, he was where he'd been a lifetime ago, when he'd been cocky, invincible, wrapped in his mission like a Kevlar vest, when he'd wanted her with a clear, clean heat that she'd felt, too.

The little boy gave a sharp cry, shattering the spell like a rock through glass. Daniel had a tape dispenser in one hand and held out the finger of the other. It had a dot of blood on it. His shoulders rocked with sobs.

"Oh, sweetie," she said, going to him, dropping to

her knees to pull him into her arms. "What is it with you and tape? Did you forget the teeth were sharp?"

She kissed the finger and recited a Spanish poem, while Daniel shuddered into quiet, watching her mouth form the words. *Sana, sana...* something *de rana. Frog,* he thought was *rana,* then something about *today* and *tomorrow.* His high school Spanish had faded from disuse.

The words flowed through him like warm water, though. Spanish was a sensual language anyway, but there was more here. The words felt like a love spell cast between Mel and her little boy.

Mel stood and Daniel wrapped himself around her like a starfish, legs around her ribs, arms around her neck, head tucked under her chin. *"Cálmate,"* Mel murmured in a tone so soothing Noah felt his own gut unclench a little. She returned to Noah. "Weren't you on the way to work?"

"Yeah." He jolted, looking at his watch. "And I'm about to be late." He lifted his gaze to her face. "But we need to talk."

She regarded him quietly, considering that. "I think we just did. We're fine on our own, as I said." Her jaw was tight and her shoulders back, determined. *Stay out of this.* That was what she was telling him.

Not so fast. He needed to sort this out, figure out what he wanted to do about being a father. "I'd like to come by tonight, if that's all right."

"Tonight? If you want to catch up, the two of us, fine, but I'm not open to discussing any arrangements about Daniel or anything."

"That's fine," he said. *For now.* "What time?"

"After I put him to bed, I guess. Say eight?" She

wrote her address on one of her cards and handed it to him before he left.

God almighty, he had a son.

If he'd known, would he have come back? Offered to marry Mel? Given up his career for her and the baby the way Paul had done for Cindi?

Of course not. As Mel had well known. This world of teaching a little person to walk and talk and use the toilet and get along with others, this dropping everything to soothe an owie, was not for him.

But then he wouldn't have believed it was for Mel, either. Not for a while anyway. The Mel he'd met almost two years ago had been ambitious and driven. Yet here she was, a single mother, acting like it was the most natural thing in the world to turn her life over to a child.

And he wanted her. There was that. Reacting to Mel had made him feel more normal than he'd felt in a year.

He wanted Mel. And he had a son.

A little boy with a dimple and curly hair and a thing for office supplies. What the hell was he going to do? Break into their lives or run like hell? Mel seemed to want him gone, but Noah was stubborn enough to hold out awhile longer.

"*BASTA,* DANIEL," MEL said, trying to hold in her frustration. Acting impatient with him only made him go slower. "Eat the ravioli, *mi'jo,* don't play with it. Sheesh." She tried to scoop food into his mouth, but he only spit it out.

Mel and her mother had been held up by bookkeeping snags at Bright Blossoms, so the schedule was shot. Mel's days were stacked dominoes. One bump and it all tumbled down. If she'd had Noah's number, she would have canceled, but she'd been too stunned to ask for it.

He was due any minute, and Daniel was not only still up, he had tomato sauce everywhere—hair, ears, neck, elbows—so she couldn't skip his bath. Besides, routines were important for a child as sensitive and active as Daniel.

Her pulse was racing and she was sweating like mad. She was excited to see Noah, but she was too frazzled to enjoy it. Being a mother did not mix well with being a woman. Or having *needs*.

Noah had instantly reminded her of both.

She should have offered a quick lunch, which she managed occasionally with her best friend Alice and, once in a while, with her buds from *Arizona News Day*. Besides, she went to bed early. Half the time, she was asleep by nine-thirty. No, she definitely did not have time for *needs*.

Her attraction to Noah was still the same, but he seemed changed—haunted and sad, his smile only a shadow of the cocky grin she remembered. Had Iraq caused that? She knew soldiers suffered for years from battle trauma.

"Melodía?"

She turned. Her mother leaned against the counter, clearly feeling weak. "*Mamá,* you should be resting."

"I am tired of the bed." Irena smiled, her face pale as caramel. Her mother hid her pain and fear from Mel as much as she could. Her fibromyalgia flared more often and more painfully since the chemo, so every day was a struggle. "I will feed Daniel now. You put on the lipstick. And wear your pretty gold hoops. Look nice for him."

"It's not a date, *Mamá*." Her mother had picked up Mel's reaction to Noah's reappearance and would be a dog with a bone about it until this visit was over, maybe longer.

"He comes to help you, no?"

"No, *Mamá*. For the last time, I told him we don't need help." He might offer money, but she would politely decline. Money implied involvement and that wasn't what either of them wanted.

"You are such a burro, *mi'ja*. You fight *una cosa buena*."

"A good thing? The man does not want a child. You should have seen his face when he realized Daniel was his. Pure horror."

"He was surprised. So was your father when I told it to him."

"And we saw how well that turned out."

"I should not have let him slip off so easily."

"A father is not an animal you trap."

"I was too much about being the strong one, to show him I was *independente* and proud. You missed having a father."

"He didn't miss having a daughter, that's for sure." When she was little and he visited, he would promise to come more often, but he was a busy man, helping people all over the world. *Other* people.

He sent cards and gifts on her birthday, then checks, sometimes late, sometimes not at all. Then five years ago, he'd married a woman with young children and took an administrative job in Washington, D.C.—settling down for the family he *wanted,* not the one forced on him by accident.

Whenever she thought of that, Mel got angry all over again.

"Men need practice. They need reminders. And they

need memories. Give Noah some, *mi'ja.* It is right. This is our blessing."

Mel sighed. "Not the St. Margaret crap again."

"What a terrible word you use. *Crap.*" Her mother, who was only religious when it suited her, had been praying to the patron saint of single mothers from the moment she'd heard Mel was pregnant. St. Margaret rested beside the *Virgen de Guadalupe* shrine in the small alcove in the living room and her mother kept candles burning constantly, which made Mel roll her eyes.

Gracias a la Santa Margarita, she'd said when she heard that Noah had returned, clasping her hands in prayer, looking so Old World that Mel thought for a moment they'd been transported to some adobe mission dripping with candle wax.

"Noah is a good man. And strong. Give him this chance." In the old days, her mother would never get pushy about men with Mel. This was her illness talking. She wanted Mel to have someone if the worst happened to her.

The thought made Mel's stomach swirl with acid. "You don't know any of that about him," she said. "You're guessing and hoping."

"I know how you talk of him. I see your eyes shine. Now, go…put in the curl for your hair like when you go out with your *amigas.*"

"Like I've done that lately." She hadn't gone out with friends since Daniel was a newborn. She'd learned her lesson then. She'd had so much fun she'd almost forgotten she was a mother. She'd returned to a sobbing baby. Her mother had run out of expressed milk and Daniel had refused the formula. The bar had been too noisy to hear her cell phone ringing.

That had brought Mel up short. She had to focus on Daniel. He would not suffer in any way because he had a single mom as his only parent.

Now Irena sat at the table and picked up a spoon. "My big *muchacho* is going to eat, eat, eat for his *abuela* now. *Abuela* law. *Muy serio*." She gave Daniel her stern face and he laughed, rapt, an opportunity she used to give him a mouthful of ravioli. "And eye shadow," her mother said. "Show off your pretty eyes."

"You never fussed for a man, *Mamá,* when you were young. You were political and fierce, not flirty." Irena had dated off and on over the years in the U.S., but never for long and never seriously.

"We have many sides, we women. Show this one to Noah. You have no life but work and Daniel and me."

"I have too much life." In fact, she'd love time to put up her feet occasionally, instead of plowing through relentless to-do lists.

"I'll meet your *novio,* then leave you. You are lucky I am so modern. When I was a girl, we were watched always. Never *solos* with boyfriends."

"He's not a boyfriend. It's too late for a chaperone anyway. I needed one that weekend. Now, the bun's out of the oven."

"The bun? Daniel, a *pañuelo?* This joke I do not like, *mi'ja.*"

"It was one crazy weekend, that's all."

"And from it came Daniel."

Who is a miracle—a fact she'd never tell her mother or the woman would fill every inch of wall space with candles honoring the patron saint of the infertile, whoever that was. "Noah was an innocent bystander."

"A bystander? He did more than stand by, I think."

"Stop." She covered her ears. "I'm not discussing sex with my mother."

"You must take more time for yourself, *niña*. As a woman. Never you go out with a man, always baby this, baby that. *Es mal*."

"I'll put on mascara, okay? And change my top." It had spaghetti on it anyway. She headed down the hall, feeling her excitement grow. She did want to see him again. That weekend glowed golden in her mind. Since then, she'd slept with only one other guy. It had been early in her pregnancy when she'd been wistful about her life changing. It had been a mistake—boring—and it had made her miss Noah even more.

She'd felt so close to him. He'd seemed to truly care, to listen with his whole soul. The sex had been scary good. Her stomach still quivered at the memory. She had felt the same rush when he stepped into her studio, instantly returning to those nights—the touches, the words, the connection as strong as handcuffs. If Daniel didn't exist, if she were single, would she sleep with Noah again? In a heartbeat. But Daniel was here, so that was that.

She donned a red silk tank top and, to please Irena, the gold hoops. Mel's hair looked lifeless, so she turned on her curling iron. She would bet Noah thought she'd sacrificed her soul by giving up her career. The least she could do was show him single moms could look hot.

NOAH WALKED INTO PAUL and Cindi's kitchen for supper a couple of hours before he was due at Mel's. When he wasn't in bed with a migraine, he ate with the family, bringing pizza or Thai takeout as his contribution.

He'd been thrown off all day at work by thoughts of Mel and Daniel. In fact, he'd overwritten a document, losing five hours of work on a story about the new Sun Devil coaching staff.

"Mmm, smells great," he said to Cindi, who was pulling a hot pan from the oven. "Lasagna?"

"Yep." Cindi was a petite powerhouse, smart and driven, with flashing eyes that missed nothing, so different from her lanky, laid-back husband. But they made it work somehow. "Just adults tonight. Emma's pouting because I wouldn't let her eat Lucky Charms, even though, quote, 'milk has cal-sum that builds back the rotted teeth.'"

"She's going to keep you guys hopping," he said. "I'll set the table." He filled the water glasses, loaded the salad bowls with greens and distributed the silverware and napkins. Paul joined them and they began eating with Emma's distant wails as background music.

A few bites in, Noah cleared his throat. "So, evidently, I'm a father."

Paul and Cindi dropped their forks with simultaneous clanks. "What?"

"Remember Mel Ramirez, Paul?"

"Sure. She drove you to the hotel after your talk."

"And stayed the weekend."

"You dog." Paul shook his head, making his shaggy hair flop.

"Paul!" Cindi slapped him lightly on the upper arm. "You slept with a student, Noah?"

"She was twenty-five and a graduate, okay? And we had…a connection."

"I'll bet it was a real meeting of the minds," Paul said, tipping his water glass in Noah's direction before taking a drink. "I'd heard she had a baby and left *News Day,* but I had no idea that you were—"

"Her mother owns Emma's day care place and she's

got a photo studio there. That's where I saw her and the
kid. His name's Daniel and he'll be a year in a couple
of weeks."

"You're just finding this out now?" Cindi's eyes were
wide.

"I missed her text when I was in the hospital in Germany."

"So she did reach out." She took a bite of garlic bread
and chewed thoughtfully. "And what are you going to
do?"

"Not sure yet. I'm going over to talk to her in a bit."

"So...Noah Stone, baby daddy," Paul crowed.

"Don't rub it in."

"I think it's great." Paul's sentimental streak usually
amused Noah. Not this time. "It'll be good for you."

"I'm not a family guy, Paul."

"When it happens to you, everything changes." Paul
kissed his wife's hand. She blushed. It was sweet that
Paul could make her melt. She was usually such a no-
nonsense person. They were a solid couple.

"What was Mel's reaction?" Cindi asked, serving
him more lasagna.

"Shock at seeing me—she felt bad that I didn't get
her message. But as to the kid, she practically warded
me off with a cross, like I was a vampire."

"Maybe she's giving you an out," Cindi mused.

"Mel doesn't bullshit. She seemed pretty firm." He
took a bite of food, thinking it through. "I can't get past
the fact that if I hadn't run into her, I would never have
known."

"And...?" Cindi prodded.

He paused, fork in the air. "And that's not right." He
felt the truth of the words. "I'm not ready to walk away."

They went silent as the idea settled in, taking slow

bites, drinking water, glancing at each other, opinions swirling and settling.

"So how will that work?" Cindi asked. "Will you stay in Phoenix? Share custody? Are you still attracted to her? Will you get together as a couple?"

"Jesus, Cin, slow down," Paul said. "He barely found out there's a kid and you've got him in a Hallmark special. He needs to see what feels right, how he fits in."

Cindi shook her head. "That is so touchy-feely, Paul. Since you started teaching, you've gone soft as butter." But she was smiling. Then she turned to Noah. "She's a single mother. Never forget that. She wants what's best for her child. Whatever you do, don't get her hopes up."

"The only hope she has about me is that I'll leave them alone," he said, not happy about that, he realized. Mel was as beautiful, fresh and full of fire as he remembered. Simply seeing her made him feel better.

She'd changed, too, though. She was softer somehow. And when she looked at that little boy, her face almost glowed. That's what parenthood did, he guessed. Well, motherhood anyway. Fathers didn't have to change at all. He knew that firsthand.

He remembered dogging his dad's heels, handing him tools when he worked on the muscle cars he loved, asking questions, showing off what he'd read, trying to impress the man who barely tolerated his presence. Some men weren't cut out to be fathers. The odds were good that Mel was correct—the best thing for Daniel might well be for Noah to stay the hell away.

CHAPTER FIVE

A HALF HOUR LATER, Noah pulled up in front of the ranch-style house where Mel lived with her mother and Daniel. *His son.* The thought still sent shock waves through him. And the kid was nearly a year old. Noah had missed it all—Mel's pregnancy, the birth, all the growth milestones since then.

Stupidly, he felt left out.

Noah tucked the box of LEGO he'd bought under his arm. Who knew Circle Ks sold toys? He'd stopped for gas and spotted the item. He knocked on the door, looking forward to seeing that sweet, smiling boy again.

Through the door came an ungodly wail. Well, not sweet and smiling all the time. The door opened and an older woman, shorter than Mel, but clearly related, said, "Noah, *bienvenido.* I'm Irena." Her dark eyes held the same humor and intelligence as Mel's, though there were dark circles beneath them. She looked tired.

"Pleased to meet you, Irena."

Daniel's crying came from deeper in the house. A fat sheepdog groaned to his feet and waddled over to sniff Noah's crotch.

"Paco, no!" Irena said. "So sorry. This one is *tan flojo* unless he can trouble a visitor."

Tan flojo meant *so lazy,* he remembered. "I don't mind." Noah patted the dog's head. With a happy sigh,

Paco dropped to his belly on the tile, legs splayed so Noah had to step over him to enter the house.

"Our hope is only that if a thief comes, perhaps he will break his neck falling over Paco."

Mel approached from the kitchen, a sobbing Daniel propped on her hip, his face smeared with orange goop.

"We're running late," Mel said loudly enough to be heard over the crying. "I still have to bathe him. Maybe we should reschedule?" Something was amok with her face. Then he realized she had makeup on only one eye and only half her hair was curly.

"I've got time." He held up the box of LEGO. "I got these for him."

"You didn't need to bring a gift." She smiled uncertainly.

"Maybe he'll cheer up." He started to tear open the box.

Mel stopped his hand. "I'm sorry, but he'll swallow the pieces. He doesn't have the fine motor skills yet." She showed him the corner of the box: *for ages 6+.* "But later on…they'll be great."

Irena approached. "Give to me Daniel," she said to Mel. "Go to finish getting ready."

"But you should rest, *Mamá.*"

Her mother thought this over. "*Sí,* I should. Here." She thrust the wailing Daniel at Noah, who braced him against his good arm. "Be of use."

"He's too fussy for a stranger," Mel objected.

"Noah is no stranger. The *papá* calms. *Véte.* Go." Irena shooed her daughter toward the hall.

"He likes to be jiggled," Mel said to Noah, watching him as she backed away, looking worried that Noah couldn't handle the task. She had a point.

Daniel paused the tears long enough to consider the

stranger holding him like a sack from Kroger's. The kid
smelled like canned spaghetti and something else—like
fabric softener, only more human.

"If you're thinking stranger-danger, I'm harmless. I
swear."

Not buying it, Daniel gave a piercing wail.

"Hey, now, don't cry, little man." Noah bobbled him
against his hip, except the kid's head kind of flopped
around on his skinny neck. It could snap so easy. The
whole setup seemed fragile as hell. There should be a
helmet, he figured, until they grew neck muscles—or
quit falling down. Noah cupped his hand around the
kid's skull to prop it up, deciding to walk around to see
if that helped.

He took a step, but hit Paco's soft belly. His bad leg
gave a little, so he lunged for balance.

Daniel blinked, then smiled. Hmm.

"You liked that?" Noah leaned Daniel out on his good
arm, bracing him with the other, and took a turn.

Daniel considered the sensation, then grinned. He
wanted more. *All right.*

Noah did it again. And again. Daniel gasped for
breath and squealed each time. Noah kept spinning,
switching directions, going faster, then slower, changing it up. Daniel shrieked with delight.

"What are you doing?" Mel said from across the
room, her eyes wide.

"Making him laugh," Noah said.

She joined him. "He's supposed to be winding down
for bed, not going on a carnival ride." She stood close to
take Daniel back, her arm brushing Noah's chest. Their
eyes met and attraction whip-cracked between them.

"You look great, Mel," he said. Her hair fell in soft
curls to her bare shoulders, the skin looking like vel-

vet. Her lips shone red and her eyes were dramatic with thick lashes.

"Thank you." A blush flared in her cheeks, making her even prettier. She caught her lip between her teeth the way she did just before she climaxed and Noah became instantly hard.

He glanced away and stepped back.

"I'll be as quick as I can with his bath and bedtime," she said, "but there's a routine we go through."

"Take your time," he said, happy for a chance to get blood flowing above the waist again. He watched her leave the room.

Then Irena crooked a finger at him from the hallway. "Be of use," she said. He followed her down the hall and she motioned toward the bathroom, where he heard rushing water.

He braced for the panic he felt in small spaces, but the room was brightly lit with a high ceiling, so he relaxed again.

It looked like a toy store had exploded inside. There were toys and buckets and plastic animals everywhere. The tile above the bathtub was covered with shapes and sea creatures and letters.

In the tub, Daniel was chewing on a duck-shaped sponge. Mel was on her knees, one hand bracing Daniel's back, the other testing the water. Her pants stretched tight across her backside, making him want to put a hand there to see if it felt as good as it looked.

For God's sake, he was ogling a mother bathing her baby. Her forced his gaze away and said, "Can I help?"

Startled, Mel twisted toward him. "No!" She caught herself and softened her tone, "It's really a one-person job."

He sat on the closed toilet lid to rest his leg.

Mel had her attention on Noah. Behind her, Noah saw Daniel reach for a red bucket, slip and start to fall, so he lunged across Mel to catch the kid before his head struck the faucet. Doing so, he connected chest to chest with Mel. Water splashed them both.

Clearly flustered, Mel shut off the water and scooted Daniel into the middle of the tub. "You see what I mean. It's crowded in here." Water had turned her shirt bloodred and revealed the lacy outline of her bra. He could smell her perfume, too, and it made him a little dizzy.

"Yeah," he said. "I guess it is a little tight. I'll see you out there."

When she emerged, it was only a few minutes later and he rose from the sofa. "That was quick."

"I let my mother put him to bed." She smiled nervously. "You're all soaked and splotched. That'll teach you to stay out of the battle zone."

Battle zone. Instantly, his mind flashed to a memory. He sat in the HMV, as it moved between the cluster of buildings. His scalp prickled. He had the coppery taste of fear on his tongue. Then windshield cracks… Bullets pinging the front grill… His ears ringing… Fighting with the door handle… Daggett grabbing him… Shouts… Fuller crumpling to the dirt…

Fear settled in Noah's chest like black crows on a winter tree.

Mel noticed his reaction and her eyes went wide. "Oh. Did that remind you of…Iraq? I didn't think. I'm sorry, Noah."

"Forget it. It's stupid. It's nothing." But he was sweating and a sharp pain slashed through his head, as though someone had split his skull with an ax. He hated that he'd reacted and that Mel had seen. He pressed his palms to both sides of his head and dropped to the sofa.

"That's not nothing." She moved closer. "You're in pain."

"You got aspirin?"

She fetched him water and pills.

He took them, then tried to smile.

"Would an ice pack help?"

"This should do it." He leaned his head back. "The ones that hit fast and sharp don't last long if I treat them quickly."

"You have worse ones?"

"The migraines. Yeah. But I don't get them as much anymore." He gritted his teeth against a deep stab of pain and fisted his hands.

"I'm so sorry."

"Not a big deal." He didn't want her pity. He was pissed. He thought he was done with out-of-the-blue episodes. "So who's religious? You or Irena or both?" He motioned toward an alcove shelf where candles were lit in front of statues of the *Virgen de Guadalupe* and another holy figurine.

Mel blushed. "Neither, really. Religion is like a wishing well to my mother. The St. Margaret is hers, but *La Virgen* is mine. The church we went to when I was a little girl had a beautiful statue and the priest told the story of her appearance in Mexico in such a memorable way. She gives me comfort, I guess."

"So what's the story on St. Margaret?"

Her smile was sheepish. "She's the patron saint of unwed mothers."

He grinned. "So Irena's, what, praying for a husband for you?"

"Mothers worry. What can I say?"

"Yeah, I get that." He looked at her again, drawn to her dark eyes and dramatic mouth. She had such strong features. Like her personality. "So Daniel's asleep then?" he said to stop himself from staring at Mel.

"Should be. He needs his bedtime routine or he fights to stay awake. It's like he thinks he's missing out on a party."

"That came from me. My mother used to bitch about me staying up late."

"He doesn't like a lot of clothes on at night, either."

"Me, neither."

"I remember." Instantly, their gazes locked. Mel's top shivered as her breathing quickened. So did his.

Abruptly, Mel averted her gaze, fiddling with her fingers. "He sleeps like you, too—all spread out. He gets warm, I guess. You should see when he's teething. You'd almost think he has a fever."

"Teething is tough?"

"He fusses some. It helps if I give him a frozen wash-cloth to bite on."

"Sounds like you've got being a parent nailed."

"No way. You're never sure. Every day is different and there is no clear path." She was twisting her fingers hard.

"You're nervous," he said. He stilled her hands with his, linking fingers. She relaxed beneath his touch.

"I don't know how to act around you."

"Act however you feel, Mel. My headache's fading," he said, still holding her hands. "Thanks to the aspirin—and seeing you." She smelled of baby soap and her perfume and he was glad to simply sit beside her. "For the past year, I've been wandering, I guess. In my life and in my mind."

"I'm so sor—"

"Please don't feel sorry for me. My point is that this is nice." He lifted their linked hands to his mouth and kissed the back of one of hers.

"Noah," she breathed, shaking the way she had the first time he kissed her—so hard their teeth had rattled against each other. Need poured through him as it had two years ago, washing away everything since then, like highway crud beneath a desert downpour.

He'd felt weighed down since Iraq, as if he still wore casts and thick bandages around his skull, still hobbled on crutches, afraid to cough or laugh for the pain. He wasn't one to cling to the past. He knew how to step lightly in life, but somehow he hadn't been able to shake those shadows, that regret, that guilt.

Here with Mel, he felt lighter, easier in his skin, more himself. He pulled their joined hands to his chest and leaned in.

She made a tiny sound and her lips parted. He had to kiss her, if only to remember how she tasted, so he pressed his mouth to hers, holding still, waiting for her to react—to pull away or stay.

With a fierce sigh, she grabbed the back of his neck and yanked him tighter against her. Stay. Definitely stay. He smiled against her mouth. Mel didn't do things halfway. She'd been so impatient for him to enter her that first time, he'd had to nearly tie her down so he could explore her body's curves and swells, her velvet skin, the warm, wet need between her legs.

Her tongue found his now, pressing it, dancing with it, eager as his own. Noah fell back on the couch, taking her with him, their lips still together. One of her legs moved between his, sliding across his erection.

He reached beneath her top, his fingers under her

bra, pushing it out of the way to fill his hands with her full breasts.

"It's been so long," she moaned.

"Yeah." He moved one hand to where her thighs met, finding her through the fabric of her pants.

"Oh…oh…." She rolled to the side to give him better access.

Squeak.

They froze. Mel reached behind her hip to pull out the source of the noise—a rubber chicken.

"Daniel's?" he asked, but a snort made him look over to find Paco, eye level with them, staring. "Yours?" He held it out.

The dog took the chicken daintily in his mouth and lumbered off.

Mel sat up and straightened her shirt. Noah sat beside her. She glanced at him, then away. "I guess the chemistry's the same."

"Yeah." He watched her profile, a million thoughts in his head.

She looked at him. "But we're not."

"No." He was far from the man he'd been. She was weighed down, too, but in a good way, by the child who was her whole world. Two years ago, career and ambition had connected them. What tied them now?

The unintended collision of sperm and egg, to put it in crude biological terms. An accident, but a child had resulted. Daniel. And that changed everything.

"I wish we could go back. I do," she said. She touched his face, desire sparking in her eyes for a moment. "But it's not possible."

He looked at her. "If I hadn't walked into that day-care place today, would I ever know about Daniel?" The idea hollowed him out, disturbed him in ways he didn't fully understand.

"Would you have looked for me?" Her words had an edge.

"Before the attack, I intended to. I thought of you a lot over there. But after what happened…"

"So probably not," she said abruptly, not wanting to hear whatever excuse he had, he could tell, so he didn't give her one.

"But I did run into you and now I know I have a son. That won't change. That's forever."

She stared at him, her forehead creasing with concern. "I know that as his biological father you have certain rights, but I hope that you'll respect what I'm trying to—"

"Stop. Mel." He locked on to her gaze. "You're the parent here. I would never interfere with how you raise Daniel." He gave a rough laugh. "I've never been much of a boyfriend, let alone a father."

She smiled, almost with sympathy.

"But I can't just walk away," he said, more firmly than he had with Cindi and Paul.

"Yes, you can," Mel said as firmly. "You didn't want this, you didn't sign up for this or—"

"But it happened." He let that settle in. "What were you going to tell him when he asked why he doesn't have a dad like all the other kids?"

She looked truly uncomfortable now. "That when he came along, he was a surprise and that you and I cared about each other, but not in a forever or family kind of way. And that you respected my wishes and—"

"And what? Walked out of his life? See ya later, gotta jet, hope you get through college okay? That's not right, Mel, and you know it."

"I haven't thought it all through, okay? He's barely a year old. I don't know what might happen later on."

It dawned on him what she meant. "You could get married. Right." That idea didn't set well at his caveman core. "But he'd be the stepfather, not the biological father. You'd still tell Daniel about me. He'd want to know."

He kept picturing Daniel's face when Noah had spun him around and he'd squealed, his dimple popping, his eyes lighting up. That little boy would demand the truth about everything he cared about.

"I figured I had time, okay? Don't forget I thought you'd signed off already, that we'd never see you again. I'm as caught off guard as you are."

"You're right." He released his anger instantly. "Still, I'm his father and I should be there for him."

"I'm sorry, but I don't see how that would work. Do you? You're in Phoenix to help your grandmother, right? Will you be staying long?"

"I've got the ASU job at least through the end of the year. After that...I have no idea." He wished he were surer of his situation. He wasn't about to make promises he couldn't keep. "I can call. I can visit."

"I know you want to do the right thing, Noah. My father felt the same way. He visited. He promised to do it more, but he never managed. He wasn't part of my life and it was awful." She looked so sad he wanted to crush her into his arms and promise to fix it.

"It hurt like hell," she continued. "I couldn't understand why he didn't want to be with us. How could he forget me? Being in limbo, living with maybe-next-time hopes that got crushed over and over... It was agony. It would have been better if he never knew about me. I don't want Daniel to ever feel that pain." Her eyes shone with unshed tears and fire.

"Neither do I," he said.

"Then go, Noah," she said softly. "Get on with your life and we'll get on with ours. Sometimes the right thing to do is to walk away."

He looked at her, his thoughts splintering in all directions. He'd had a piss-poor father, so he knew the pain of not being enough, of dying for attention, for proof that he was loved. He'd hated being that needy, even as a kid. He wouldn't want that for Daniel, either. Noah was his father's son, he knew that cold. Restless, career-driven, selfish. He'd make a lousy dad.

He *wanted* to do the right thing, but that didn't mean he could manage it. Still, some stubborn part of him would not leave this alone.

"I need to think about this. We both do."

"I have thought about it. I won't change my mind. I can't afford to."

"A minute ago, you were ready to rip off my clothes and now you want me to leave and never come back?"

"I'm human, Noah." Her expression seemed sad. "But I have to see beyond my own needs to what's best for Daniel. So do you." She lifted her chin, determined.

"It's late. I should go." There was no use arguing with her any more tonight. He patted her leg and stood.

She walked him to the door.

"I am glad I ran into you today," he said softly. "It would have been a mistake not to track you down. It's good to see you again."

"I know." Her gaze raced over his face. "It's been a long time since I— Well, let's just say I don't get out much." She sighed. "And if it were only me, no Daniel…"

"Yeah?"

"We'd be in bed right now," she said.

The possibility thundered through him, making it hard to think.

"I wish it weren't so complicated." Her face kind of crumpled.

"I know." He pulled her into his arms and rested his cheek against her hair, breathing her in, stealing the pleasure of her body pressed against his for one last moment.

"You have to go," she said, pushing out of his arms, clearly reluctant.

"I'll call you," he said.

"I won't change my mind."

He leaned in and kissed her. He couldn't help it.

"I'm not kidding, Noah." Her eyes were so big in the moonlight.

"I know you're not."

"Good night." But when she shut the door, she was smiling.

Noah turned toward the street. It was a muggy July night and crickets buzzed loudly. He looked up. Monsoon clouds were darker shapes against the indigo sky lit by a full golden moon.

Alone in the night, his mood abruptly sank. Maybe he should walk away. It was what Mel wanted and Daniel wouldn't know the difference. Not until he was much older and Mel would give him that speech.

The idea made Noah feel dead inside.

He pictured Daniel in his crib, legs and arms spread wide. Did Mel sing him that Spanish rhyme about the frog to put him to sleep?

I can call. I can visit. That had been an empty offer and he knew it.

Let it go. It would be simpler for everyone. His life was in flux. But something held him here, stubborn and stuck, and he knew he wasn't done yet. Maybe Mel wasn't, either.

CHAPTER SIX

THE NEXT MORNING, MEL headed into the kitchen to fix breakfast, yawning and exhausted. She'd stupidly lain awake for hours, reliving those couch moments with Noah. The years had melted away and she'd felt again like a newly minted photojournalist sleeping with a man who shared her passion for the truth, for the *story,* in words or pictures.

That weekend she'd felt so carefree. It seemed like a lifetime ago. *Carefree* was out of her vocabulary now. She was a single parent of an active toddler with an ailing mother and she didn't dare forget that for a second.

She found her mother making oatmeal and Daniel gnawing on the box of LEGO he'd dragged off the kitchen table, where Mel had left it.

When she'd gotten him out of bed, he'd fussed until she twirled him in a circle the way Noah had done. He'd squealed with delight.

Guys roughhoused more, she realized. Daniel would need masculine influences in his life, for sure. But it couldn't be Noah. Noah was not a family man. He'd told her that from the beginning and she believed him.

He was different since Iraq, too. *Wandering,* he'd said. Lost. That's how he seemed to her. The words *battle zone* had slammed him with a brutal headache. That suggested emotional turmoil to her.

She remembered that in his statements to the press

he'd taken blame for his capture. Military experts had ranted about the irresponsibility of allowing media on the front lines of battle. That had to have hit Noah hard. He wasn't even reporting now. That had to be part of what he meant about *wandering*.

He'd get back to it, she knew. That was who he was. Even if he wanted to be stand-up about being a dad, there was no place in Noah's life for that.

In the end, Mel and Daniel would get hurt.

If a man were to be seriously interested in her, he would have to love Daniel as much as she did, want to be with him every day. Daniel would be his whole world, not a quick phone call on his birthday or a check for Christmas.

I can call. I can visit. Everything in Mel knew that would not work. She'd lived through that. She didn't want to make Daniel live it, too.

Once a little time passed, and the reality set in, Noah would realize she was right. Noah was nothing if not a realist and he knew his own limits.

She put the LEGO on the refrigerator so Daniel couldn't reach them.

"You have a nice time, you two?" her mother asked.

"We talked, if that's what you mean."

"You have color in your cheeks. I think more happened than talk."

She turned to grab some juice to avoid answering.

"But he comes again to see us, *sí?*"

"It's better for Daniel if he doesn't."

"But what about for you, *mi'ja?* What is better for you?"

"Not Noah. He won't be here long." She went to the cupboard for a glass.

"Perhaps he stays on, now that fatherhood comes to him."

She spun on her mother. "Stop it. Please, *Mamá*. Noah is not father material and he knows it. We both know it."

"He will learn."

"You're making wishes again." She'd been right to tell Noah to stay away. And when he called her, she would say it again.

"I understand your fear, *mi'ja*. It was hard for me when you were small and we were alone in a new country. I spoke little English."

"You were strong and brave. I loved that about you. I learned from you."

"I hid how hard it was."

"You didn't need a man to be complete and neither do I." She knew that, for all his good intentions, Noah would behave as her own father had. They had the same love of travel, the same career obsession. History would repeat itself and she wanted nothing to do with it.

"Not to be complete. To be more. *Más rico*." *Richer.*

Mel rolled her eyes.

Her mother flinched and bent, holding her stomach.

"What's wrong?" Mel rushed to her side, bracing her with one arm.

"A little pain is all." Irena forced a smile.

"Maybe you should rest today. I don't have a lot in the studio—a couple of portraits, some prints to show a client. Marla and I can juggle the desk."

"There is a new couple coming to see—for when their baby comes."

"I can handle the tour, *Mamá*. Don't worry."

Her mother sat heavily on the chair, in too much pain to hide it. Irena suffered in silence far too often.

"I think you should go to that support group the nurse told us about." It was for people living with cancer. "You can go and let your hair down."

"Let my hair...?" She put her hand to her thick braid.

"It's an expression. It means to be yourself and not hold back."

"I don't need a group to be myself, *mi'ja*. This I cannot escape." She patted Mel's hand.

"And I don't need a man for my life to be *más rico*." She patted back.

They smiled at each other, recognizing their separate stubbornness.

"I'll go with you to the first meeting, how's that?" Mel said.

"I suppose that would be all right."

"Eh, eh," Daniel said, reaching up for Mel to hold him. He leaned back against her arm, clearly wanting another of Noah's spins.

"Already, Daniel misses his *papá*," her mother said in mock sorrow.

Holy hell. As if her own confused feelings weren't bad enough, both her mother and her child were rooting for more time with Noah.

The stupid, dreamy part of her had felt a twinge when she saw Daniel in Noah's arms, spinning around, both of them smiling so big. It was the hopeless fantasy of being a couple—parents together, loving their child— a normal, happy family. But it was impossible.

She'd seen utter horror in Noah's eyes when he first realized who Daniel was. He'd looked so trapped. If he'd been a fox, he'd have chewed off a leg to escape. First reactions were the truest. *Remember that, chica.*

"Okay, drama queen, we're here," Noah said, parking in front of Bright Blossoms a few days later.

"I'm a *princess,* Uncle Noah. *Mommy* is the queen." Emma rolled her eyes at his ignorance. "And you are not my friend today." She clutched the scuba goggles she'd brought for "show day."

"Sorry, but friends don't let friends eat too much sugar."

"It was a *secret!*"

Cindi had asked about the purple stain on Emma's dress from the day Noah had met Mel and Daniel and Noah had confessed his foul deed. Cindi had not been pleased. *Do not submit to emotional blackmail, Noah. Have a backbone. She's three years old, for God's sake.*

Now Emma refused to take his hand, marching ahead of him into the building.

He'd offered to bring Emma to day care for a selfish reason. He'd left a message with Mel about getting together again, but she hadn't called back. She no doubt hoped to wait him out, but he wanted a little more time with Daniel. And with Mel, truth be known.

Irena was at the check-in counter and smiled at him. "Noah, hello. And, *señorita,*" she said to Emma, pouting at his side. *"Qué pasa, chulita?"*

"Uncle Noah is mean, Missus R."

"I ratted her out with her mother about extra Popsicles."

"Uh-uh," Irena said, winking at him. She wagged a finger at Emma. "*Tu* mommy knows best. What have you there?" She pointed at the goggles. "Is that for show time? *Córrale, mi' ja.* Run, so you don't be late."

Emma turned and scampered off, putting on the goggles as she went.

"So my daughter gives you the brush-off, *sí?*" Irena

said. "That is how you say? *Brush-off?*" She flicked her hand, as if shooing someone away.

He laughed. "Pretty much, yeah."

"But you are the father. That is not proper. I try to talk to her of this."

"Mel's looking out for Daniel the best she can." The words came out slowly and even as he said them, he hated the truth they represented.

"You, too, give yourself no chance?" Irena gave him a quelling look.

"Anyway, I want to talk to Mel about another visit. Is she here?"

"This morning, no. She has a photograph outdoors." She hesitated. "But, you know…I have the good idea. Tonight she comes with me to a meeting. She thinks to bring Daniel, but he will fuss. I was going to ask one of my girls, but it must be you instead who will watch over him. Be of use, Noah. Okay?"

"You want me to babysit?"

"And after, you and my daughter will talk more."

"I doubt Mel will be down for either idea."

"But she is wrong. My daughter needs your *chistes*— your jokes, Noah. She smiles with you. Since Daniel, she is serious always. Also, since my illness. I make her feel too low."

"You're sick?"

"*Sí,* I have cancer. The treatments make me tired. Melodía worries."

"I'm sorry to hear that." It explained how tired Irena looked and why Mel had told her to rest the other night.

"So, you will come tonight? Dinner, six o'clock. I make my famous enchiladas."

"As long as you clear it with Mel, sure."

"*Sí, sí. No hay problema.*"

"Then it's a plan." He smiled, not sure he actually knew what he was in for with the babysitting, but he'd give it a try. "Which room is Daniel in, by the way?" He might as well take a peek at the kid.

"In the second playroom. He is *muy mimada,* very spoiled, by my girls."

He spotted Daniel right off, as if he were outlined in white light. He was smaller than the other kids, but strong, Noah thought. He was patting the back of a sobbing girl holding a headless doll.

Then Noah noticed Daniel was holding the head. Uh-oh. Had he decapitated the doll and was now apologizing for it? What a scamp.

Daniel was his son. His *son.* With his DNA and his dimples. He would probably hate asparagus and V-necked sweaters and love snow, flat pillows and driving fast. Would he be a good writer? Or would he have Mel's artist's eye? Or both?

Noah turned to go, still smiling, but the minute he stepped out the door, reality hit him. *Get over it. You were an accidental sperm donor. You never wanted kids and you'd be a terrible parent, just like your old man.*

Sure, it looked easy now, when Daniel was cute and his needs were simple, but what about later on, when life got tough? When he got hurt or sick? When a girl broke his heart or his best friends ganged up on him? Or he started beer-bonging or doing drugs or screwing up in school? What the hell use would Noah be then? If he were like his dad, next to none.

No, being a father was far more than spinning a baby around a few times until he giggled or noticing how much he looked like you.

That was ego shit for sure.

Maybe this babysitting gig would clear out that fuzzy

fantasy for good and he'd be happy to do what Mel wanted—leave and not let the door hit him on the ass on the way out of their lives.

"WHAT DO YOU MEAN you got a babysitter?" Mel asked her mother. "Without checking with me? Who is it? Someone from Bright Blossoms?"

"You will be glad. You'll see."

"If Daniel gets restless in the meeting, I'll walk him outside." Daniel had terrible separation anxiety, something she'd hoped he would have grown out of by now.

"This is better, *mi'ja*. Trust in me."

"Okay, I guess." If a babysitter made her mother more confident about going to the meeting, Mel would not object.

On top of hiring a sitter, her mother had insisted on making her special enchiladas, which kept her too long on her feet. She'd set out the good china, too. Sometimes her mother made her nuts.

Mel got Daniel into his chair and bibbed him up. He was into squishy foods lately, so she'd prepared vitamin-fortified oatmeal with some squash she'd chopped up with butter and a little brown sugar to cut the sharpness.

She had set both warmed dishes on Daniel's tray when the doorbell rang. The sitter was early, but that would give Daniel more time to get used to her.

She opened the door to…*Noah?* He held a bunch of orange star lilies in one hand and a neon-blue tricycle in the other.

"*You're* the babysitter?"

"Surprise!" her mother called from behind her. "I said you would like."

"I'm a surprise?" Noah looked past Mel to Irena.

"I decide this is best." Her mother beamed as if she'd pulled off the best stunt ever. "He comes to bring Emma today so I ask him this favor."

"Okay if I come in?" Noah asked.

Mel had unconsciously blocked him. "Sorry, sure." She stepped back.

"Just in time for supper," Irena said. "I make plenty."

Mel rolled her eyes. That explained the complicated dish and the china. "You schemed with my mother?" she asked him.

"She swore she'd clear it with you."

"Well, she didn't."

"Anyway, here." He held out the flowers. "The colors reminded me of you."

"They're beautiful," she said, taking the bouquet. "And is that for Daniel?" She motioned at the tricycle, which he'd set on the floor. Kids didn't ride tricycles until they were two or three.

He caught her look. "What? Does he already have one?"

"Not yet, no. He's a little…young."

"So he'll grow into it. Every kid needs goals."

"You don't have to bring presents every time you come over." She hesitated. "Not that you'll be coming over again." She stopped herself. "That didn't come out right. I mean, there's no expectation that you'll—"

"Mel," he said softly, taking her by the arms, "your mom asked me to watch Daniel tonight. That's all that's going on." He held her gaze, reassuring her. "I brought a gift, since I struck out on the LEGO, okay?"

"I don't mean to be defensive." She simply knew she didn't dare get comfortable with any parentlike behavior from Noah. She could feel the happy-family fantasy ready to pop into her head at the smallest sign.

At that moment, Daniel let out a howl of distress from the dining table.

"Dios mio!" her mother exclaimed, running to check him.

Mel saw Daniel must have touched the pan of enchiladas her mother had taken from the oven. Mel rushed over, Noah at her side. Her mother was at the refrigerator, getting a stick of butter, but Noah grabbed ice from a water glass and pressed it to Daniel's fingers.

Startled, Daniel stopped crying and stared up at Noah. He braced himself to shriek, then seemed to realize the pain was gone. His small shoulders relaxed, his face lost its grimace and he gave a watery smile.

"Gotta watch out for hot stuff in the kitchen, buddy," Noah said.

"I'm so sorry," her mother said. *"Qué idiota!* I was not thinking. I am too much hurrying. Tonight, this meeting, it makes me so *nerviosa....*"

"It's okay. It was an accident." Mel was jolted by her mother's admission. Irena had always been sturdy as a tree in a crisis, but she was evidently more shaken up than she'd let on. Mel hoped this support group would offer the comfort her mother didn't seem willing to ask for from her daughter.

"Let Mommy see, *cariño,*" Mel said to Daniel, examining his hand, which looked so small against Noah's broad palm.

"It's just red, no blistering," Noah said. "Mild first degree. He's fine."

"So, you're trained in first aid?" she asked him, so close she could see the flecks of gold in his brown eyes. They were both leaning over Daniel.

"I was a lifeguard in college. Does that qualify me for the job?"

"Depending on how recently you renewed your certification," she joked. *"Sana, sana,"* she said to Daniel, and kissed his finger.

"That's part of that rhyme. Something about a frog, right?"

She smiled, surprised he'd remembered. "Tadpole. *Colita de rana*—basically *little frog's tail.*" She recited the poem, translating it line by line.

"That's very sweet."

"It's very Latino. Stoic, but hopeful, I guess."

Noah watched her for a long moment, as if caught up in what she'd said, until her mother motioned him to sit at the small table. She filled his plate with a generous serving of enchiladas.

"This looks great," he said. With his deep voice and size, he seemed to take up a lot of space in the small kitchen. He winked at Mel, then took a bite. "Mmm," he said.

"Eh, eh," Daniel said, reaching for Noah's plate.

Noah fed him a bite. Daniel grinned up at him. "Best enchiladas, ever, am I right?" Noah said. "This is great, Irena."

"It is recipe of my *mamá.* She had a small *restaurante* in San Vicente. When I first came to the north, I sold tamales downtown."

"Mel told me the story of how you came to the U.S."

"She did?" Her mother shot Mel a look. "You told this to Noah?"

"It…came up. When we met." Her mother would see that as evidence that Mel cared more for Noah than she'd let on, since the story was so private.

"You were brave to smuggle those photos across the border."

"I never forget the man's face when he give them to

me. *Do not fail,* he say to me. And in the end, he is lost. Killed like so many."

"Like you would have been, *Mamá,*" Mel said, her throat going tight at the thought. "You were lucky to escape. We both were lucky."

Noah didn't speak, just held her mother's gaze—respectful and serious. Mel saw her mother take that in, saw the connection between them, so much said without a word.

Finally, her mother broke the silence. "My only regret is that my experiences make my daughter to decide to take dangerous pictures. She almost was shot, did you know this?"

"I wasn't in danger, *Mamá.* I told you that." She looked at Noah. "I took pictures of a dogfight in Tucson for a *News Day* story."

"Those people who fight the dogs are *animales.* They shoot the *perritos* who lose. You think they wouldn't kill a nosy photographer?"

"I was careful. I had Dave Roberts with me and pepper spray."

"Pepper spray against a shotgun? *Chulita.* She thinks she protects me with hiding the truth, Noah. She must always to be strong, my daughter. Though I am proud that her photos make change to the law."

"That's an exaggeration," Mel said, flushing. "After the story came out, there was a state bill to tighten the punishment for dogfighting, but it was already in the works before that."

"But you contributed. Photos stop you cold, remember? Make people see what they'd rather ignore? Someone smart once told me that." Noah's gaze held her close, admiring and sexual at once. Her entire body tingled.

"Melodía is sad not to be with her newspaper now, but I am happy she is safe and that I see her and my grandson every day."

"That's the silver lining, I guess," Noah said.

"Of course, it would be better with a husband," her mother said with a dramatic sigh, "but *así es la vida.*"

"*Mamá,* please."

"I am only saying that we make the best of what happens, no?"

"*Así es la vida,*" Noah said, clearly fighting a grin.

"See? Noah agrees," her mother said, playing innocent.

Noah burst out laughing. Mel blew air up through her bangs.

"And you," her mother said to Noah, "you write stories in dangerous places, too. Melodía tells me you are famous for this. And we see on the news that you got so hurt."

Noah's smile disappeared instantly and his expression went wooden. "I don't write stories like that now," he said so flatly it was as though a wall had shot up between him and the rest of the table.

"More enchiladas?" Mel asked to cover for the moment. "*Mamá,* you should tell Noah about your dream— Bright Blossoms."

"Yeah," Noah said. "How did you get started?" He shot Mel a look of gratitude for the subject change and took another helping.

"Always, I want this. I have just my Melodía, no more *niños,* and I begin in my home with *vecinos*—neighbors. I take the classes to learn child development and how to make a business and I grow until I can rent a space. And so it goes. *Así es.*"

Noah asked more questions and her mother answered eagerly. Mel enjoyed seeing her animated, her eyes twinkling, her hands moving. Noah was able to get her talking in more detail than Mel had ever heard, explaining how her approach had drawn clients from nearby offices, as well as the neighborhood, and how she chose and trained her caregivers.

Again, Mel had that risky feeling of coziness. As though Noah belonged here. Their little family, enjoying dinner together. And later, Noah and she would make their way to bed, to make love, bodies moving as one, Noah's mouth on hers, his hands in all the right places....

So insane. Dios mio, what was wrong with her?

Mel glanced at the clock. "I'd better make some notes for you about Daniel—his routines, emergency numbers, all that."

"For two hours I need notes?" Noah asked.

"Things happen fast with kids. He burned his hand in a few seconds." She hesitated. "We won't be that far away, so maybe my cell number is enough." She handed him one of her cards. "If you have any questions, call. *Any* question. *Any*time."

"If I can't figure out the TV remote, I'll give you a ring."

She rolled her eyes. "Let's hope that's the worst problem you face."

"I go to get my purse." Her mother left the table.

"I'll handle his bath and bed when I get back," Mel said to Noah. "As it gets closer to eight, do quiet activities so he's not too wound up for bed."

"So no paintball or joyriding?"

She smiled. "Give him a snack. Some Cheerios or half a banana, but peel off the strings. And nothing with sugar."

"No sugar. Got it."

"When you wipe his face and hands, use warm water on one of the soft cloths. No soap. He's afraid of soap in his eyes."

"That's because soap is for sissies, right, big guy?" He held up his palm for a high-five.

Daniel surveyed him, blinking.

"You don't know how to high-five?" He shook his head in mock dismay. "Pitiful, Mel." Noah lifted Daniel's pudgy arm and patted his palm. "That's a high-five. You'll need it, along with some hand grips, a few wrestling moves and a chest bump to be considered a true dude. Let's go again. High-five." He raised his hand for Daniel to slap.

He did it.

"Excellent!" Noah said.

Daniel beamed and held his hand up for another try.

This was a good time to slip away, Mel decided, while Daniel was focused on Noah. "Bye-bye, Danny. We'll be back soon. Mommy loves you!" she said cheerfully, giving him a quick kiss on the head. She motioned for her mother to join her at the door.

"Mah...Mah!" Daniel called to her, his voice sharp with alarm. He rocked up and down in his chair, wanting to go with them, his little face full of panic.

"Mommy will be back soon," she said brightly, but his fear was a knife to her heart. "You have fun with Noah, okay? He has separation anxiety," she explained. "Keep him busy and he should be okay in a few minutes."

"I've got this," Noah said, trying to be encouraging, though he looked startled by the outburst. "No worries."

Mel hesitated, but her mother tugged her out the door. She was right, of course. It was only two hours. How bad could it get? She was afraid to find out.

CHAPTER SEVEN

DANIEL'S FACE WAS ALMOST purple as he wailed for his mother in such desperate grief Noah's heart went out to him. Separation anxiety, huh? Sounded like a fancy name for the misery of childhood. A couple of high-fives weren't going to do shit for this. "If she were my mom, I'd miss her, too, chief."

Dinner was clearly over, so he would clean the kid up. Noah tried to lift him out of the chair, but his legs got caught beneath the tray, making him cry harder. "Jesus, it's like dinner prison here." By the time he'd wiggled the kid out, he was quietly blubbering and looked scared of Noah.

"I'm on your side, little dude. I swear."

The kid's face was a mess, so Noah set him next to the kitchen sink and used the bib to swipe off the biggest chunks. One look at that crumpled face with huge tears rolling down and Noah decided to forget the water, too. "So what if your face looks like a car crash. Life's messy."

He carried Daniel into the front room and sat with him on his lap to fish out toys from a big basket, wiggling one after the other in his face, while Daniel sobbed, his little shoulders shaking, his breaths shuddering out.

Poor kid.

Meanwhile, the dog was acting weird. He stood on

the tile by the front door and whenever he caught Noah's eye, he gave a keening whine. He wanted out? He
had a dog door, didn't he?

What about a walk?

Of course! Noah would take Daniel and the dog for
a walk to the park at the end of the street. Fresh air…
movement…perfect.

He located a leash on a hook by the back door, tucked
Daniel into a football hold and set off, leaning back
to slow Paco and preserve the strength in his bad leg,
which already throbbed. Even then, they were almost
galloping. Worried that Daniel's brain was getting
sloshed, Noah put him up on his shoulders like dads at
the zoo. Daniel squealed with delight.

Score. Noah smiled, as the boy curved himself
around Noah's head, clapping Noah's face so that Noah's vision blinked on and off as soft palms covered
first one eye, then the other.

He couldn't believe what a relief it was to make the
kid happy and how awful it felt to make him cry. He
had new empathy for Mel. When Daniel had objected
to her departure, she'd looked like she'd taken a punch
to the gut. The whole parenthood gig was no cakewalk.

They went along like that for a while until Daniel
seemed to tense up, then groan. What was wrong now?
Noah was about to take him down to check when a god-
awful smell dropped over him like a poisonous fog.

"Damn, you off-loaded supper, didn't you?" he said,
while Daniel slapped Noah's cheeks playfully. "That's
deadly. I don't get how you turned a delicious meal into
toxic waste."

He'd have to change the kid, for sure. It was definitely first aid, judging by the smell. He started to turn
back, but Daniel said, "Mo…mo," bouncing up and

down on his poop-laden backside. Noah kept going. He had a little time, he figured, before the mess damaged Daniel's bottom.

At the park, Noah put Daniel on the ground and maxed out Paco's leash so the dog could wander and sniff trees. The kid was barefoot, but that should be okay. Noah had rarely worn shoes all summer as a kid.

Whenever Paco got near enough, Daniel gave him a pat, getting a slobbery lick in return, which made him giggle hysterically. Daniel seemed to laugh as easily as he cried. Was it normal to cry so much? Was he overly sensitive? Mel and Irena wouldn't baby him. They'd teach him to be strong and independent, Noah was certain. But what about the guy Mel married?

That thought made his gut roil. The dude better be solid. Patient and loving. And he'd better adore Daniel. Noah consoled himself with the fact that Mel was no fool. She'd pick a good one.

By the time they got back to the house, the fumes were making Noah's eyes water. It was easy to spot Daniel's room as the one painted red, blue and yellow, with circus stuff on the walls. He found what appeared to be diaper central—a table with shelves that held disposable diapers, wipes and creams.

He laid Daniel on his back on the plastic pad and waited for him to shriek, but the kid grabbed his feet and looked up at Noah like he expected him to know the drill.

Noah noticed a string dangling from a mobile over Daniel's head. When he pulled it, "Twinkle, Little Star" played and the circus animals turned in a slow circle. Daniel smiled, showing two tiny teeth on the bottom. What a great smile he had. He would be a charmer.

Time to get rid of the biohazard in the kid's drawers. "Okay, amigo, one diaper change coming up."

The mess turned out to be surprisingly neat and it all went great until Noah started with the fresh diaper, when Daniel kicked and bucked and complained. No way could he go commando until he was potty-trained, so Noah kept at it. With all the moving around, it took a few tries to get the tabs properly sealed. He gave up on the overall straps, tucking them into his pants.

Back in the living room, Daniel wanted down to play with his toys. Noah had to take a leak anyway. "Hang here a sec, okay?" He dashed to the john, where he had to pry a clip contraption off the lid. He was finishing up when he heard a bang and a cry.

In the kitchen, Daniel sat sobbing with a red mark and a bruise on his forehead. He must have been going for the cereal box on the table and banged into the leg. They should really look into that helmet idea.

Noah carried the Cheerios and Daniel, still sniffling, into the living room and sat on the couch, with the boy under his arm. "How about some news?" Noah clicked the remote to CNN.

He watched a piece about the federal deficit, then one about some bio fuels and something on stem-cell research. Daniel chewed on Cheerios and a stuffed penguin he clutched.

The next story made Noah freeze. Two marines had been killed by an IED in Afghanistan. *Steady,* he told himself, feeling his muscles tense and his breathing go shallow. *It's the news. It's not happening to you. Stay calm.*

His eyes flicked away from the screen and he closed them, taking slow breaths. Twinges and stabs started up in his skull like a distant thunderstorm.

You're better than this. You're past this. He noticed his leg muscles were so tight his thighs trembled. He had to get control. He had to watch Daniel, for God's sake. If he slipped into panic, he'd be lost.

Anchor yourself. Focus. He forced himself to feel the couch cushion beneath his ass, to see the table before him, the walls beyond. His gaze snagged on the shrine with candlelight flickering on the face of *La Virgen*. He remembered Mel saying the saint gave her comfort, so he kept his eyes there and took deep, slow breaths. After a bit, calm began to pour through him. *You got this.* Yeah, he did.

He glanced at Daniel, now chewing on a jingling ball Noah hoped didn't belong to the dog. "How about some cartoons?" He clicked to the cartoon channel where a buxom nurse examined a big-eared blue creature who drooled over her chest. Hmm, this is what kids watched these days?

He leaned back against the sofa, grateful for the progress he'd made. Over the months, he'd been desensitizing himself to war news, watching a few more seconds each time, talking himself down from the fear, the panic, the crazy, racing thoughts.

That *battle zone* moment with Mel troubled him—not only because she'd seen his reaction, but because he'd been hit by a memory of Iraq, too. He'd learned to fight them off, since they brought brutal headaches in their wake.

The day of the attack had become a blur and he intended to keep it that way. When he'd read that Captain Carver had been forced into retirement after the investigation, Noah had written a letter to the Army in his defense, which the Army ignored. Carver's fate was Noah's fault, too. Another crime he had to live with.

Of his hospital stay, he remembered little. He re-
called General Nelson's words about the harm Noah had
caused. And he remembered visiting Emile Daggett in
the hospital.

His head, like Noah's, had been wrapped in gauze,
the bruises on his face fading to yellow, his scrapes
scabbed over. He'd recognized Noah, but stared coldly
at him.

When he didn't respond to Noah's halting apology,
the nurse tried to say Daggett's brain injury made it
hard to speak, but Noah had read him loud and clear.
He didn't give a shit about Noah's regret. Noah didn't
blame him one bit.

Later on, he'd written to him. He'd also written to
Fuller's family and to Chuy and Bo to express his regret for putting them in harm's way.

Bo, the driver, had emailed back:

We were soldiers. We did our jobs. I sleep at
night.

Chuy, the sharpshooter, had called to cut Noah un-
earned slack. *You were just a crazy-ass civie whose
ass we had to save.* He'd ended the call inviting Noah
to visit him. *Call ahead,* cabrón. *Won't be no Humvee
escort for you in my hood.* Emile didn't respond.

Abruptly, Noah realized Daniel's ball no longer jan-
gled. The little boy was gone. He jumped up. "Daniel?"
The sound of splashing led him to the bathroom, where
the kid was using the toilet as a birdbath for the penguin.

What if he'd fallen in? Kids could drown in a ta-
blespoon of water. Electricity poured through Noah.
That annoying clip had been there to keep Daniel from
drowning. He'd let his attention wander and the kid
could have died. Mel was right. Things happened fast

with kids. Parenthood was not for sissies. He looked at his watch. It had barely been two hours. It felt like days.

ALL THE WAY HOME FROM the meeting, Mel kept glancing at her mother. Tears glistened in Irena's eyes. They'd stayed late so Irena could talk longer with a couple of the women.

Mel had been the only family member in attendance. The seven women and three men had talked about healing, about hope, about their fears and a lot about how exhausting it was to hide their struggle from loved ones.

Most of the time, her mother had sat very straight, her only sign of distress the way she gripped and twisted the bamboo handles of her bag. Finally, Mel had leaned in to say, "Don't hold yourself back. This group is for you. However you feel, whatever you need to say."

She'd squeezed Mel's hand. As if given permission, tears slid silently down her cheeks.

Off and on, Mel's mind had wandered to what was happening at home with Daniel and Noah. She'd fought the temptation to call and check. They were returning forty-five minutes later than she'd told Noah. She hoped he didn't mind and that Daniel hadn't cried long.

As she turned into the driveway, her heart began to skip beats. Partly, it was anxiety about Daniel, but it was also seeing Noah again. Guiltily, she'd liked knowing he was in her house waiting for her.

Inside, the television blared with gunshots and yelling. Toys were scattered across the living room and there was a tipped-over box of Cheerios on the table, the little Os in clumps on the surface and scattered on the floor.

Daniel was asleep in the crook of Noah's arm. Noah was out, too, his head to one side, hair flopped over,

looking so protective of Daniel and so sexy to her. Mel's
blood throbbed in her veins.

"Qué suave," her mother said. *How nice.*

It was. Very nice.

"I go to bed now," her mother said wearily. "Thank
you, *mi'ja.* I am happy you know how this goes for me.
I wish only for you not to worry so very much. *No te
preocupes. Lo que pasa, pasa."*

Don't worry. What happens, happens. The stoicism
may have come from her mother's Salvadoran roots or
maybe her sturdy soul, but it was not an attitude that
came easily to Mel. She worked hard to shape the world
her way. She didn't simply let things happen.

"I'll do my best, *Mamá."* Her best to hide her worry
anyway. She pressed her cheek to her mother's face and
breathed in her rosewater lotion—a smell that had always comforted Mel, along with her mother's soft Spanish songs. She wanted only to be that kind of comfort
and support to her own son. And to her mother during
her illness, however it went, easy or hard.

After her mother left, she studied the two males on
the sofa. Daniel's face was streaked with dirt and the
remains of supper. His overalls were filthy and the bot-
toms of his feet were black. He'd been outside barefoot,
risking his tender feet. Good grief.

On the TV, cartoon superheroes were battling, so
she flipped off the set. Noah jolted at the silence, then
hunched over Daniel, an arm out, as if to ward off a
blow. He looked terrified.

"Noah? It's me."

He jerked to check on Daniel, then relaxed, himself
again. He wiped his face with a hand. "We were watching cartoons. I drifted off, I guess."

"How did it go?" She held her breath, hoping for the best.

"We took Paco for a walk to the park. We played. We ate. It was a party."

"I can see that." She nodded at the mess around the room.

"If the neighbors hadn't called about the loud music, the police wouldn't have showed up, either. All in all, a totally bangin' time."

She smiled. "Speaking of banging…what happened to his forehead?" She could see a raised bruise beneath his curls.

"Dance battle, but he *owned* those b-boys."

"Noah…"

"Okay. He hit his head on a chair leg. Like you said, things happen fast." He looked suddenly serious. "You really can't look away for a minute. I don't know how you do it." She noticed he was rubbing his leg, so it had to be hurting.

"Don't forget, I've had a year to train and, you know, grow eyes in the back of my head and a third arm for juggling."

Noah smiled. "It's nice to see you joke." He dug in with his gaze. "Your mom says you're too serious these days."

"That's possible," she said, realizing that at the moment she felt like her old self, more relaxed, more, well, carefree. More like the Mel she'd been when she met Noah. It was nice, fleeting though it was.

She reached down to lift Daniel from Noah's body, leaning close, her hair falling against Noah's face as he shifted to accommodate her.

It was just the two of them with a sleeping child between them. *It's an illusion,* she reminded herself, ignoring the warmth coursing through her, the sense of rightness, that stupid family fantasy again.

She noticed Noah had cereal stuck to his cheek and picked it off.

Misreading her gesture as sexual, he caught her hand as if to kiss it.

Heat spiked through her. "It was just…" She showed him the oat circle. She remembered his hands, how warm they'd been, how insistent on her body. She'd never had a man study her so closely in bed.

Smiling, he ate the O from her fingertip, his tongue just brushing her skin. Electricity intensified the heat already burning through her.

"I've probably got those things all over the place, if you want to check." He nodded down at his belt, and the bottom dropped out of her stomach. Desire caught her in a swift wave, totally inappropriate while she stood with her sleeping son in her arms.

She adjusted Daniel on her hip, then noticed her hand was damp. Looking down, she saw a wet spot on the couch and a blotch on Noah's shirt. "Uh-oh."

Noah followed her gaze. "The diaper tabs must have come loose. He wasn't that wild about getting changed and I had to retape the thing a couple times. I'll pay to have your sofa cleaned."

"Don't worry about it," she said, realizing how surreal this moment was. Two years ago, she'd been having sex with a rock star of a reporter and now he was offering to clean pee off her couch.

She lifted Daniel over her shoulder. "Anyway, I've got to put him to bed. We've kept you too late." She made as if to leave the room.

"I'll wait for you," he said, his eyes holding hers steadily. He'd said the same thing the other night, while she finished the bath. *I can wait. Take your time.* They were the words of a loyal, patient man who would be there whenever you needed him. But how could that be Noah?

"I won't be long," she said, breathless as a girl expecting her first kiss when she returned. "He's pretty much down for the count."

What was she thinking? Her emotions were high from the support group meeting, the sight of the baby in Noah's arms, both of them asleep, that warm family glow and this man she'd missed, whose touch she'd longed for all these months.

Crazy, crazy. Don't even think it. Stepping into Daniel's room steadied her a bit. While she changed him and put him to bed, she tried to block off all that lust and longing. Sure she wanted Noah—now. Long-term, it was impossible and pointless. By the time she stepped into the living room, she'd resolved to say a chaste goodnight and be done with Noah.

Then she saw him. He was naked to the waist, scrubbing the sofa, the soft lamplight turning his sliding muscles to shivering gold.

Holy moley, she was only human.

"You don't have to… Please stop," she said. *In fact, if you don't, I'll throw you to the couch and maul you.*

He rose and turned to her. "I rinsed out my shirt, so I thought I might as well give the sofa a try." They stood close, almost embracing. She could smell the orange of the dish soap he'd put on the towel and his cologne and clean sweat and oats and…*oh, just look at that body.*

Then she noticed several small reddened scars on his shoulders. They had to be from Iraq. Ice zipped through her at the thought.

"You okay?" he asked her, reading her alarm.

"I'm fine," she said, lifting her eyes to his. Pure heat shone at her from their depths. She was certain hers matched his, degree for degree. "Maybe I'm not so fine. Maybe I'm in a little trouble here."

"I'm right with you." His fingers brushed the edges of her hair, then grasped something he held out—another oat ring.

She ate it from his finger, her tongue flicking his skin.

"You're playing with fire, lady." He shifted his body so their hips nearly touched.

"Then I should stop." She sighed and stepped back.

"Ah." He eased away, too. "So how did the meeting go? What was it about anyway?"

"It was for cancer survivors. I wanted her to have a place to talk freely."

"Your mother told me she was ill. Is she in remission?"

She shook her head. "We're not sure yet. There were some new growths, so she had a second surgery. She has fibromyalgia, which complicates the treatment."

"This has to be tough for you." His gaze never wavered. He was not intimidated by her emotion, nor did he pity her.

"It's difficult to see her so scared. She's always been a rock. It's…hard."

"Come here," he murmured, and pulled her into his arms, as though it was the most natural thing to do, as though they'd been doing it for years. She wrapped her arms around his bare back, his muscles sliding beneath her palms.

"I probably smell pretty ripe," he said.

"No, you don't. You smell like you." She rested her

cheek against his chest and let herself feel the comfort of his arms around her.

"You, too," he said, breathing her in. "You smell great. Have you ever had a Zombie?"

"A what?" She looked up at him.

"It's an old-school tropical drink that's sweet and peppery. That's what you smell like to me. It's red, too, which is your color. Try one and you'll see."

Suddenly, the moment shifted from comfort to desire. Noah's eyes held her captive. Her breathing went shaky and so did his. Need rushed through her and she didn't want to fight it.

Noah ran his hands down her back, hesitating at her hips, then slid the last few inches to grip her backside. He hauled her against his groin, letting her know her effect on him. She sucked in a breath.

"Yeah," he said shakily. "Me, too." His eyes burned into her with a single question: *Do you want this?*

Absolutely. Sex would feel so good. Her body longed to melt into his, to live again that glorious weekend when hope had been so high, when their futures had been bright as klieg lights before them.

She could feel the hard, fast beat of Noah's heart against her breasts, his ribs swelling and subsiding faster with each passing second. Why the hell not?

A trickle of reality broke into her brain. She had a child and a very ill mother. Noah had been through hell in Iraq. She was preoccupied and worried and he was damaged and lost.

Worse, they had Daniel between them now. Nothing was simple anymore. Even if it could be only sex for tonight, there would be a price to pay. She needed regular hours, she took no breaks. With her mother's health so fragile and her little boy depending on her, every action had consequences.

"You're having one hell of a debate in there," he said, tapping her temple. "Give me the summary graf."

"It's the butterfly effect," she said. "The ripples. If we go to bed we'll get no sleep and it's already late. Mornings start at six. And there's Daniel to consider. And my mother..."

"And St. Margaret." He smiled wryly.

"It's...complicated." But her body was screaming, *Go for it. Take a break—a private moment for the two of you. Deal with the ripples later.*

"You're right," Noah said, bending to capture her mouth in a slow kiss, as if to say, *Look what we're passing up. Taste how sorry we'll be.*

His lips were soft but strong, his tongue just there, separating her lips slightly, offering more, but not being pushy, letting them both feel how much they wanted this.

She broke away. "That's not helping."

"Sorry," he said, cupping the side of her face tenderly. She leaned into his touch. When he let go, he opened his palm to show her a piece of cereal resting there. "My souvenir." He tucked it into his jeans pocket. "I should let you get some sleep." He went to grab his damp shirt and met her at the door.

"Thanks for tonight, Noah," she said. "For watching Daniel."

"I enjoyed it. I'm glad I got to spend time with him."

"I should have made sure you got my text about him. It wasn't fair of me to leave you hanging."

"In a way, it was better you didn't reach me. I was in no shape to respond. I'm not sure I'm much better now." His eyes took on a faraway look.

Slowly, he came back to her. "Still, I meant that text. I knew you'd do great at whatever you tried. You're a great mother and you've got a great kid."

He's yours, too. But saying so would only make this harder. "He is pretty amazing, isn't he?"

"Yeah. He is." The affection and awe in Noah's eyes matched her own. Who else, besides her mother, could feel the same pride? It was lovely.

Then sadness washed across Noah's features. She knew why. He would be going for good this time.

"You'll get back to reporting, right?" She wanted to cheer him up.

"That's my plan. I'll start with some freelance pieces to be sure I've got my chops back, then get hired somewhere."

"National Record?"

"Not sure they'll want me. I didn't leave under the best of terms. I'll see what's out there. In this market, who knows?"

"There isn't a news outlet that wouldn't want Noah Stone."

"My last story lined bird cages months ago, Mel. My recent notoriety hasn't helped. The military's been arguing against wartime embeds ever since."

"That doesn't reverse your achievements. Your Pulitzer, your—"

"I'll find a spot," he said, cutting her off. "Don't worry about me. Maybe I can get a stringer assignment for a big paper. I have a friend who worked short-term for *News Watch,* the investigative-journalism foundation."

"That would be right up your alley."

"Right up a lot of people's alleys. We'll see."

"Whatever you decide, I know you'll do great."

"Like I said, we'll see." A muscle ticked in his jaw. He was tense about this. Finally, he backed down the stairs. "See you, Mel."

He put on his shirt, still damp, she could see, leaving it unbuttoned and flapping as he walked away. She wished she could call him back. She'd liked how she'd felt with him. It was like remembering herself again. Pregnancy and her mother's illness had turned her world upside down, and since Daniel's birth, she'd been focused completely on raising him. With Noah, she'd been a woman again, and she liked that. She liked remembering the photographer she'd been—and would be again once Daniel was older.

But the happy-family fantasy was too dangerous to risk more time with him. She'd made the right choice—stopped this before someone got hurt. Mel first and, down the line, Daniel. She turned around to clean up the mess in her living room. The mess in her heart would take a while longer.

CHAPTER EIGHT

NOAH JERKED UP IN the dark, gasping for breath, his heart slamming into his ribs. He'd yelled. He could tell that, could feel it in the set of his jaw, the roughness of his throat. He was shaking and his teeth chattered. He'd had the nightmare again.

You're all right. You're in bed, not a battlefield. There are no dead soldiers here, only you, shaking and sweating like a fool.

He fell back on the mattress and forced himself to take a slow breath, fought his heart back to normal rhythm. The pillowcase was damp and he realized he was drenched in sweat, hence the chattering teeth.

Damn, he hated this.

He closed his eyes, but his brain took him straight to the dream. There he was, running, trying to carry someone. Men shouted. Shots zinged. Bullet holes appeared between the eyes of the men he ran up to. What was happening? What was he doing? A downward glance. The rifle, heavy in his hands. Chuy's sniper rifle. Noah at the trigger. He was the one. Horror washed over him. He was the killer here.

Stop! He sat up, slapped his feet to the floor, digging down with his toes to ground himself. He leaned forward, elbows on his knees, and pressed his palms to the sides of his head. The metallic taste in his mouth told him he'd bitten his tongue again.

Damn. He pushed to his feet, left the bedroom to pace the tiny living room of Paul's guesthouse. Back and forth, back and forth, forcing his thoughts away from the dark pit they wanted to slide into.

He was tempted to go for gin, but that was no solution. He'd cut back on the booze since returning to Phoenix. That, too, was part of his healing. He stared out the window. A cold moon blasted the desert trees with a relentless silver light.

Suddenly, he thought of Daniel, saw his round-cheeked face, heard his helpless giggle when Paco licked his face. What a great kid. Sweet. Smart, too, he'd bet. How many teeth did he have? Two on the bottom. Yeah.

Noah would miss him. He'd only spent a couple hours with the kid, but he would miss him.

And Mel. He would miss her, too. Thinking of Daniel and Mel settled him, cooled his anxious fever, squeezed out the remnants of his nightmare. Blowing out his breath in relief, he lay on the sofa, hoping to sleep.

When pale sunlight broke through the thin curtains a few hours later, he sat up slowly, groggy, his head thick with fog.

Thinking would not be easy today, but he would not miss work because of an attack. He was done letting the nightmares and flashbacks control his life. And he *was* better. Early on, the noise of a trash pickup sent him ducking for cover, the smell of bus exhaust made him puke up his guts.

That part was over.

He made his shaky way to the shower and gutted out a cold one to stave off the headache that usually followed a bad night.

He stopped in Paul and Cindi's kitchen for some of

her fresh-ground coffee and found her emptying the dishwasher. "How did the babysitting go?" she asked, straightening with an armload of plates.

"Not bad." He decided to keep it light. "Except I screwed up the diaper and ended up with pee on the sofa."

"I bet Mel loved that."

"She didn't mind so much." She'd been flirting with him at the time. He'd liked that. He reached for a mug, then saw Cindi watching him. "What?"

"Nothing. Just your tone. You had fun, didn't you?"

"Don't sound so surprised. And, yeah, I did. The kid was cool. And it was good to see Mel again." She'd felt right in his arms and tasted like heaven. He'd missed her dig-in gaze. Her mind. Her body. Definitely her body. He hadn't realized how much.

"So there's still chemistry. Interesting…" She turned to put the plates in the cupboard.

"What's that supposed to mean?"

"Nothing, but…are you going to pursue something with her?"

"No. There would be…*ripples*. That's how she puts it."

"That's true for single moms." She sighed. "A woman I work with is divorced with a toddler. She's always frantic, always juggling. Any glitch throws her off—a flat tire, a sick babysitter, a rush project at work."

"Mel's mother isn't well, so Mel helps with the child-care business, plus runs her own photo studio, along with raising Daniel, so, yeah, it's intense."

"So…what did you decide to do?"

"Leave them alone," he said, but it made him feel empty inside. "I won't be here long. I don't know where

I'll end up. I can't promise to visit. I can't promise much at all right now."

"And that's what Mel wants? For you to leave?"

"Yeah." Though she seemed sad to say goodbye, reluctant, struggling to do what she saw as the right thing.

"Hmm." Cindi shut the cupboard, then considered him, not quite happy with what he'd said, it seemed. "So tell me more about Daniel."

"He's a great kid. Small, but strong. He's got a sense of humor, you can tell already. He's got this little giggle.… Anyway, I taught him how to do a high-five. He picked it up quick, too, so I'm sure he's smart."

"Show me his picture. You got one, didn't you?"

"No. I didn't." That startled him. "And Mel's a photographer, no less. I need a photo, don't I? I'll ask her for one…yeah." By phone or in person? The possibility cheered him.

Emma bounded into the room dressed in a neon pink glittery swimsuit, her equally pink and glittery backpack on her back.

"Emma, you are *not* wearing that to school," Cindi said calmly.

"But this is what I *feel* like wearing. You said wear what you *feel*."

"I mean, from school clothes. That is not appropriate, except on Water Day. And pick up your room or you'll get a frownie face on the chart."

"You get a frownie face on *my* chart, Mommy. For being *mean*. Can Noah drive me to school? Please, please?"

"I'm not going downtown today, kid, sorry," Noah said.

"That sucks!"

"Do not say *sucks!*" Cindi said. "And apologize to Noah."

"I'm just distapointed."

"And...?" Cindi demanded.

"I'm sorry, Uncle Noah," Emma said glumly. "Okay?"

"Next time, Em," he said.

"Next time takes for-*ev*-er." She sighed, then flounced off.

"Even with two parents, it's no picnic." Cindi patted her stomach. "When this one gets here, Emma will seriously run off the rails."

"You're good parents. You'll make it work."

She smiled at him, then jolted. "Hey, if you're heading to ASU, could you drop this prescription off with Paul?" She held out an envelope.

"No problem. I've got a little time." Later in the morning, he had an interview with the head of the nanotechnology department, part of a series on ASU's cutting-edge programs. His job was to make academic and scientific rhetoric accessible to alumni, boost their pride and get them to pull out the checkbooks when the fundraising drive started up.

When he got to ASU, Paul was in class. Noah read his posted schedule and headed to the room intending to slip in and out. But when he stuck his head in the door, Paul looked up from the small group and said, "Noah! Come in."

"Just dropping this off." Noah held out the envelope.

Paul took it. "Your timing is perfect. We were going over techniques to coax reluctant interview subjects to answer tough questions." He turned to the class, sitting in a semicircle, their laptops, papers, Starbucks cups and water bottles in front of them.

"This man is an expert. He was on the Pulitzer team that broke the Florida pain-clinic scams. Best of all, he's one of our own. He graduated from ASU with me."

A murmur went through the group.

"Noah Stone, meet my advanced reporting class."

He nodded in greeting.

"Talk to us about techniques that work well for you," Paul said. "If you've got a minute."

"I'm sure you've laid out what they need to know."

"Yeah, but I don't have your war stories. Give us an example."

Noah smiled. "Let's see. We got stalled on the pain-clinic story when the two main doctors clammed up. I used a basic move on the first guy. I put away my note-pad and recorder, so he thought we were done. As I got up to leave I said, 'I bet you had a good laugh when the police caught your partner's wife shoving bogus pre-scription pads in the glove compartment.'

"He laughed and told me what an idiot his partner was. I'd picked up that he was dying to vent about the guy. It was total ego. He wanted me to know he was the smart one."

The students stared at him, rapt. His mission had been so clear in those days, his mind sharp and focused. With everything in him, he wanted to feel like that again. "The guy kept saying 'This is off the record, right?' I never answered, but he was too far gone to notice. Never underestimate human vanity or the need to confess—to even the most heinous acts. He gave me all I needed to nail him with a big smug grin on his face."

The students laughed.

"Here's a tip. When you have a skittish source with a great scoop, don't bring a notepad the first visit. It's casual, you're just talking, getting background. Keep it all in your head, bookmarking what you want to pursue later. Once he trusts you not to burn him, you can go deeper. And never burn a good source. All you have is your credibility. Never jeopardize it. Ever."

The students scribbled in notebooks or typed on their laptops.

"It's not only being a good listener, either. Shrinks listen. Friends listen. You're an investigator. You need people to tell you the last thing they want to tell you, so you have to know how to lead, to guide, to apply just the right pressure at just the right time."

"And that's a skill you can learn?" Paul said, prodding for more.

"Sure. As long as you have good instincts. You need empathy, too. You have to be able to suspend judgment. Like a novelist, you have to put yourself in the shoes of even the sleaziest dirt bag. It's actually a seduction, when you think about it."

He warmed to the topic, gripped the top of the chair he stood behind, leaned forward as he spoke. "You need to establish quick intimacy. Revealing something embarrassing or personal about yourself is a good start. The natural response is to share in return and that builds trust."

"Like what you did with that gangbanger series?" Paul said.

"Now, that was a truly scary dude who'd murder you as soon as look at you, but he was arguing on the phone with his mother, and I got the vibe that she still called the shots, even though the guy was in his twenties. So I mentioned that my mother was always nagging me to make more money and get somewhere in life.

"He laughed and called me a pussy, then he told me that after his dad was killed—both his parents were bangers—his mom put him on the worst corners to sling product to teach him to be a man. So that broke the ice and he answered any question I threw at him after that."

The students were enjoying this, shooting glances at each other.

"Now, my mom would hate being compared to a gangbanger, so for the record, she never nagged, she only *encouraged*."

Their laughter lifted his spirits. He was glad Paul had dragged him in here to talk. He felt better suddenly—as though he'd been dog-paddling in deep water, exhausted, nearly drowning, when his feet found the bottom and he could walk to the shore.

"Your best weapon is silence. Ask the tough question and then wait, maintaining eye contact. Nine times out of ten, the social discomfort will make the person blurt something incriminating."

Heads nodded. Laptop keys clicked.

"You all are taking notes, but really, you'll get the feel for it. Listen to Paul. He'll steer you right." He stepped back. "Anything else before I go?"

"Yeah," said a kid with a goatee and trendy glasses. "Could you tell us about Iraq? Was it worth it? Getting held hostage, I mean, to get the story?"

The question hit him hard. Noah hadn't dealt with it in months. He took a deep breath and said what he had to say. "I sacrificed caution to follow a hunch and caused injuries and a death, along with damaging the peace effort in Iraq." He paused, letting his words sink in, feeling that cold ache start up again. "Never forget there are consequences to what we do. Some are deadlier and more regrettable than others. I wore blinders that day. Keep your eyes open and your heads on straight and you won't make my mistakes."

The students took that in with a respectful silence.

"We'll let you go," Paul said, standing to open the door for him. "Thanks for your time."

"Good luck to you all." Noah managed a smile and got out of there.

Weak in the knees, he found a bench. At first, talking to the students, he'd forgotten Iraq, slipped free of the weight of guilt he carried to share his passion for reporting.

But he had no business forgetting what he'd done. He was no J-school role model. He was a cautionary tale, a warning about self-serving hubris and obsession and he'd better keep that front and center here on out.

When he finished with his ASU work that afternoon, Noah found himself flipping through the newspapers and magazines he'd stacked up to read. After that student discussion, his synapses were firing fast and hard, like a kid with attention deficit disorder who'd taken his first dose of Adderall.

The mass of print didn't squiggle before his eyes as in the past. His mind didn't wander off or want to give up. He flipped pages, skimming headlines, speed-reading nut grafs. He was hunting down a story, he realized, just like the old days.

His gaze landed on a political brief about Sheriff Sam Pasamonte, the fame-obsessed Arizona sheriff who'd made a national name for himself as a law-and-order tough guy. Noah had followed the man's celebrity hunt over the years. He remembered that *Arizona News Day* had taken him on and he'd retaliated by briefly arresting the publisher on trumped-up charges.

This story declared the man under federal indictment over charges of abuse of office. Noah's attention spiked. Bullies with political authority were a particular hot-button for him. The end of the piece mentioned that Sheriff Sam had recently walked away from a reality show he was slated to star in. When asked why, Sheriff Sam had no comment.

No comment? Sam Pasamonte? That guy loved to be quoted—the more outrageous the question, the better he relished answering. Something was off. And why would such a publicity hound give up a starring role in a TV show?

The familiar tingle started at the back of Noah's neck, surged down his spine and lit up his insides. He was hot, onto something, totally focused, in full pursuit. He hadn't felt this way in so long. He wanted to weep with relief. For the first time in a year, he was dying to investigate. He had questions to ask, leads to follow, people to talk to, research to do.

It was almost visceral, his reaction, as if the neural pathways in his brain he'd carved over the years had at last opened up again, sparking and crackling with energy and purpose.

I am back.

At last.

His first task was background. He called up clips on Pasamonte from the internet. There were thousands, but he quickly sorted the wheat from the chaff. Noah wondered if Connie Keller, his old contact, a longtime sheriff department secretary who knew where all the bodies were buried, still worked there. He'd call her first.

The sound of a vacuum cleaner made Noah look up. The office was deserted. It was seven o'clock. He'd lost track of time. He had two pages of notes—people to call, data to chase, backstory to gather. He'd been focused, driven, like the old days. That felt good. No, great.

He'd even jotted notes on two other ideas that intrigued him. The rush on bids for solar plants and wind farms had the potential to pull in scam artists, involve developer collusion and bid-rigging. And problems with privately funded prisons had cropped up here and there across the country. Corners were being cut, sweetheart deals made with officials, probable kickbacks and bribes. Someone needed to look at the big picture, pick up the patterns, make sense of the patchwork quilt of troubles. Exactly the kind of work he did best.

Maybe he still had nightmares and migraines, but he was ready to get back to the work he was born to do, the work that made his life worth living. The work that had been everything to him.

Yeah. He wanted to punch a fist in the air. He wanted to dance, break out champagne, climb Squaw Peak and shout into the desert sky, *I'm back.*

More than that, he wanted to call Mel. He hadn't told her how low he'd felt, how afraid he'd been that he was finished in the business, but she would understand the fire burning in his gut now. Mel would get it.

Except, he couldn't call her. He'd said goodbye.

Damn.

What about Paul? Sure. Paul would celebrate with him. In his quiet way, Paul had been rooting for this since he saw the beat-down Noah at that bar in New Mexico. He would talk to Paul. On the way home, he stopped at a drugstore for notepads, file folders and a printer cartridge. At the checkout counter, he noticed something ingenious he could have used while baby-sitting Daniel. It was called KidMinder. It was kid-friendly, mom-pleasing and age appropriate. Best of all, Daniel could use it now, not five years down the line.

No harm in dropping it off, right? It was on his way home. While he was there, he could ask Mel for a photo of Daniel. And tell her about his breakthrough.

Ten minutes later, he rang the bell and Mel flung open the door. "What are you doing here?" She sounded flustered, but there was color in her cheeks and a light in her eyes, so he knew he wasn't totally unwelcome.

"I bought something cool you can use with Daniel." He held out the KidMinder. "It was tough trying to hold on to Daniel and the dog at the park, but with this you can easily control him, keep him out of traffic or away from the stairs or give him more slack."

"You bought him a *leash?*" She burst out laughing. "He's not a dog, Noah. When I take him and Paco out together, I use the jogging stroller. Here." She opened the coat closet and showed him a baby seat on wheels.

"That would work. Sure."

"Thanks, though. It was a nice…thought."

"Right." Their gazes caught and held. He needed to say something more. "Also, I was thinking that I need a picture of him. A photograph."

"A photograph? Oh. Of course. I should have offered you one already." She blushed sheepishly. "I'll print up some and leave them for you at the counter at Bright Blossoms. That would be easiest, I think."

"Sure. I drop Emma off on Friday."

"I'll have them ready then, no problem."

"Okay then. Good." He felt like an idiot standing there. Was he going to blurt, *Guess what, I'm working on a story again* like an overeager kid?

"Was there something else?"

Before he could reply, he heard a delighted shriek

and Daniel popped out from behind Mel to quick-step toward Noah, powdered sugar on his face, a wad of dough in one fist.

Noah knelt down to greet him, feeling a pinch in his chest. Daniel held up his hand for a high-five and Noah patted his sticky palm. "High-five, little dude."

Daniel held out the glob.

"It's a sopapilla," Mel said. "Mom just made some. You don't have to—"

Noah ate Daniel's offering. "Yum," he said, though it tasted kind of grimy.

Daniel clapped his hands in delight.

"Noah!" Irena said, standing behind Mel in the doorway. "Come in for sopapillas. I make *muchos muchos.*"

"Okay with you?" he asked Mel quietly.

She nodded, giving him an uncertain smile.

Inside, Irena held out a plate of the pillow-shaped fried pastry sprinkled with powdered sugar.

"Thanks," he said, taking one from the top.

"Uh…uh…uh." Daniel was holding up his arms to Noah, fingers wiggling with urgency.

"You want up?" Noah put down the pastry, dusted his fingers, then hauled Daniel up onto his shoulders, while Mel hovered, hands raised, as if spotting the kid on a high wire.

"I won't let him fall, Mel. This is how we did the walk."

"Whee!" Daniel crowed, grabbing fistfuls of Noah's hair and yanking.

"Ouch. Not so hard on the reins, cowboy."

"No pulling hair, *Danielito,*" Mel said, reaching up to stop his hands.

Daniel bucked on Noah's shoulders, then twisted toward the door. Out of nowhere Paco appeared to nudge Noah's crotch and whine.

"They want another walk, I guess," he said, tickled that they'd remembered last night's fun as fondly as he had.

"It's bath time, Noah. It's too late for a walk."

"We'll make it quick. How's that? Just around the block."

Daniel shrieked with joy. "Ba…ba…ba!" he called, which had to be *block*. The kid was sharp as a tack.

Mel considered her son's excitement. "I'm going to regret this, I'm sure, but go ahead. Fifteen minutes, but only Daniel. Paco stays."

"You want to come? It'll be fun.…"

"Just hurry back."

"You don't know what you're missing."

"Go already." She was fighting a grin.

Noah set off with Daniel on his shoulders, feeling pretty damn good. He liked being with the little boy, liked making him happy. The block passed quickly and when he rounded the corner for the house, Mel was waiting in the doorway. As Noah headed up the walk, Daniel began to squawk, "Mo…mo…mo," bucking on Noah's shoulders.

"Sorry, kid. We made a deal. Fifteen minutes," he said for Mel's benefit.

"It's bath time, Daniel," she said firmly, taking him down.

"No…no…no!" Daniel shrieked, reaching for Noah. It was pitiful.

"You like your bath, remember?" She spoke loud enough to be heard over Daniel's yells. "Say good-night to Noah now."

"Noooo," he shrieked, still clamoring for Noah.

Noah's heart flipped over. "Sorry, big guy."

The boy's shrieks turned to heartbroken sobs.

"He's overtired. And he's not good with transitions. This is how it goes when we break the routine. Shh, Daniel, shh." She swayed back and forth. "You're making this harder, don't you see?" The crack in her voice told him she didn't just mean for Daniel. "We agreed, Noah. This is why."

Daniel was sucking his thumb, tucked against his mother's chest, miserable.

Noah hadn't thought this through. He'd only wanted to make Daniel happy, but he'd ended up making him cry. He could see down the line how that would go. Noah would miss birthday parties and picnics and soccer games. Would the kid wait at the window, hoping in vain for Daddy to show? Noah couldn't bear putting pain in those big brown eyes.

"You're right," he said. He touched Daniel's head, the hair soft, the scalp warm, the skull so fragile. The little boy turned tear-filled eyes up at him. A sharp, searing pain shot through him.

"I'll get you the pictures," Mel said, a catch in her voice. "This has to be goodbye. It's for the best."

"Yeah," he said, his jaw tight. He touched her cheek, then dropped his hand. Around Mel, he forgot how much he'd changed, too. "It is."

Then he walked away, with the smell of Daniel's scalp still on his fingers, the sight of him in Mel's arms etched so deeply into his brain he wouldn't need a photograph to remember either of them at all.

AT THE DESK IN HER STUDIO, Mel flipped through the pages of the photo book she'd prepared for Noah, fighting the lump in her throat the entire time. He'd had to ask for a picture of his own son. Why hadn't she thought of it?

Clearly, she hadn't really accepted that Noah was out of their lives. He'd come by with that stupid leash and her heart had leaped in her chest.

He's changed his mind. He wants to stay, become a family.

It was so stupid, but the mental snapshot of Daniel on Noah's shoulders had stayed in her head, taunting her ever since.

Daniel deserved a daddy.

But Noah was not a good risk. He'd told her long ago that he was too selfish, too career-obsessed for a family. He'd said his father should never have married and that Noah never intended to. Family was everything to her and to him it meant little. His family had failed him, in a way, so he'd concluded it wasn't worth the trouble. At least, that was how she'd interpreted his attitude.

You took a small hurt to avoid a bigger one later, right? That was the mature thing to do. When you had a child, you had to be mature. There was no room for error or selfishness.

One day, if she found the right man, he'd be someone who hadn't had fatherhood sprung on him, who knew and loved Daniel, who wouldn't have to crowbar him into his life the way Noah would have to.

Ever since Mel told her mother that Noah wouldn't be back, Irena had been lighting big, fat pillar candles at the St. Margaret shrine and letting out giant sighs. Irena was convinced all Noah needed was time with Daniel and Mel and he would decide to stay. She thought Mel had pushed him away.

Maybe she had, but Noah sure as hell hadn't fought her over it. He knew she was right, too.

Mel closed the book and set it on top of the two other copies she'd ordered—one for Irena, the other for her father, who'd sent an extravagant basket of baby items after her mother called him about Daniel.

Every time she thought about her dad, she felt the old hurt. Nothing he could do now would fix that for her, not a college fund for Daniel, not a weeklong visit, not a long letter of apology. Nothing would erase that empty feeling of not being enough for him, of not mattering, of being forgotten.

It wasn't rational, but it was real. If she let things happen with Noah, that would be Daniel's future. She could not bear that.

She found herself hardly breathing. She'd felt heavy with sadness since they'd said goodbye. She missed Noah. And after spending so little time with him, it was ridiculous. The truth was that she longed to be with him again, to feel the way he made her feel. She wished she'd taken photos of him, tried to capture that knowing smile, those see-all eyes, the sense that he understood her, knew her, truly cared about her.

She'd spent an embarrassing amount of time replaying his kisses and touches. She had photos in her head, though, that she'd automatically composed, the details vivid. The wince from his bad leg when he'd crouched to greet Daniel, the way his dimple flashed when he laughed, how the gold flecks in his eyes glistened when he looked at his son.

Stop this. Let it go. You're an adult.

And sometimes adulthood just plain sucked.

The studio door jingled and she turned to see Jen Steiner, her next client, walk in. She was beautiful, in her thirties and wore a stylish summer hat. She was here to order prints of her little girl. She joined Mel at her computer and picked up the photo book. "Is this your son? Can I see?"

Before Mel could speak, she began turning the pages. Mel had enjoyed looking through the photos herself. Lived day by day, Daniel's growth and development had been imperceptible, but seen through the pages of photos, the changes were dramatic.

And Noah had missed it all. Would the book make him feel better or worse about that? She wasn't certain. Since Iraq, he seemed more guarded to her, his emotions tucked away.

"He's darling. Look at that dimple and those curls."

He looks just like his father. But all she said was, "Thank you very much. Shall we look at your proofs now?"

Jen oohed and aahed at the photos, which Mel presented in a slideshow. "I couldn't believe how you got her to hold still and smile. Every one of these is fabulous. I'm going to order far too many prints. I hope you're happy."

"I'm delighted."

"And you don't charge nearly enough for how good you are."

She smiled. "I'm building my business, so I want to be reasonable."

"Lucky for me." Jen hesitated. "Speaking of that, I have an idea. The entire Steiner-Markowitz clan is gathering in Tucson next weekend. My sister was going to ask a friend to take pictures, but I want something more professional. Would you do it? You'd take formal shots, plus candids. We'd host you. I can guarantee you'll get tons of orders."

"That's a great offer, but I don't think I could manage a weekend. I have Daniel to consider."

"Can't your mother watch him? This would mean on-going business in Phoenix. One of my nieces is about to announce her engagement, so she'll need a wedding photographer. I know my family will love your work."

Mel looked at her. The job would definitely be a client builder. Jen's family was wealthy and well connected. Bright Blossoms had a big insurance bill coming due soon, too. "I'll have to talk to my mom. Her health's a little uncertain…but if I can work it out, I'd love to shoot your reunion."

"Great. Let me know by Friday, okay?"

"You bet." Mel took Jen's print order, then walked her out. Back at her desk, she started to close out her computer's photo folders, when her journalism portfolio caught her eye. She played the pictures as a slideshow, her student work followed by her *News Day* shots. There were the Yaqui Easter parade shots and the graffiti collages Noah had admired, photos from a story about pawnshops, some from the human-smuggler story and, her favorite, a shot of a pit bull where the dog's whole soul showed in its eyes—fire and fight and sorrow and pride.

She missed taking news photos. She adored Daniel and wouldn't change a moment of the past two years, but she did miss the old Mel and all she'd hoped to achieve. Noah had reminded her of the glory days.

She would return to it, once Daniel was in school, but by then would she be behind the curve, out of date? Would there even be a local job for her, with newspapers shrinking every day? She wouldn't be able to travel even then, so chasing world-changing shots across the globe might never be possible.

Oh, well. She sighed and clicked the folder closed. Back to real life. She noticed an email from Alice asking if Mel needed her to bring anything to Daniel's birthday party on Sunday.

It was a good thing Mel had ended things with Noah before the party. Talk about awkward. She couldn't have invited him. The only person who knew he was Daniel's father was Alice, and Mel had no intention of telling her Noah had returned. Alice was too romantic. The last thing Mel needed was one more person lighting candles in front of St. Margaret for her.

CHAPTER NINE

"Thanks for helping out with Em," Paul said Friday morning, joining Noah at the kitchen counter for coffee. Cindi had already left for an early appointment and Paul was on his way out, too.

"Happy to help. Emma's my bud. Aren't you, Em?"

"Scrambled eggs are yucky," she said. Noah's job was to supervise her breakfast, then drive her to Bright Blossoms.

"Do what you can," Paul muttered to him, standing at the coffeepot. "Many have fallen before you."

"We'll work it out, no sweat."

His friend looked him over, then sipped his coffee. "Think about what I said. The grant money's sitting there."

"I will." Paul had offered Noah a stipend to mentor the advanced reporting students Noah had spoken with. They wanted to write more ambitious pieces for the university newspaper and needed advice. Noah was considering the offer.

"You've got that story rolling, which is great, but I think you'll find working with students rewarding." When Noah told Paul about his breakthrough, the guy had practically hugged him. He'd clearly been concerned. "I'm really glad for you," he now said quietly, resting a hand on Noah's shoulder.

"Yeah. Thanks." Maybe Paul had gone soft as Cindi

had charged, but Noah felt lucky to have a friend who cared so much. In fact, Paul and Cindi felt like family to him. Or how family was supposed to feel. His own mother's guilt over how she thought she'd failed Noah as a child kept her distant. At least, he assumed that was why. Maybe she flat-out disliked him as a person. As unhappy as she'd been, she'd done her best, he believed. As had his father. He didn't blame either of them for how things turned out.

Still, spending time with the Stocktons, feeling their affection and concern, he felt as though there was a place for him here. Almost a home. Hokey, but true. Friends were the family you chose, right?

After Paul left, Noah sat down to negotiate breakfast with Emma as swiftly as he could manage. The next few days would be hectic. This weekend, he not only had a yard sale at his grandmother's place, he needed to sift through pages of public records on Sheriff Sam to prep for an interview with a former staffer from the Attorney General's office who had crucial information. He wanted to reach out to *Arizona News Day* for background on their old stories, too.

Mel might be a help with that, but he'd promised to leave her alone.

When he dropped Emma off, he would get the photos of Daniel and maybe peek in on him in his day-care room. The thought of never seeing the boy again sank his spirits too low. This way, he could taper off....

Ten minutes later, Noah said, "This is my last bite, Em," and finished off his scrambled eggs. The deal was if she ate her eggs bite-for-bite with him, she'd get a toaster pastry for the road. The girl had a future in labor negotiations.

Emma sighed, scrunched up her face as though she had to eat poison, then took her last bite.

"Great, now brush your teeth, grab your backpack and you can pick out the treat you want."

Noah stood to get more coffee. Picking up the carafe, he glanced at the TV on the counter Paul had left tuned to CNN, the sound low. To Noah's shock, his own face filled the screen. It was his official *National Record* photo. His heart lurched, his hand jerked and coffee splashed the counter, his legs and the floor.

He put down the pot and upped the sound with shaking fingers. The story was about a reporter who'd been captured in Afghanistan and the anchor was comparing the incident with Noah's in Iraq.

No. Not again. He froze as the image shifted to the footage of himself and Emile Daggett being loaded into an Army helicopter on gurneys. At the sight, Noah's insides convulsed and nausea sent him half stumbling to the small bathroom off the kitchen, where he emptied his guts.

Trembling, he rinsed his mouth at the sink and splashed his face.

Then, like a blow, a memory struck, the force of it making him sink to floor, braced against the wall. He fought against it, but it was too late. Pictures filled his head.

Noah lay on his side, the taste of blood and dirt in his mouth. His ears rang, his mind flickered. A rifle jabbed his ribs...agonizing pain... He got to his knees, knives seemed to slice his broken leg. Emile kneeled beside him, bleeding from his face and skull... On the ground, Reggie Fuller, eyes blank, a black spot between his eyes the only clue as to why he lay so very still.

And Noah and Emile were next, Noah sensed with a dull horror.

Think about your life, he told himself. Remember the best of it.

Instead, what played in his head was: I can't write this story because I'll be dead.

Then it was over, his mind black. Noah leaned his head against the wall, shaking, gasping for air. *Stop it,* he told himself. *Don't think about it.* His scalp tightened and tingled, signaling a freight train of a migraine heading his way.

"Was it the eggs?" Emma stood outside the bathroom door, backpack half on, staring at him with wide eyes. "They made you upchuck? Will I do it? I hate to upchuck. It burns my throat so bad." Big tears formed in her eyes.

"It wasn't the eggs, Em. Something on the news made me sick."

"Like seeing a surgery, you mean? All bloody and stuff?"

"Like that, yeah."

"Mommy hates Daddy to watch TV when we eat. You shouldn't do it."

"I'll remember next time." He forced a smile. "Teeth all brushed?"

"See?" She displayed her teeth in a wide smile.

"Grab one of those Pop Tarts and we'll go." He wiped up the coffee he'd spilled on the counter and floor, loaded a plastic bag with ice to wrap around the base of his skull, which sometimes staved off the headache. He had to fight this. He had no time for a setback now.

"You can have a bite," Emma said, holding out her snack. "It's cinnamon. My favorite flavor. It's the very last one." She was clearly torn about sharing it.

"That's okay. You earned it, fair and square, Em."

"I did," she said, slipping her hand in his, ready to go.

She kept up a distracting chatter all the way to Bright Blossoms, for which he was grateful. He couldn't get the metal taste out of his mouth.

That was the first time he'd remembered those seconds kneeling with Emile, waiting to be shot. His heart was still racing and sweat made his hand slide on the steering wheel.

Would he remember more? Why hadn't they been shot? They'd been held captive for hours. What had gone on then? How had the rescue come about?

His reporter brain wanted to know the whole story. The rest of him, which valued his peace of mind and protected the progress he'd made, wanted never to remember.

"Uncle Noah? Did you hear?"

He drew his attention back to Emma. "Yeah?"

"I said that Pop Tarts are better than Popsicles, right?"

"Oh, uh, yeah. Less drippy. Sure."

The reception desk was empty, so he took Emma to her class, then headed down the hall. In Daniel's room, a caregiver was holding Daniel on her lap, singing the birthday song. On his head was a paper crown. Behind him, the calendar had a cake with Daniel's name on it pinned to Sunday.

Daniel's birthday was Sunday. His *first* birthday. Noah's heart squeezed. Mel had told him the date, but he'd forgotten. Damn.

He had to get a gift, no question. Mel would say it wasn't necessary, but so what? In fact, watching his little boy clap his hands in glee as the song finished, he made a decision. He would send a present every year, no matter where he ended up. That was something he *could* promise. And once he had some cash, he'd designate an automatic investment into a college fund for Daniel. Mel would have to accept that. He was the kid's father no matter what.

When he got to the ASU office, he braced himself for questions from people who'd seen the CNN broadcast. He knew the pundits would go at it again about the proper role of reporters in war. He'd been labeled a hot-dog journalist heedless of the risks he'd incurred. He'd agreed, but that didn't mean he wanted to rehash it all.

He slogged through the day, which felt gray and cold to him, though it was bright and sunny outside, his head aching, but not badly enough to send him to bed, thank God. Only two people brought up the incident and he was able to mumble something about his recap being part of the news cycle and escape more questions.

By the time he headed out to Apache Junction to set up for the yard sale, he was exhausted, soaked in sour sweat and his mind was murky, his spirits low. At least he'd be alone in the house that night.

Sometime on Saturday, he would bring his grandmother over from the assisted-living place he'd helped her move into so she would feel part of the event. He'd hired a couple of neighbors to help him price and sell the goods.

At midnight, he jerked up from the daybed in his grandmother's sewing room, his body rigid, face damp with sweat, the nightmare fresh in his head: the soldier heavy on his shoulder, legs burning with pain…men falling…shouts…the gun in his hands…his own bellow of horror.

When would he be done?

When his cell phone alarm went off at five, he was relieved to notice the headache he had was mild and he was tolerably alert. The sale went well all day Saturday, so that by Sunday noon, Noah was hauling what remained to Goodwill and the dump, his grandmother delighted with her profits.

He'd have to do the final cleanup of the house later on, since he wanted to buy and deliver Daniel's birthday gifts that afternoon. He hoped Mel wouldn't fight him over the presents. She needed to know he was serious about honoring the little guy's day every year.

MEL CLIMBED DOWN FROM the ladder to survey her handiwork. Red, yellow and blue balloons and streamers decorated the patio, along with a happy birthday banner. She'd set small tables here and there and covered them with circus tablecloths. Money was tight, so she'd done it all on a shoestring, borrowing the low plastic slide, the toy castle, the big punching clown and some climbing blocks from Bright Blossoms for the kids to play on.

This was going to be fun. Casual and simple.

She checked her watch. Right on schedule, despite some last-minute hassles. All she had left was to put helium in a few more balloons, wake Daniel up from his nap and get him and herself dressed. Her mother was off picking up two of her cancer-group friends.

Right before the party started, Mel would bring out the chips, dips, salsa and veggies for the adults, the fish-shaped crackers and animal cookies for the kids. The hot dogs, burgers and fixings waited in the fridge. She'd loaded an ice chest with beer, soda and juice boxes and she had wine at the ready.

The dining-room table looked fun with its circus

tablecloth and Daniel's small clown-face cake. She'd
made it from scratch for him to mangle and eat as he
saw fit. Around it were two dozen cupcakes decorated
with confetti for the children. Three flavors of ice cream
waited in the freezer.

She'd charged her camera and her mom's camcorder.

That was everything, right? She went down her mental checklist: decorations, food, drink, entertainment,
Daniel's cake, the cupcakes, the— *Uh-oh.* She'd forgotten the cake for the adults. The *pièce de résistance.*

She'd splurged on a Very Berry Chocolate Supreme
Cake from Best Desserts Bakery, which had won Best
of Phoenix three years running. She had to pick it up
before the bakery closed. Yikes!

She checked her watch. She had twenty minutes for
a fifteen-minute drive. Damn. Her mother was at the
far end of the valley by now. She tried Alice, who lived
close to the bakery, but got no answer, so she ran for her
shoes and purse. She'd have to wake Daniel and bring
him with her.

Grabbing the bakery reminder from the fridge, she
dialed the number to beg them for a few minutes' grace.
As the call was ringing through her doorbell sounded.
What now?

The phone to her ear, she pulled open the door and
found Noah there.

"Noah?" she said.

"Nope. Barb," snapped the woman on the phone.
"Wrong number."

"No. Wait! Don't hang up," she said. She lifted a
finger at Noah, telling him to wait a sec. "This is Mel
Ramirez. I'm supposed to pick up a cake and I'm running late. Will someone be there for, say, an extra ten
minutes?"

"Ten minutes…? Maybe. Come to the back."

"Okay. Got it. Back door." She clicked off and smiled apologetically. "I'm sorry." What was he doing here? He had a large Toys "R" Us bag and a box under his arm. Surely her mother hadn't said anything about the party to him.

Noah took in the room behind her. "You're having a party?"

She flushed. "Yes, but I forgot the cake, so I've got to get it before the bakery closes."

"Yeah, I heard. Ten minutes." He lifted the bag. "I'm just dropping these off. They all got great reviews for kids Daniel's age."

"You shouldn't have," she said, accepting the bag and box. "I'm sorry I didn't invite you, but I thought—"

"That it would be weird, yeah." She thought she saw a flash of hurt in his eyes.

She felt an answering stab, but she had no time to deal with that. "I'm sorry, but I've got to wake Daniel up from his nap and go, so—"

"Why don't I get the cake so you don't have to wake him?"

"Really? I mean, it would help. I still have a few things to do—"

"All I need is the address, Mel."

She handed him the reminder slip and watched him drive away.

She'd accepted an armload of gifts from the man, then sent him off to fetch the cake for a birthday party she'd deliberately not invited him to.

She felt like a world-class jerk.

By the time he got back, Mel had set out the food, finished the balloons and gotten herself dressed. "Thank you so much," she said, following him to the table where he placed the big box.

Together, they lifted out the two-tier cake decorated like a big top with clowns and balloons. Noah licked a dab of frosting from his finger. "Yum."

"I know. They make great cakes." She looked at him. "Stay for the party, Noah. You should. Really."

"That's not a good idea," he said, though something flickered in his eyes. Wistfulness? "You need anything else? Ice? More balloons?"

The baby monitor crackled and Daniel called out.

"He's awake," she said. "At least stay so Daniel can open your presents." She looked at her watch. "There's time."

"Yeah?" He cleared his throat, clearly not wanting to sound too eager, but he followed her into Daniel's room, where the little boy stood holding the crib bars, waiting to be lifted out.

"Happy birthday, *mi'jo.* It's time for your party." His face was soft from sleep and he cuddled against her when she carried him to the changing table.

"So I get to see a pro at work." Noah loomed over her, watching closely as she changed his diaper. "So, is it normal to have such minuscule equipment?"

"*Ay, Dios.* You men and your penises. He's normal, though the doctor never got out the tape measure. They grow proportionately, so don't worry."

"Good to know," he said, grinning. "I wouldn't want him to be at a disadvantage with the ladies." He waggled his eyebrows. Daniel craned his head to grin up at Noah. "Right, big man? Or should I say, proportionate man?"

Mel took Daniel's special birthday shirt off the shelf where she'd put it.

"That's a cool shirt," Noah said, fingering the brightly woven shirt her aunt had sent. "This from Salvador?"

"Yep. My aunt sent it for his birthday celebration."

She put on the shirt, tugged on denim shorts, then took a comb to his tangled curls. He squawked right away, hating the hassle.

"The curls can be a pain, little dude," Noah said. "Try dreadlocks when you're older. Much less painful, I swear."

"I'll remember that," she said. She picked Daniel up. "Shall we see what Noah brought you?" She led the way to the living room, where they sat on the floor and Noah dumped the items from the sack.

"Toy camera," he announced, taking it out of its box. "So he can be like his mother." There were buttons to push, rotating pictures and several sounds. "The reviews said it's durable and holds the child's interest for a long time."

"The reviews?"

"Yeah. I checked online before I hit the store."

Daniel glommed on to the gift, slapping at the spinner, then squealing. "Looks like a hit," Noah said. He picked up the second package. "Now, this is a CD player to do kiddie karaoke with. It's officially for two-year-olds, but a mom in the store raved about it for her younger daughter."

"It looks like fun," Mel said, her throat tight, thinking of Noah in the store poring over the best toys, asking nearby moms for advice.

He held out the third box to her. "These are for the bath. Peel-off stickers like what you've got, but more for boys." They were a roadway and cars.

"That is very cool," she said. "He'll like this."

"The last one's my favorite." He grabbed the big box and opened it. "It's a wagon he can push and put crap into. It comes with blocks, but on the review, a single mom said it got her kid into the habit of picking up his toys, so cleanup became a game. Plus, I figure it'll keep him from falling when he walks."

"What do you mean? Daniel walks quite well for his age."

"Are you kidding? He teeters bad. Face-plant about to happen. Personally, I think he needs a helmet, but you're the mom." In seconds, he'd put the legs on the frame and set the wagon upright.

"You did too much," she said.

"They should last him and he'll grow into the karaoke. Like the trike and the LEGO." He stopped and she realized he was thinking that he wouldn't be around to see him play with the items.

He lifted his gaze to her face. "I'll be sending gifts every year, Mel. I promise. Later on, when I'm more cash-fat, I'm setting up a college fund."

"Noah, you don't need to—"

"I *want* to. I insist. If I have to, I'll file papers about it." He was teasing, but she heard bedrock determination in his voice.

"Okay, then. That would be great." His determination moved her.

"Good."

Daniel was still engrossed in the camera, clapping his hands and bucking up and down when each picture flipped and made a sound.

"He likes it, huh?" Noah flat-out beamed. It was so cute, Mel had to fight the urge to laugh out loud. Noah gave the wagon a push and pull. "And this is very sturdy. And safe. There were recalls of similar toys because of a key box that stuck out. This model's okay."

"It's great, Noah," she said. "Really great. Hang on." She jumped up to get her camera and came back to snap some shots of the two of them.

"Can I get prints? You can put them with the photo you already did."

"You didn't pick up the pictures?"

"Not yet. Friday didn't start out well." His tone, abruptly dark, made her remember the newscast she'd seen.

"Was that because of what happened in Afghanistan? I saw the news."

"It threw me off some." His jaw tightened. "But I got past it."

She could tell he didn't want to talk about it, so she left the subject alone. "Actually, I made you a book of photos. It's at the front desk."

"A book?"

"Yeah. I've got a copy here I can show you." She discarded the boxes and sack on her way to her mother's room and brought back the photo book.

Noah smiled at the cover shot of Daniel on the ABC block. "You took this the day I came. I remember the green paint on his face. Looks cute."

She nodded, then opened to the first picture—Mel holding Daniel after his birth.

"Wow. So tiny. And you look beautiful." He looked up at her face, taking her in so closely she blushed. He looked at the next photo of her mother taken in the hospital room. "Look at Irena. Her grin's so big you can hardly see her eyes." He laughed at the next shot of Daniel in his carrier, Paco staring down at him. "Paco looks stunned."

"We had just walked in the door. He was checking out the intruder." She flipped the page. "But a minute later…" Paco was dropping his rubber chicken into the carrier.

"The passing of the chicken, a Ramirez welcome tradition?"

"Exactly."

Noah slowly turned the pages, studying each picture of Daniel crossing milestones—lifting his head, smiling, crawling, sitting up by himself, sitting in the tub, eating solid food, cruising and finally walking. He asked for details from each picture. She saw him swallow hard a couple of times. The muscle in his jaw kept ticking and ticking.

Finished, he closed the book. "This is great. Like being there. Thanks."

I wish you had been. To keep from saying that, she said, "I'll keep sending you photos, if you want. Wherever you end up. Just always get me your address when you move." Her voice was stupidly shaky. It wasn't as though anyone was dying, but she realized she faced another goodbye.

They both looked at Daniel, who was now putting blocks into his blue wagon. "It's hard to believe he's a year old," she said.

"It went fast?"

"And slow."

"Important stuff feels that way—fast and slow." He watched her for a long moment, then sighed. "I should leave you to your party. You sure you don't need anything else?"

"We're set, I think."

Noah moved to Daniel. "Happy birthday, big guy." Daniel didn't look up, still enthralled by his toy.

"Daniel, say bye-bye to Noah." She had to force the words out.

"Don't interrupt him. I'm glad he likes it that much." Noah pushed to his feet and went to the door. Mel followed.

This would be their third goodbye and she dreaded it worst of all.

"Where's Irena?" he asked, lingering in the doorway.

"She's picking up friends from her group."

"How's her health?"

"She seems tired lately. I think she's pushing herself too hard."

"Strong people don't like limits. Do they, Mel?" He winked at her. "Are you doing too much?"

"I've been busy in the studio, but that's a good thing. I have a big job coming up—a family reunion that should bring in more clients."

"That's good to hear."

"Yeah. I need to grow my business. We've got bills to pay." Except now her mother seemed so tired Mel worried that leaving Daniel with her for the entire weekend might be too much.

"You sound concerned."

"I'm not," she said, forcing away her doubts. "I just want it to go well."

"With you behind the lens, how could it not?"

"You always make me feel talented."

"That's because you are. Don't forget that."

Their gazes locked and she felt the old connection. She missed talking to him. She realized she hardly talked to anyone about her life these days. She should make more time to get together with Alice.

"So who's coming to the party?"

"My friend Alice and her boyfriend, friends from

the department store where I used to work, some people from the *Arizona News Day,* the caregivers from Bright Blossoms, some kids. Maybe thirty-five people altogether."

"Do any of them know about me? That I'm Daniel's father?"

"Only Alice. But she doesn't know you're in town."

"So what *did* you tell people?"

"Not many asked. I'm a private person. If they did, I said I'd been involved with a man and that it hadn't worked out. I didn't use your name because people know who you are and I didn't want to raise eyebrows or start gossip."

"So you were guarding my rep? Noah Stone, journalist and baby daddy?" His smile held sadness.

"Ma…ma…ma…uh…" Daniel had crawled over and pulled himself up by Mel's capris. He raised his arms, wanting to be held. She propped him on her hip.

"Happy birthday, little dude," Noah said. He planted a kiss on Daniel's head, then sniffed his hair. "What is that amazing smell?"

"It's great, isn't it? Natural baby perfume. *Eau de bebé,* I guess. From the first day, he smelled like that."

Noah smiled, then looked at her intently, like he was memorizing her face. "You look great, Mel. Like I said, red's your color." His eyes dropped to her chest. "It's probably inappropriate to picture you naked right now, but that's what I'm doing."

His words burned through her. "It sure doesn't help me stay calm."

"Can't help myself around you." After a few seconds, Noah seemed to shake himself out of the moment. "Anyway, good luck with your party." He backed down the steps, watching her.

"You want a cupcake for the road? I made them from scratch. They're no Very Berry Chocolate Supreme, but they're moist. Buttercream frosting."

"I should take off. Have fun. Relax if you can."

She couldn't stand it anymore. "Don't go, Noah. Stay for the party. You're a friend of mine. So why not?"

"You sure?" He considered the idea. "Actually, if *News Day* people are coming, I'd like to talk to them about a story idea I've started on."

"An investigative piece?"

"Yeah. It's on Sam Pasamonte."

"Wow, that's great, Noah."

"It is. Actually, it's the first time I've felt clearheaded enough to really dig in again and write. It feels like a breakthrough…like I'm finally back."

"I'm so glad to hear that." She stepped out on the porch, wanting to hug him, excited and relieved. She'd been worried.

"I knew you would be," he said softly. He took a step toward her again.

"Then you have to stay." She paused. "For your story."

"You twisted my arm." He climbed onto the porch, looking pretty pleased about it.

"And, talk about timing, here comes my editor." She nodded behind him to where Randall Cox and his wife were coming up the walk.

"I am so sorry we're early," his wife said when they reached the porch, "but everything's on a deadline to my husband. I'm Peg Cox. And is this the birthday boy?" She leaned toward Daniel, too closely. "What a cutie pie. Look at your fancy shirt. Pretty warm though." She glanced at Mel.

"If he gets overheated, I'll change him," Mel said

while Daniel tucked his face into Mel's neck to get away from the stranger.

"Randall Cox, *Arizona News Day,*" Randall said to Noah.

"Noah Stone," he said, shaking Randall's proffered hand.

"Yeah," he said. "They've been recapping your ordeal over there."

"Can't fight the news cycle, I guess," Noah said, clearly wanting to change the subject. "I'm glad to meet you. *News Day* made me want to be a reporter."

"That so?"

"Oh, yeah. It broke the big stories, hogged all the awards. Very inspiring. How long have you been ME?"

"Three years now. I was in Detroit. *Free Press.*"

"This must be a change."

"Yeah, but Phoenix has interesting issues and I'm the big dog out here, so I like that."

"And I was so sick of snow I can't tell you," Peg said. "Here you go." She handed Noah the gift bag, as though he was a host, and walked past him into the house. Noah shrugged at Mel. She shrugged back. They followed the Coxes inside. For better or worse, Noah was at the party.

Her mother and her friends arrived next. Irena's grin split her face when she saw Noah, so Mel pulled her aside to warn her not to introduce him as Daniel's father. She did the same for Alice when she came. Her friend's eyes went wide. "So does this mean you two are—"

"No. We're not. He's passing through town. End of story. We'll talk later."

Alice sighed. "We never talk, Mel."

"I know. It's my fault. I'm just—"

"Too busy being a mom." She turned toward the crowd in the living room where Noah stood. "He is *hot*. And he keeps staring at you."

"Let it go, please," Mel said.

"For now. But *just* for now. We're talking if I have to schedule a photo shoot for my nephew to buy some of your time."

"I could use the job."

"You are hopeless, but I'm not giving up on you yet."

The house was soon full of people laughing and talking and children playing. Noah circulated easily, especially among the reporters, who seemed to gravitate to him. Mel took snapshots as she shifted from group to group, moving invisibly the way she liked, quickly composing each shot, capturing personalities and atmosphere as best she could. She always felt more at ease behind a camera. Her studio was rewarding, but she loved the challenge of candid work—having to adjust lighting and angle, depth of field and shutter speed depending on the background, the light, the movement of her subjects, counting on her instincts, moment to moment.

Irena had taken charge of the video camera, mostly following Daniel, who was tagging along after the older children. They were kind to him, letting him go down the slide with them, helping him slug the inflated clown or pushing him in Noah's wagon.

When it seemed time to eat, Mel grabbed the dogs and burgers from the fridge. Noah came up from behind her. "Would it help if I ran the grill for you?"

"That would be great," she said, handing him the tray. "Go for it."

She realized the two of them might be creating the false impression that they were a couple. Noah had greeted people at the door, accepted gifts, distributed drinks and now he was cooking the food, a beer in one hand, amusing the guests, acting completely at home.

Yikes.

Noah's gaze met hers and she felt so good she didn't care about false impressions at all. All during the party, he'd been catching her eye with a wink or a smile or a nod of encouragement. It was exactly like they *were* throwing the party together. *Don't get used to this,* she reminded herself sternly. *Don't think what you're thinking.*

The adults settled in to eat, while the kids abandoned half-eaten food to shriek and chase each other.

When it was time for the cake, Mel placed the small clown cake on Daniel's tray. He first buried his fists in it, twisting them like handlebars, then leaned tentatively forward for a bite. He picked his head up, eyes wide, mouth circled in white-and-red frosting, as if he couldn't believe his luck.

"That's the idea, sweetie," she said, leaning in for another snapshot as he clapped his hands and crowed, flinging frosting and cake left and right.

She noticed that her mother's friend Gloria was now holding the camcorder. Her mother sat beside Daniel, looking pale. Come to think of it, she'd been sitting in that same chair for most of the party. Her fibromyalgia must be acting up. She'd seemed so tired lately.

"Shall I bring out the grown-up cake?" Alice asked.

"Sure." She pushed aside her worry to help Alice serve pieces to everyone, who oohed and aahed and asked for the name of the bakery.

A few minutes later, Noah joined her, his cake plate in his hand. "This cake is amazing. You try it yet?" When she shook her head, he held out a forkful.

"Wow, that is good," she said as the cherries, berries and moist chocolate merged and swirled in her mouth.

"No kidding. This alone is worth sticking around for."

"Are you glad you stayed?" she asked him.

"Are you?" He really wanted to know, she could tell.

"I am. Very glad."

"Good." He smiled. "Alice tells me she can't believe no one has noticed Daniel has my hair and my dimple."

"It's bad enough they think we're a couple, with you grilling the food and handing out drinks and chasing Paco away from the kids' leftovers."

"And the fact that I can't take my eyes off you." He took her arm and pulled her closer to avoid a collision with running children.

His words made her stomach bottom out. He was taking her all in, holding her with his gaze as though he never wanted to let her go. Her legs went liquid the way they had that first night.

"Alice also told me you're no fun anymore."

"She exaggerates."

"Really? When do you relax, anyway?"

"After Daniel's in bed...when I don't fall asleep first. I'm relaxing now."

"I haven't seen you sit down once and, believe me, I've been watching. Those pants make your butt look amazing, by the way."

"Thank you," she said, her face going hot.

"Come here." He took her by the hand through the kitchen to the patio where he sat her down, took her camera strap from around her neck and placed her legs on a chair. She felt instantly better and let go a breath she'd evidently been holding.

He ducked into the house and returned with an

opened beer and a piece of cake, which he put on the table. "There. Drink a beer, eat some cake and catch up with your friend." He motioned Alice over. "I'll keep track of Daniel."

"Thank you, Noah," she said.

He backed away, watching her, then turned for Daniel, who was heading for the slide.

"Interesting," Alice said. "So, the man fetches you food, puts your feet up and is taking care of your child so you can talk to a friend. And you want him out of your life…why?"

She groaned. "Because it's not real. He'll be gone soon. And it's not what either of us wants." *And because I've begun to want it more than I dare admit.*

CHAPTER TEN

WHEN THE DOOR CLOSED on the last guest, Noah found Mel in the kitchen, Daniel on her hip, covering the remains of the fancy cake with plastic wrap. She looked so good to him. The red top with skinny straps went great with her tan and he liked how she'd curled her hair in soft waves that bounced on her shoulders. Those pants showed off her shape so well it hurt to watch.

"Hey," he said softly. "You doing okay?"

"I'm beat, but I think it went well."

"Looked like everyone had a good time. Especially this guy." He patted Daniel's head and the boy reached for him. Noah took him onto one hip.

"That hurts your arm, doesn't it?" Mel asked. "I've seen you wince."

With her eye for detail, he wasn't surprised she'd noticed. "It gets sore, but not like it used to." He spotted a smear of red frosting near Daniel's ear and wiped it away. "You have a good time?" he asked.

Daniel lifted his small hand. *He wanted a high-five.* Noah gave him one, his insides going as soft as the frosting on the cake. This kid was so great.

"Seemed like you talked to a lot of people," Mel said to him.

"I did. Yeah." It had been strangely easy, as though he'd dropped into some guy's life, with a wife and a kid and a house and a dog. Even a mother-in-law. He hadn't minded that much, either.

"Did you talk to Randall about your story?"

"Yeah. Dave Roberts, too. They're going to help me out with their notes and sources. We've got a meeting set up." He'd been pleased at how well that had come together.

"That's great, Noah. I'm glad you're back to writing."

"Me, too. And Dave told me you seriously kicked butt on that dogfight story. He said they wanted to turn you both away until you raged at Dave like he was your boyfriend screwing up your date, so they let you in."

"I couldn't believe they bought that."

"Dave says you were seriously *intrepid.*"

"He said that? Intrepid?" She grinned. "That's high praise from him."

"I'm not surprised. I knew you'd be great. He wants you back, he says."

"I miss it a lot. But I can't even think about it until Daniel's in school." She sighed and he saw for a moment how tough the sacrifice had been for her. He could never have done what she did.

She was a much better person than he was.

Much better. And now he needed to leave her be.

"I'd better take off." He handed Daniel to her and they walked together to the door.

"I'll put the prints from today with the photo book," she said.

"That'd be great." He wished he'd taken the camera away from her to get a few photos of her, too. Damn, he would miss her. "Thanks."

"I guess this is it. Goodbye for real," she said, her

forehead creasing, as though she didn't like the idea. He sure as hell didn't.

Before he could say so, there was a thud from the kitchen, followed by a dish hitting the floor. Someone had fallen.

They ran to the kitchen, where they found Irena sprawled on the tile on her side, a broken bowl and a smear of salsa near her hand.

Mel dropped to her knees beside her mother. "*Mamá!* Can you hear me?" She set Daniel down and the boy crawled toward the living room.

Irena didn't respond.

"Looks like she fainted. Maybe get a damp towel." He put her legs over a tipped-over stool to get blood to her heart and brain. Her clothes were not constricting her at all, at least.

Mel pressed the cloth to her mother's face and neck. "The doctor said she might become anemic. Maybe that's why she fainted. Should we drive her to the hospital or call an ambulance?" Though her eyes were scared, Mel spoke calmly. That was Mel. Solid, even in a crisis.

Irena's eyes opened and she blinked. *"Qué pasó?"* She started to sit up.

"Don't move, *Mamá*. You fainted. Does anything hurt?"

"Lo siento, mi'ja," Irena said, grimacing. She grabbed her abdomen.

"Your stomach? Is that all?"

Her mother nodded.

"You'll need to talk to the doctors, Mel," Noah said. "I'll watch Daniel while you drive Irena to the hospital."

"Are you sure?" Mel said. "I don't want to impose."

"Mel. Please."

She gave him a steady look. "I'm glad you're here."

"There's nowhere else I'd rather be."

A few minutes later, Daniel cocked on his hip, Noah watched Mel and her mother drive away, wondering what exactly he'd meant when he'd said those words. They sounded way too dramatic, way too significant, way too...*permanent.*

Don't get her hopes up, Cindi had warned him. She was right. It had been the heat of the moment, the urgency of the crisis. Surely Mel would realize that, right? Surely that was all he'd meant to say.

MEL WAS SO TIRED BY THE time she pulled into her driveway from the hospital that turning the steering wheel made her arms ache. It was after ten and she was exhausted. Her mind was sluggish, her spirits battered, her face tight from fighting tears and panic.

Then she noticed the light in the front window and her heart lifted a bit. A dark, empty house would have sunk her even lower. Even better, Noah and Daniel were inside. She couldn't wait to see them both, and she was too damn tired to give herself a hard time about that.

She pulled into the garage and turned off the car, resting her forehead on the steering wheel while she took slow, deep breaths. She wasn't about to walk in and burst into tears. She'd held back during the E.R. wait while the doctor examined her mother, then explained the need for tests, and while Irena got situated in a room. Mel could hold back long enough to say good-night to Noah and put Daniel to bed. After that, she had all the time in the world to cry.

When she felt calm enough, she stepped into the house and Noah rose from the love seat and came to her, a finger to his lips. She saw that Daniel slept on the sofa, blocked from falling by the backs of two kitchen chairs. "How is she?" Noah asked.

"Dehydrated. They think that's why she fainted. But her white count is elevated and they don't know why. It's causing her abdominal pain, they think. They want to keep her for a few days for tests. Her oncologist will see her in the morning. They gave her a heavy-duty painkiller and she's asleep, so they sent me home."

"How are you holding up?" The kindness in his face did her in.

"Not so good," she choked out, and walked into his open arms. Tears slid down her cheeks, but she refused to sob. What good would that do?

"You're scared. That's natural, Mel. She's stable, the doctors are looking after her and there's nothing you can do right now except get some rest."

She nodded against his shoulder. He was right and it was a relief to hear. Her spinning thoughts stopped. Nothing had changed, but she felt better with Noah's arms around her, his heart beating steadily against her own.

"Did you eat?" he asked after a few seconds.

She shook her head against his chest.

"Let me heat you up a leftover hot dog."

The idea sounded wretched, but when he set the plate of chips, carrots and a microwaved wiener in front of her, she realized she was starving. She wolfed it down, drinking the ice-cold beer he'd opened, and felt strength returning to her body. She felt less shaky. Noah watched her eat every bite. She looked around and saw the party debris was gone. "You cleaned up."

"I figured you'd feel better coming home to a picked-up house."

"Are you for real?" She reached out to pretend to pinch him.

"Just channeling Irena—*be of use.* You feel any better?"

"I do. Thanks. I'd better put Daniel in bed."

Noah followed her to the couch, where she scooped Daniel into her arms. He hardly stirred as she settled him against her shoulder.

"He did some hard partying," Noah murmured. He went with her to Daniel's room where she changed his diaper and T-shirt and put him into his crib without waking him.

Noah stood beside her, looking down at the sleeping boy. "Happy birthday, little dude." He glanced up at her. Reading her face, he put his hand over hers on the top bar of Daniel's crib. What was he telling her? She was afraid to guess. They left the room together and Mel flipped off the light and pulled the door partway closed.

"Is there anything else you need before I go?" Noah asked her quietly.

Go? He was going? Panic flew through her. Once Noah left, she would face a sleepless night of worry. She dreaded that.

Noah stood tall beside her, safe and reassuring. Whether or not he could be a steady father to Daniel, he'd been exactly what she'd needed today—a second set of hands at the party, watchful eyes on Daniel while she went to the hospital. He'd straightened her house, fed her and comforted her. She wasn't used to being helped, but Noah had made it seem natural and right.

Being with him now felt natural and right.

He looked at her *that way,* the way he had that long-ago weekend, with pure desire, and it made her breathless. If they went to bed, she could escape from dread and fear for the night.

"Yes," she said, "there is something else." She looked at him. "I need you to tuck me in."

"Tuck you...? Mel." A shudder passed through him and his eyes flared with abrupt lust. "Are you sure?" She could tell he hadn't expected this.

"I want to go back to that weekend when the future was bright, when it was just you and me, talking and laughing and making love, when there were nothing but good things ahead of us." Her voice shook.

He took her hand and kissed her palm before bending to sweep her into his arms. "Point me to your room."

"End of the hall," she breathed, clasping her hands around the back of his neck, watching his eyes burn at her, feeling her heart pound, wanting what would happen next more than she'd wanted anything in a long, long time.

STANDING OVER THE BED, holding Mel in his arms, Noah leaned in to capture her mouth for as gentle a kiss as he could manage when he wanted to rip off her clothes and bury himself inside her.

I need you to tuck me in.

The words had been a flash fire turning whatever restraint he had to instant ash. *Take it easy,* he warned himself. Mel needed to be taken care of, and he was the lucky man who got to do it. That meant controlling himself, no matter the effect the woman had on his brain, his heart and his parts.

His quick impression of the space was fire and serenity: hot colors, red spread covered with bright pillows...low, simple furniture...gray walls filled with framed photos...the smell of her perfume.

Bracing her against his good arm, he tore down the covers with the other, sending pillows flying. Setting her on the mattress, he helped her out of her top, leaving her in a white bra. She reached for his shirt buttons, but he stopped her hands and yanked his shirt over his head. Screw the buttons.

Mel looked him over. He saw her eyes hitch here and there on his scars, but he focused on her, unclasping her bra and tossing it to the floor.

Her bare breasts sent lust pouring through him. "You are so beautiful," he said, bending to kiss the top of one, then the other, feeling the shiver of arousal that passed through her. He forced himself to go slow, to enjoy every inch of her, to give her all the pleasure he could manage. He pressed his tongue against her neck, felt the quick throb of her pulse.

"That feels…so…so…" She gave a soft exhalation, as if she'd let go of a rope and was falling free. "Just… so…"

He smiled, moving to her collarbone, then kissing his way to the ball of her shoulder, down her arm to the bend of her elbow, a spot that made her giggle softly. He grinned against her skin, kissed down to her palm, then teased each finger with his tongue.

She squirmed beneath him and bent her knees, shifting her hips. Next she would dig her heels into his ass. She wanted to yank him into position as she had that weekend: *Here*…now *there*. *Right* there and just like *that*.

But he didn't want to succumb to her rush this time. She'd given herself over to him and he would make her glad she had. He wanted to soothe her, as well as excite her, and to honor every part of the body he remembered with such pleasure.

Sensing his resolve, Mel surrendered, letting her legs drop to the sheets, trusting him to get her where she needed to go.

He returned to her breasts, cupping them, warm and heavy in his hands, familiar, but changed, too—fuller, the nipples a darker brown—but still beautiful. He ran his tongue around the edge of a nipple, then sucked the tip the way she liked, loving how she arched against his lips.

"Just like that," she breathed. He moved to the other breast, tracing the nipple with his tongue, making her moan. "And that…definitely *that*."

He forced himself to move on, knowing if he focused on one lush spot too long, he'd be done for. He kissed his way down the valley between her breasts to her abdomen, shifting down the bed.

She lifted her head to look at him. "What are you doing?"

"I want to taste you."

Her eyes flared and she bit her lip, falling back onto the pillow.

Pleased, he scooped her hips into his palms, pressing his thumbs against the tendons high on her thigh. With his tongue, he found her clit, wet and swollen, sweet and salty as he remembered, her flesh like delicate velvet.

"Dios mio," she said. "You have no *idea*…how *good*…that *feels*."

"Oh, I think I do," he said, smiling against her, kissing her there, then teasing her with his tongue as she tensed and pushed against his mouth, gripping his hair with both hands. Seconds later, she convulsed into a climax, saying his name in a faint gasp.

He held himself still, as he knew she preferred, until the waves had finished with her. Except, her body began to quake again. He pulled himself up to her face and found her crying with a smile on her face, tears spilling down her cheeks. "I don't know why I'm crying. That was amazing. This is stupid."

"Pent-up feelings, Mel." He pulled her onto his chest. "It's what you needed to do." He stroked her back with the tips of his fingers, knowing she loved the sensation. "It's all good."

"I don't know what I'll do if my mother dies."

He felt a wave of shared pain at her words. "You're a strong person," he said, knowing that was true. "Whatever happens, you'll handle it." Also true.

Her shoulders shook for a few more seconds, then she seemed to calm down. "I'm glad she's had this time with Daniel."

"She adores him, that's for sure."

"I found out I was pregnant the same day she learned she had cancer," she said softly. "I don't think I told you that."

"You didn't. Damn. Talk about timing."

"No kidding. Plus, I wasn't supposed to be able to get pregnant. My fallopian tubes are scarred. The doctor told me I'd need in vitro fertilization to get pregnant. That makes Daniel kind of a miracle."

"Proves there were some determined swimmers in there."

"Relentless, like your reporting," she said. He felt her smile against his chest. "I hated leaving my job, but I have no regrets about Daniel, especially if my mother—" she gulped "—doesn't have much time."

He stroked her hair and kissed her neck, wishing he could take away her pain. "I think you're very brave, Mel. *Melodía*. I like how that sounds."

"I guess it's better than *Mel-o-dy,*" she said, saying it in a mocking, singsong voice, "but it's still lightweight."

"A pretty name doesn't make you weak. Maybe you can be Melodía or Melody and still be a kick-ass mom and an intrepid photographer and a together woman. Just a thought."

She raised her face to smile at him. "So, now you're a life coach?"

"All part of my tuck-in service. Whatever you need, Mel."

"How about what you need?" she said, her eyes abruptly ablaze.

"I'm good. Tonight is about you. Aren't you sleepy?"

"Not one bit," she said, sounding as energetic as she'd been that weekend—boundlessly enthusiastic, endlessly inventive.

"Mornings start early around here, remember?"

"I don't care right now." She rose to straddle him. "And neither do you, I can see." She looked down at his erection.

"That's because all the blood from my brain is otherwise occupied."

She positioned herself over him. "Let's go with that for now."

Maybe it would be better if she slept, but Noah was only human. He buried himself to the hilt in her warm core. She sucked in a breath.

"Is this good?" he asked, moving her up and down, taking each stroke slowly, like rolling ocean waves.

"You know it is. It's perfect." She bit her lip. "I missed you—this." She amended her words quickly, looking at him to see if he'd caught her slip.

He stilled himself and stopped her hips. "I missed

you, too, Mel." He met her gaze, wanting her to absorb the words. "More than I let myself know."

"I'm glad," she said, falling forward onto his chest. He held her close, pressing his mouth to her neck while they rocked together, climbing the hill to fly off the top, so high and far he never wanted to land.

Careful now. Don't get carried away.

But he was escaping, too, slipping into the time before Iraq, when being together in bed had been more than enough for both of them. No questions, no ripples.

Except the pregnancy they hadn't known about. That had turned into a tidal wave, washing away all that had been easy between them forever.

And after this? In the morning? There would be ripples, all right. How far they would reach remained to be seen.

"SHOULD I GO?" Noah's voice caught Mel as she was drifting off. She'd been reveling in the experience of having Noah spooned around her, just like her pregnancy fantasy. His words were a stab of light through a protective curtain.

She turned to see his face. "Probably. But I don't want you to." They'd stolen a moment and she wasn't ready for reality to bear down on them again. She checked the clock, then groaned. "One a.m. That leaves five hours of sleep if we fall off right now. I want to visit the hospital before I go to work."

"Would it save you time if I took Daniel to Bright Blossoms?"

"It would simplify things."

"Then I'll do it. You've got a lot on your shoulders right now—your mother's illness, her business, yours and Daniel. Let me help you."

"But you're busy, too. You've got your job, your grandmother's house and that freelance story to pursue."

"Far less than you, Mel."

"I don't want you feeling sorry for me. I have friends who can help me. I'm not bereft. I can manage." Though among her friends, she was the one who gave advice, suggested solutions and pitched in to implement them. At least that's how it had been before Daniel.

"Let me help you."

She looked at him, wondering exactly what yes might mean.

"You're thinking about the ripples," he said. "Don't. Let's get through this crisis. Forget the rest for now." Something in his face made her want to give in, stop fighting to run the show. With all she faced at the moment, it felt good to trust Noah, to let it all go.

"Okay," she said softly. "We'll get through this and put the rest on hold."

"Good." He lay back down and snuggled up to her, spooning them tight, his hand on her breast, their bodies a perfect fit, breathing as one. It felt so very right. They'd fallen into place like puzzle pieces in a happy-family jigsaw.

Uh-oh.

Alarm bells clanged in her head. This was dangerous. This was addictive. The solution was obvious. Put the brakes on sex. That way, she could handle Noah's help until her mother recovered and be ready to say good-bye when the crisis was over and reality set in again. It was her best hope, she knew, so, with a sigh of regret, she said, "But the sex has to stop."

"What?" Noah tensed, gripping her more tightly, more wonderfully.

"Tonight was an escape. Tomorrow we're back to real life. It's the only way this will work."

"Okay, if that's what you want," he said, kissing her neck. "No more sex." It sounded as though he was smiling.

She shifted to look at him. "I mean it, Noah. I'm serious."

Noah opened one eye. "The longer you talk, the less you'll sleep."

"I'm not kidding."

"I know that," he said, but she could tell he didn't believe her. She'd have to prove it to him. She only hoped she'd be strong enough.

"I WILL BE HERE ONLY a few days, *mi'ja*," Mel's mother said to her the next morning from her hospital bed. She was struggling to keep her eyes open. "The doctors want my blood count up…and be sure the pain… *está controlado.* And it is—" her eyelids drifted closed "—*mucho mejor.*"

"That's because you're on morphine, *Mamá.* Don't try to protect me. I need to know everything the doctors said."

"I jus' tell you everything." Her mother blinked, sitting up higher in the bed, trying to stay alert. "The infection they fix and wait to be sure. I have this pretty room and nurses who are so kind. *Todo está bien.*"

"Okay, I guess." So far, so good anyway.

"And you? You slept, *mi'ja.* I see in your face."

"I guess I slept."

"You are pink now. *Qué pasó?* Is it Noah?"

"Why would you think that?" She felt herself go bright red.

"He stays long at the fiesta. He looks always at you. *Algo pasó, verdad?*"

Something happened, right? There was no use trying to hide it from her mother, so Mel confessed, "Noah stayed last night, okay? He wants to help us get through your illness, to help with Daniel."

"And you? To be with you?"

"No. That's…not possible. He'll be around until you're better."

Her mother beamed, brightening the dimly lit room with her smile. "I know this. All while I am here so ill, I feel in my heart not to worry." She put her hands in prayer and looked upward. *"Mil gracias, Santa Margarita."*

"Oh, stop. St. Margaret doesn't bless premarital sex and we both know that. You use the saints like wishing on a star."

"Do not speak ill of the faith of my parents." Her mother beamed.

"I don't know what I'm doing, *Mamá.*" She sagged against the chair.

"You do what is in your heart." Her mother patted her hand. "That is good. Always, you are here." She tapped Mel's skull. "Planning, thinking. Too much." Her mother patted Mel's breastbone. "Here is your good guide."

"I can't believe you're sick, but you're giving me comfort."

"You with that smile are comfort for me."

"I guess that's good." Mel felt so overwhelmed. Noah had been acting like a husband and father from the moment he knocked on the door the previous afternoon. They'd slept together and had amazing sex, maybe more amazing than before because they knew each other better, had experienced more in life, or maybe just because they'd been fighting the urge since he'd returned.

Either way, things had changed between them. Was it real? Was it good? Did she even want it? Her head spun like Daniel during Noah's merry-go-round game. Their feelings for each other had intensified, sure, but that didn't change the reality that Noah would not stick around. And even if he did, he could never be the kind of father Daniel deserved. It wasn't in him.

She left the hospital for Bright Blossoms and the day flew by while she juggled her studio and her mother's duties. Before she knew it, it was 6:00 p.m. She wanted to stop by the hospital to see her mother, who was holding her own, the nurse had told her when she called, her pain mostly managed. She and Daniel would eat at the hospital.

When she rounded the corner toward her mother's room, she saw the door was open. Inside, Noah sat on the guest chair. On her mother's tray was a potted plant with flowers and a Spanish magazine.

"Hey, Mel," he said, rising to greet them. "Hey, buddy." He raised a palm to give Daniel a high-five, then leaned in to kiss Mel.

She tensed, uncomfortable because of the intimacy Noah had assumed between them. Like sex, it could give her a false sense that they were a couple, rather than friends getting through a crisis.

Noah seemed taken aback by her stiffness. "I wanted to see how Irena was doing and connect with you and Daniel," he said, eyeing her closely.

"That was nice of you."

"He brings me flowers and a magazine," Irena said, clearly loving this.

"And I'm down for watching Daniel this weekend," Noah said.

"You're what?"

"I tell to him about Tucson," her mother said. "Your job there."

"Oh." She hadn't thought through her week and what her mother's illness meant about the Steiner-Markowitz reunion shoot. "I should probably cancel it. I need to be here for you, *Mamá*."

"You cannot cancel now," her mother chided. "They count on you."

"It's no problem for me," Noah said. "I'm happy to help."

"I don't know. I'll have to think about it."

"In the meantime, do you want me to get takeout for supper? I've got an interview tonight, but I can grab you some food."

"That's okay. We'll eat here at the hospital. Go to your interview."

"You sure? Because I can easily—"

"I'm positive. I'll walk you to the elevator." She wanted to clear the air without her mother overhearing. At the bank of elevators, she said, "About this weekend, I know you're trying to pitch in, but—"

"That reunion means money, plus referrals. You told me yourself. You can't cancel, Mel. And I can handle it, like I said."

"An entire weekend? Meals and baths and bedtimes and cranky fits? No breaks in the day unless he naps, which he rarely does if his routine's off. You don't know what you're offering."

"Then show me," he said. "Train me. Babysitter boot camp. We've got the rest of the week." He pushed the down button on the elevator.

She studied him. Could he possibly mean that?

"I said I'd help you through the crisis, remember? This is where it counts. Give me tonight to do research and shape an outline for the story, but after that I'm all yours."

It would solve a problem and the weekend was important. She hated letting down a client. "You should think about it, Noah. It's a whole weekend."

"I have. I don't make promises I can't keep."

"All right then. Thanks."

He leaned in and kissed her softly, heat flaring in his eyes and speeding along her nerve endings. "I can come by later tonight. It'll be late—nine or so."

She shook her head. "Not a good idea. We agreed on babysitting, not babysitting with benefits."

"If you change your mind..." He mimed holding a phone as he stepped into the open elevator. He grinned at her as the doors closed between them.

He wasn't making this easier. It was a relief not to have to juggle Daniel and her job and Bright Blossoms and her mother's hospitalization all alone, she had to admit, but the family fantasy hung in Mel's head like the wisps of a delicious dream. She valued self-sufficiency. It was basic to who she was. If she lost that, where would she be?

NOAH SLUMPED AGAINST THE back of the elevator. What had he gotten himself into? Without missing a beat, he'd convinced Mel he could handle Daniel *all weekend long.* He'd be on duty 24/7. It would take more than a long walk and a few handfuls of Cheerios to keep the kid content. Once Daniel figured out it was amateur hour, he'd dial the separation anxiety to max volume, no question.

Noah had gone overboard, throwing himself into Mel, Daniel and Irena's lives as if he meant to be husband, father and son-in-law to them. It had been the postcoital glow, along with some subterranean longing to be like everyone else, to find a long-term place for himself with people he loved who loved him back. That had come from the relief of beginning to feel normal again, no doubt, but it was hopelessly unrealistic.

Mel was right to doubt him. What if, while he watched Daniel, he got slammed by one of the headaches that sent him to bed in the dark with an ice pack for two days? The thought made sweat pop over his body even in the air-conditioned chill of the lobby.

No. He would not let Mel down.

He'd promised to help her out and he would do it. He would ask Cindi and Paul to be his backup, insurance against any physical dive he might experience, and he would get all he could from babysitting boot camp with Mel. Maybe he'd read up on child care beforehand. As a reporter, he always prepped in advance. He'd do that here, too.

CHAPTER ELEVEN

TUESDAY NIGHT, MEL LEFT Daniel in his high chair to answer the door.

"What do you think of this?" Noah said, holding out a DVD in a rental case. It was called, *What to Expect from Your Child, birth to 3.*

Her heart tightened. He was doing his best, that was clear.

"What?" he said, reading her face. "Overkill?"

"No. It's very sweet. I appreciate that you're trying so hard."

He fished a small steno notepad from his pocket. "For notes."

"You won't need that," she said, leading him to the kitchen and handing him what she'd typed up. "This has all the daily details."

He flipped over the first sheet, then the next and the next. "Four pages? Should I take this personally?"

"Better safe than sorry. So you'll know everything." She bit her lip, realizing she'd probably overdone the detail. "This is the first time I've left him with anyone." Her throat tightened at the thought.

"I get it, Mel." He moved in to smooth her hair from her cheek. "I won't let you down."

"I know you won't." She almost leaned up to kiss him, but Daniel banged his spoon on the tray, reminding her she'd promised not to get physical with Noah again. "Anyway, we're doing dessert now." She put a plate of watermelon, strawberries and blueberries on Daniel's tray, then explained the food she would prepare in advance—rotisserie chicken, noodle casserole, a slow-cooker roast with vegetables she would leave Friday morning for dinner that night.

She showed him the sippy cups and baby plates, the jars of toddler food for emergencies or trips to the park. When she turned around, Daniel was tossing strawberries to the floor for Paco. "When he feeds the dog, he's finished. If you serve him grapes, be sure to cut them in half so he doesn't choke. That goes for any food. Small bites always."

"Got it," Noah said. He listened politely, smiling and nodding, while she talked and talked, nervous and jumpy and very aware of how close Noah stood, of how good he smelled, and how his eyes roved her body the entire time.

"Okay, moving on to the bath. Bring the printout so I cover all the points." She motioned for him to follow her down the hall, Daniel in her arms.

NOAH SAT AGAINST THE wall at the far end of the tub, his legs stretched so they brushed Mel's body, his head swimming with dos and don'ts, be-careful-ofs and re-member-tos.

He kept losing his train of thought watching her. She was so damned sexy. Now her breasts swayed as she knelt over the tub, rinsing Daniel's hair. The little boy fussed and wiggled, while she deftly poured water, all the while explaining, warning, listing and describing things to Noah, her voice husky and tender, almost hypnotic, her fingers gentle and nimble. He watched her thigh muscles shiver and tighten.

What was that about soap versus shampoo? Maybe he'd give the kid one good bath right before Mel got home and be done with it.

"He really likes the peel-on road and cars you gave him," Mel said, nodding as Daniel placed a school bus onto the black plastic strip of road.

"Look at that. He put the bus right at the intersection. Pretty smart."

"I think that's accidental. But wait until we read to him and you'll see how verbally advanced he is."

"That's no surprise with you as his mother."

"And you as his father." Their eyes met and held. They were Daniel's parents. Mel and he. Together. It was a strange feeling. Cozy and claustrophobic at once. Again, he felt like he'd been dropped into someone else's life.

"There, done," Mel said finally, lifting Daniel out of the water. "Can you grab that towel for me? Hold it open?"

Noah yanked the blue towel from over his head and opened it on his lap so Mel could put Daniel there, a soft weight on his legs and against his chest in the steamy, soap-fragrant room. Mel knelt close to dry Daniel's body and scrub his wet hair with the thick cloth, her movements vibrating against Noah's body, her lips nearly close enough to kiss, light flashing from her dark pupils.

When they went to Daniel's room, Mel laid the little boy in his towel on the diaper table and explained about which T-shirts were night shirts and why and told him the lotion was for his skin, the baby oil to untangle his hair, but only a drop or two or he got too greasy and on and on. Whatever.

Daniel looked bored, so Noah pulled the string on his mobile.

"How'd you know he likes that?" she asked.

"When I changed his diaper the other night I figured it out. I'm not totally clueless, Mel."

She colored. "I don't mean to suggest that you are. I just—"

"It's cool. You're nervous about leaving him. You like things done your way. I get it. If it makes you feel better, Cindi and Paul said they'd be my backup."

She smiled. "You know me too well."

"I think I do," he said, and it pleased him to realize it.

After Daniel was dressed, Mel carried him to a blue plush rocker recliner beside a small table with a stack of books. The bookcase against the wall held more of the thick cardboard ones, along with childhood classics—*The Velveteen Rabbit, Winnie the Pooh, Goodnight Moon, Where the Wild Things Are.*

"Would you get that stuffed dog from his crib?" she asked Noah.

He grabbed the squishy sheepdog. "This must be named Paco."

"Paquito, yes. Daniel needs it to fall asleep. Keep track of Paquito or bedtime's a disaster."

"Got it. Necessary security object." As if on cue, the stuffed dog's namesake lumbered in and dropped at Mel's feet. "So Paco's in on story time?"

"Of course." Mel took a book from the top of the stack. "He likes all of these," she said, motioning down the pile, "but this is our current number one." It was small, with pages of padded plastic. Mel opened it, but Daniel took it from her and thrust it at Noah, who'd sat beside the chair on the floor.

"He wants me to read it to him?"

"Looks like it." Mel seemed as surprised as he was. She got out of the chair and motioned for Noah to take her place.

Touched, Noah took Daniel onto his lap. Maybe this weekend wouldn't go so badly after all. He opened the book, which had objects for Daniel to pinch or beep or shake, with catchy rhymes. As Noah read, Daniel kept craning to look up at his face, maybe curious about the deeper voice.

Noah's heart seemed to be dissolving in his chest. Had to be more of that biological hardwiring, but he liked it. He enjoyed the hell out of this sweet little boy, his pudgy hands and tiny fingers patting the pages, pinching and poking the buttons and clasps and strings with utter concentration, so intent that he was breathing noisily through his mouth.

The moment was kind of magical. Noah suddenly got what Paul had said about things changing when you had your own kid. Completely against his will, Noah *did* have one. And things had definitely changed.

At the end, Noah started to put the book back, but Daniel leaned for it. "Eh, eh, eh," he said.

"Oh, you're not finished, Noah. Three readings. At least." Mel grinned.

They went through the book two more times, then Daniel reached for his mother, who resumed her seat on the chair and read him a book with farm animals, asking Daniel to point to various ones—the chick, the duck, the dog, the cow—which he did successfully.

"He nailed that," Noah said. "You think he's gifted?"

"It's too soon to tell," she said, her eyes locking with his. "But I think he's a quick learner." All parents thought their kids were brilliant, he guessed, but he figured he and Mel were right about Daniel. She put away the book.

"Now comes singing," she said to him. She was so beautiful, her eyes bright with love for Daniel, her skin golden in the lamplight. It was hard not to kiss her. And it would be hard after that to stop. "I usually start with 'Duermete, Niño Lindo.'"

"'Sleep, pretty baby'?"

"You know the song?" Her eyes lit up.

"Just how to translate it. High school Spanish."

"He likes any music, so sing whatever you like." She launched into the song, her voice soft and as pretty as her name, followed by "All the Pretty Little Ponies." Noah felt like he'd dropped into a fairy tale.

After the songs, Mel did a Spanish pat-a-cake rhyme about making tortillas for *mamá* and *papá,* the good ones for *mamá,* the burned ones for *papá.*

Daniel was enthralled. So was Noah. Mel smiled. "This is Daniel's favorite part of the day."

"No wonder. You put on a show for him."

"It's my favorite, too."

"I can see that. You're kind of glowing."

"I am?"

"Yeah. You are. Daniel's a lucky boy to have you as a mother." She had a serenity that Noah found magnetic—a complete contrast to his own turmoil, so constant since Iraq that he'd stopped noticing it.

"I think I'm the lucky one." She looked down at her son.

Noah looked at them both and thought, *And I'm the luckiest of all.*

"Time for bed," she said, rising from the chair with Daniel. She gave him a smooch on the cheek and put him into his crib, Paquito beside him. "Night-night, *Danielito, mi amor.*" The little boy's eyes drifted shut.

"'Night, little dude," Noah said. He followed Mel to the door.

"Make sure the monitor is on—" she tapped the box on the bureau "—as well as the night-light." She pointed at an outlet that had a glowing circus seal. "I keep the door open a crack—to hear better and for circulation."

In the hallway, she turned to him. "So, that's it. A practice bedtime."

He found himself staring at her mouth. They'd danced around each other all evening, brushing fingers, bumping arms and hips and legs. At the moment he could make out her nipples beneath the thin shirt and he wanted to touch them the way that made her groan until she begged him to take her to bed. She couldn't be serious about no sex. Not now. Not after all this.

"You'll sleep in my bedroom, since that's where the monitor is," she said.

"How about we practice that, too?" He leaned in to take her mouth.

NOAH'S LIPS STOPPED Mel's words and all sensible thought. All evening, the sparks and jolts of being so near him, brushing against him, had shaken her over and over, wearing her down. They were alone in the house, Daniel asleep, her mother away, in the quiet hallway lit with gold from the baseboard lights.

They'd agreed. No more sex.

But it was late and she was so tired of fighting her reactions. She'd brought Noah into their precious nighttime routine and he'd clearly enjoyed it. When Daniel gave him the book, she'd thought she'd melt right into the carpet with affection. The man was loving and gentle with Daniel, and as sexy as hell with her. How was she supposed to resist *that?*

Noah pressed her against the wall with his hips and took her face in his hands, still kissing her, sending charge after charge along her nerves. Finally, he pulled back. "What do you say? You feeling this?"

"Of course. I can't be within three feet of you and not feel this. But that doesn't mean we have to do anything about it," she said weakly.

"Remind me again why not."

"Because it's too confusing…too distracting. It messes me up."

"And makes you feel good," he said, kissing her neck. "How can that be bad?" He moved to her collarbone. "And what about the morning routine? Don't I need to see how that works?" He gripped her backside and rocked against her. He was charming her, coaxing her into what she'd sworn not to do. He figured she couldn't resist him. He had a point.

But she hadn't achieved all she'd achieved in life by succumbing to every urge. She had discipline, control, maturity. She put her hands against his chest and pushed him back.

He looked surprised.

"You're right about the morning routine, though. You can stay in my mother's room. I'll put fresh sheets on." She turned for the linen closet, acting sure of herself, hoping he couldn't tell how shaky she was.

Grabbing the set of sheets, she headed down the hall, turning back to Noah, who stared after her. "Come on. Be of use."

Together they stripped and remade the bed. Mel folded back the corner and smoothed the sheet. "There you go. I'll wake you at six."

"I'll be up." He looked at her with such longing she could hardly stand it.

"Quit that."

"What?" He blinked.

"Just…good night," she said, and left, closing the door behind her—hard. What was she going to do about Noah? She'd been a single mom for a year and managed just fine, thank you. But Noah made her want more. He made her want him—as a man and as a father to their child.

Mel woke to the crackle of the monitor and Daniel crying softly. She checked the clock. Midnight. Now and then, after an intense day, Daniel woke from a bad dream in the night. He'd likely go right back to sleep, but she decided to check on him.

She found him quietly fussing in the crib, already asleep, so she stroked his back until he stilled.

When she turned to leave, Noah was leaning in the doorway, naked except for boxers. "He okay?" he asked sleepily, running his hand over his face.

She nodded, passing beneath his arm, then pulling the door nearly shut. "I didn't know you were such a light sleeper."

"I've become one, yeah." He frowned, as if that troubled him.

"Once in a while, Daniel cries from a bad dream. Patting his back is usually all he needs. If he's standing up, fully wake, you can rock him for a few minutes, but don't let him down to play. Night's for sleeping."

"Until you reach a certain age, I guess." Noah's face had been softened by sleep and she picked up the warm spice of his skin, reminding her of the other night when they'd slept spooned together.

"That's nice…what you're wearing," he said, nodding

at her spaghetti-strapped red satin camisole and matching shorts. "The fabric looks wet." He touched the cloth against her ribs, sliding his hand up and down. "Feels nice. I like these skinny little straps." He ran a finger underneath one and eased it softly down her arm.

She leaned into the touch with a small gasp. She couldn't help it. It was the middle of the night, they were both half-asleep. It seemed ridiculous to hold out any longer. *Remind me again why not....*

Noah took down the other strap, the fabric tickling her upper arm, sending goose bumps across her skin in a wave. The bodice slipped lower, exposing the tops of her breasts, teasing her skin, making her nipples cramp deliciously.

"Mmm. Nice." A slow smile spread across Noah's face. He'd noticed her nipples. He took the bottom of her top on both sides and very slowly pulled it down, eagerly watching for each newly exposed bit of flesh.

Mel's breath rasped in and out. She was desperately aroused, standing in the softly lit hallway with Noah slowly disrobing her. Her sex was a knot of need and her legs were jelly.

One more tug and the cami sagged to her hips, the straps to the crooks of her elbows. Noah cupped her breasts in his warm palms, lifting them both. He kissed one, his tongue moving hot and slow around the tight tip, then shifting to the other one, turning her more and more liquid below the waist.

"I give up," she said, almost falling against him. "Come to bed." She took his hand and pulled him to her room, her entire body on fire for him. She wished she could pretend she was sleepwalking, that she didn't know what she was doing, but she knew full well and didn't give a damn.

Fingers flying, they rid themselves of Mel's sleep clothes and Noah's boxers and lay together, blessedly naked. They moved silkily against each other, slippery as Mel's camisole, their hands finding every lovely place, one by one, coaxing, teasing, soothing, arousing. They made love without words, staring into each other's eyes, the only sounds sighs and gasps and hard breaths as they rocked together, muscles tightening, then letting go, steady, then faster until they surged together to release.

When they'd finished, Noah wrapped himself around her body from behind, held her close and whispered, "This feels right to me, Mel."

It did. It felt right. But that didn't mean it wasn't wrong.

A CRACKLE, THEN THE sound of Daniel's voice from the monitor woke Noah with a start. He blinked, fighting to remember where he was. Meanwhile, Mel scrambled out of his arms and out of bed like a fire alarm had gone off.

Oh, yeah. He pushed up and sat on the edge of the bed, foggy as hell. They'd made love until deep into the night, drifting off what seemed like mere moments before. He stumbled into the bathroom to pee and splash his face.

By the time he got to the kitchen, Mel had Daniel in his high chair and was putting water into a teakettle. The coffeepot was already gurgling.

She turned to him, her face puffy from lack of sleep, her expression oddly frantic, not like Mel at all. "Instant rice is his favorite breakfast," she said, ducking his gaze. "You can see how much is in the bowl. Let it soak in boiling water for three minutes, then add milk to cool it for him."

"Okay," he said, hoping to hell that was written down somewhere.

"Get Daniel some milk in a sippy cup, would you? Also juice if you want. The coffee's almost done. I'm toasting a bagel for me. You want one?"

He wasn't awake enough to even know, but he realized he'd offered to take Daniel to Bright Blossoms so he'd better get with it. "Sure. Great." He went to the fridge, then poured their drinks.

Mel was babbling about what to put in the diaper bag, when Noah took her arms gently and turned her to face him. "Mel, what's going on with you?"

Her gaze shot to him. "Last night was a mistake, Noah."

"Because we started so late, right? Tonight we'll do better."

"No. It was a mistake, period." She gave a quick, confirming nod and backed away from his touch. "You're helping me and that's great." She swallowed hard. "But the rest of it is too much. We're not.… This isn't…" She blew out a breath. "Hell. What I'm trying to say is it's too easy for this to seem like more than it could ever be between us." Her cheeks, pale from lack of sleep, turned pink.

She was right and he knew it. As down-to-earth as she was, Mel wasn't immune to the dream of home and family everyone grew up with. A dream in which he had no place and could never fit. "I get you. I shouldn't have pushed."

"It wasn't only you, believe me." She sighed. "Anyway, you've got my notes. You've seen the routines, night and morning. You know where everything is—even the syrup of ipecac, right?" She forced a smile.

"In case he chews on some deadly nightshade. Check." He smiled back.

"On Friday, pick up Daniel no later than six at Bright Blossoms. Earlier is better because he gets cranky when he's hungry. I'll put the house key in the front compartment of his diaper bag, so you should be set."

"So, what, you're canceling babysitting boot camp?"

"You passed, Noah. Look for your certificate in the mail."

"Are you sure? I want you to trust me with him."

"I do. I really do. Let's leave it at that. I'll call you Friday. Thanks for everything." Her eyes flitted away. She was hiding whatever she was feeling and he respected that. His own feelings were pretty damned mixed, too.

And as it turned out, he was lucky Mel had given him the rest of the week off. It got hectic as hell for him. The work on his freelance project escalated. The *News Day* people handed over notes and contacts to help him expose Sheriff Sam. The former assistant attorney general came through with copies of budgets the man had doctored to hide election law violations that the feds were now investigating.

And Connie, the administrative assistant, was happy to talk to him about *all the unmitigated, wrong-ass crap that goes on around here.* The reality-show escapade had really upset her, especially the bogus drug raid he'd called to impress the producers. She'd given Noah a photo she'd taken of a stack of unprocessed warrants for suspects in major crimes that hadn't been served because deputies had been dragged into Pasamonte's campaign to become an even bigger celebrity than he already was.

She'd vouched for Noah with a couple of disgruntled

deputies who had seen important cases fold because of the sheriff's obsession with stardom and were willing to give him background. Noah had put in calls to them, hoping they wouldn't get cold feet before he got them on record.

He'd nailed the best angle himself. He'd tracked down the canceled reality show's producer and the woman had overnighted him the footage showing the sheriff bragging about doing precisely what he'd denied to state and federal officials. Noah would watch it over the weekend, he hoped, while Daniel napped or after he went to bed.

Friday afternoon, Noah had to talk to one of the deputies, but that put him behind on the final article for the alumni magazine. If they missed the slot at the printer's, the magazines wouldn't make it to alumni before the fundraising calls began.

By the time he'd emailed the story, it was 5:45 p.m. Damn. Bright Blossoms closed at six and he was a half-hour away. He called to warn them he'd be late. Speeding there he got a ticket, slowing him down even more.

Marla met him at the door, holding a red-faced, wet-cheeked Daniel. "He's cranky. I gave him juice and crackers, but he wants his supper."

Daniel began to complain, "Ma…ma…ma…"

"Sorry. I got hit with a ticket on the way. Can I pay you for the extra time?"

The woman shook her head. "I'm missing my son's soccer game. Money won't fix that. Just drive home safe. You have precious cargo."

"Sure. Thanks." This was firsthand experience in juggling a kid and a career. No wonder Mel was unwilling to mess with her schedule.

"We'll get you some food, pal," Noah said to Daniel,

who continued to wail as Noah wrangled him into the car seat and clicked the seat belt in place.

He turned into the first burger place drive-through he saw and ordered a burger, fries and a small vanilla shake, figuring the milk would be good for Daniel and Noah could hand him back fries as he drove. Not Mel-approved, but not bad for an emergency.

Daniel was still hollering when the food came. Noah blew on a couple fries and twisted around to hand them to him. Daniel shoved the food into his mouth, his face red and wet with tears, snot getting mixed in with the fries. Would that make him sick? God, Noah hoped not.

The car behind honked and Noah moved out of the drive-through, then handed Daniel the shake. He took a sip and his eyes went wide. *Score.*

Noah took off, careful to stick with the speed limit. He was on the freeway when Daniel yelled. Looking in the mirror, Noah watched the kid suck at the straw, then give up. Great, the shake was too thick and Noah was doing sixty-five. He could pull off, locate a spoon…

With a frustrated shriek, Daniel tossed the cup to the floor. It opened, splattering vanilla ice cream everywhere.

Never mind the spoon. Noah handed over a fry as a consolation prize, keeping his eyes on the road, but Daniel threw it away, sobbing in despair. No doubt he wanted his mother on top of everything.

Noah squeezed the wheel, gritted his teeth and kept driving.

By the time he took Mel's exit, the sobs had lapsed into sniffling and shaky breaths and when he pulled into the driveway, it was dead silent back there. Daniel had fallen asleep, a fry in one fist, a couple on his chest, vanilla ice cream streaking his shirt.

Noah just sat there in the car, AC on, engine idling, letting the kid sleep. Daniel's face looked so peaceful now. What was he dreaming about? Milkshakes he could actually drink and babysitters who showed up on time?

Noah's cell phone rang, making him jump. He popped out of the driver's seat to answer it without disturbing the baby. The caller ID said it was Mel.

"Hey," he whispered.

"Why are you whispering? Is something wrong?"

"No. Daniel fell asleep in the car on the way home."

"It's almost seven. You're just getting home?"

"We had, uh, an errand to take care of, but we're fine."

"Okay. So he was all right when you picked him up? Did he cry?"

"He fussed a little." He rolled his eyes at his own fib. "But now he's sleeping like an angel."

"You'd better wake him up."

"Are you nuts?" She didn't know how miserable he'd been.

"If you don't, he won't sleep at bedtime."

"Right. Gotcha." And he had work to do once Daniel was in bed. Still, it seemed cruel to drag him from such hard-won slumber. "So were you making sure we weren't at a strip club or was there something you needed?"

She laughed softly. "I wanted to tell you you'll run out of diapers. My bad. Get the same brand and size. I'll reimburse you. I should have left you cash, but it got hectic and I—"

"I can buy diapers, Mel."

"And check the slow cooker. I have this sneaking feeling I forgot to turn it on before I left. Which means you'll have to eat the casserole tonight. It might not be thawed. In that case—"

"I'll rustle up the grub, no sweat." He had a burger, didn't he, and a half a carton of not-yet-tossed fries?

"Also, Paquito's on top of the dryer. I forgot him when I was finishing the laundry. Daniel will need it—"

"To sleep with. Yeah, I remember, Mel."

"Also, his night T-shirts are in the dryer. I didn't get a chance to fold them."

"I'll find what we need, I'm sure."

"I know. You're a trained babysitter, right?" She was clearly trying to joke. "I just… Oh, I don't know. I miss him, Noah. Already. I know that sounds utterly nuts."

"It's not nuts. You're his mother. This is your first night away. Of course you miss him."

"You probably think I'm a neurotic mess."

"You're not neurotic. Now, if you'd told me how to fold the T-shirts, *that* would be neurotic. You're a great mom."

"With control issues," she said on a sigh.

"To some degree. But we all have those. Try to enjoy yourself. Danny and I will keep the home fires burning. How's it going down there? You started shooting yet?" He wanted to get her off the worry loop she was on.

"I start the portraits in a few minutes, then some candids at the dinner."

"You looking forward to it?"

"Actually, yeah. Jen has been trotting me room to room to meet everyone, talking me up like I won a Pulitzer."

"You will one day. I expect that."

She laughed and he could feel her relax. "Mom's

doing better. She's not in pain and she's holding down food. They might release her Monday."

"I'd be happy to bring her home if that would help."

"Thanks, but I've already put you through too much."

"It's no trouble."

"It's a lot of trouble. All of this is. No one knows that better than I." She hesitated. "Oops, they're calling me."

"Knock 'em dead, Mel."

"I'll do my best."

"You always do." He hung up, thinking about her.

CHAPTER TWELVE

MEL'S ROUTINES DIDN'T seem to work so well with Noah in charge. Upset and wanting his mother, Daniel wouldn't eat much. Noah tried spaghetti, buttered bread, even some cream of rice, but no go.

Bath time turned into full-on playtime. No way was Noah risking a crying jag over hygiene. Sunday morning he'd be sure the kid was mopped up enough to meet Mel's inspection. Somehow a bucket of water got poured on the floor, so they left the room with sopping towels and scattered toys.

Daniel seemed fidgety and anxious, clearly missing Mel. Paco seemed forlorn, too. Noah entertained them both as best he could. As it got dark, Noah watched panic rise in the little boy's face. Big tears filled his eyes and he put his thumb in his mouth, clearly trying to comfort himself.

Damn, childhood was full of traumas.

Noah read books until his throat was dry and sang a bunch of songs, but the minute he put Daniel into the crib the kid bellowed as though he'd been caged with the Minotaur. In the end, Noah rocked him in the recliner until he dropped off to sleep around midnight.

Too beat to try to do any work, Noah fell into bed, only to have the monitor crackle at four-thirty the next morning. *Four-thirty?* Damn. You'd think going to bed so late, the kid would have slept in some, but no.

Bleary-eyed, Noah got him dressed, fed him cream of rice and a banana, then lay on the living-room floor to watch him play with his new blue wagon.

Noah woke with a start to see that Daniel wasn't in the room. Noise from the kitchen sent him running. Daniel had overturned the sugar bowl and dumped a tumbler of orange juice on the floor.

Jesus Christ. To wake himself up and keep Daniel and the dog out of trouble, Noah took them for a walk to the park.

The rest of the day was a blur that included cranky outbursts, various minor calamities averted and no naps. Finally, it was bedtime. Except Daniel refused to be left alone. In the end, Noah lay on the floor beside the crib and Daniel stared at him through the bars, not happy, but not shrieking, either.

Sometime later, Noah's cell phone woke him up. He found himself still on the floor of Daniel's room. "H'lo," he mumbled, blinking in the dim light.

"Did I wake you?" It was Mel.

"I dozed off, I guess. What time is it?"

"Ten. I haven't had a minute to call, it's been so busy. How'd the day go?"

We made an ungodly mess in the kitchen, nearly flooded the bathroom and almost pulled down the bookcase on our heads. "Good. We played. We went to the park."

"I'm so glad. You have no idea what a relief that is. I was afraid he'd miss me so much that he'd be miserable for you."

"Are you kidding? We're batchin' it over here. Hella good times. Let me pay the strippers so they can leave. Can you hang on?"

She laughed with delight. "Well, that's great. Go back

to sleep. Kiss my little boy for me in the morning, okay? I'll see you early evening. Seven or so."

"Sounds good." *Seven.* Only twenty-one more hours of baby-care hell. He could handle that. He'd relieved Mel's mind and that was the point, right?

He woke in the morning to the sound of Daniel softly babbling and realized he was still lying on the floor, his head resting on Paco's belly.

Noah looked up at the ceiling. For the first time, he noticed it was painted with fluffy white clouds. *Mel.* That made him smile.

He braced for another day of chaos and tears, but by that afternoon, he was surprised to find the mood had smoothed out. After lunch, they were in the backyard and Daniel ran over to him to give him a high-five. Charmed, Noah lay back on the grass and lifted Daniel up over his head to wiggle him around. The little boy giggled and dropped drool straight into Noah's eye, but Noah didn't mind one bit.

When he lowered Daniel to his chest, Daniel patted Noah's cheeks, looked him right in the eye and said, "Dada."

Electricity flew through Noah. The kid had called him *Dada.* "That's right, buddy. I'm your dada and I always will be." He raised a hand and Daniel gave him another high-five. Warm emotion filled Noah, swirled in his chest, made his lungs feel tight and his eyes blur a little. He loved this little boy and he wanted to stay in his life. This was real, deep in his flesh, solid in his heart.

So how would that work? What exactly could he promise and what would Mel say about it? And what about Mel? He had growing feelings for her. Was he falling in love? Very possibly. And what exactly was he going to do about that?

BY THE TIME MEL TURNED down her street, her arms fairly ached to hold her son again. Her heart beat hard against her ribs and her throat was tight with held-back emotion. The broiling daytime heat had softened into a warm dusk and the sky was lit with sunset's brilliant pink, orange and purple. This was the time of day she loved to take photos, as colors deepened and light evened out, no harsh shadows or washed-out features to mar the crisp images.

When she pulled up to her house, she saw that Noah sat on the step to the terrace with Daniel on his lap. He tossed Paco's rubber chicken in a high arc and the dog galumphed out to get it.

Mel's heart felt as though it might burst in her chest. Feelings streaked through her—delight, wonder, surprise, longing—and an overwhelming sense that this was *right*. Real. This meant something.

Accepting the chicken from Paco, Noah noticed Mel's arrival. He leaned down to pick up Daniel, point toward Mel, then wave Daniel's hand at her.

Mel parked in the driveway, hopped out of the car and hurried over.

"No broken bones, see?" Noah said. "The scars will hardly show." His eyes were alight with pleasure at seeing her. She loved that. So much.

"That's all I could ask," she said, grinning. "Hey, Danielito." She held out her arms, swallowing past the tightness in her throat. How she'd missed him. He looked older in a mere two days.

Daniel pressed back against Noah's chest, suddenly shy.

"I told you she'd be back," Noah said to him. He tried to hand Daniel over, but the little boy wouldn't budge. "What's the deal?" Noah asked her.

"It's a transition thing," she said, though a wave of hurt washed through her anyway. "He's bonded to you now. He does this with Marla sometimes at the end of the day. Then he adjusts and shifts over to me. It's normal." But it hurt every time.

"Makes sense, I guess." He seemed concerned for her, she could tell. "We stayed busy, but he definitely missed you. A lot. Trust me."

She smiled at him. "It's okay, Noah. I missed you, *mi'jo*," she said to Daniel, noticing tomato sauce crusted his cheek. He had a milk mustache and his shirt was snapped crooked, but he seemed content and that was all she cared about.

He stared at her for a few seconds, then leaned out, arms outstretched. Relief washed through her—joy, too—and she took him into her arms. She kissed his cheek and neck and he giggled and patted her face.

"I missed you so much." She breathed in his smell and held him tight. "God, it was awful," she said to Noah. "I felt like my heart had been ripped out."

"I can imagine," he said, then stopped, as if caught by his own words. "Having a kid changes you," he finished softly. "Your trip go how you wanted?"

"Yeah. I got great shots and I think I've booked a wedding and a birthday party out of it."

"It's good to see you," Noah said, his voice low and serious.

"It's good to see you, too." Her cheeks heated.

"I taught Daniel a new game. We call it Blueberry Fetch."

"How does it go?"

"I toss a blueberry and he brings it to me."

"You let him eat fruit off the floor?"

"Of course not. When he brings it to me, I give him a fresh one to eat."

"First, you buy him a leash, then you teach him to fetch. He's not a pet."

"Come on. It wore him out and, trust me, he needed that. *I* needed that."

"I'm afraid to ask what else you taught him."

"Relax. It'll be a while before he can belch 'The Star-Spangled Banner.' And the armpit farts…no go, I'm sorry to say."

She laughed. "You're terrible."

"Just a guy showin' another guy the ropes."

"If you say so." She smiled. "Let's go inside. I need a shower."

At the door, Noah turned to her. "I have to warn you the place is not as squared away as you like. We did some major partying. There was an incident with a rubber duck in the toilet, but I'm pretty handy with a plunger, so we're all good there."

"Okay…"

Inside the house, she saw that Noah hadn't exaggerated much. The place was a mess, toys and clothes everywhere. The kitchen was stacked with dishes and the floor was suspiciously sticky. Paco nosed her thigh. She reached to pet him and noticed a big hunk of his fur was gone. "What happened here?"

"Peanut butter is surprisingly difficult to remove."

Her gaze fell on a pizza box on the table. "You ordered pizza?"

"Needed something to go with the beer when we watched lady wrestling."

"God. What about the pot roast?"

"You hadn't turned it on, so it's in the fridge. We, um, foraged."

"I don't even want to know what that means. I guess I'm glad I wasn't gone any longer."

"I don't know about that. We might have nailed belching the alphabet—at least the first twelve letters."

"So, you had an okay time?" she asked softly, hopefully.

"It got hectic, but it was good, Mel. Very good." Again, his face flashed with emotion. "Anyway, go take your shower. I'll give Daniel his bath."

"You've done more than enough. You can go."

"I'd like to stay."

"Really?" Their gazes caught and held. Energy flew between them—attraction, sure, but also affection, intimacy, and something new she was afraid to name. Her entire body felt lit up and she could hardly breathe.

"Yeah," Noah said. "Really."

"I would like that." They stood that way, staring at each other until Daniel squawked, impatient to move.

"Go wash up and I'll handle Daniel. There's at least one lamp we haven't broken yet." He was trying to joke, but he seemed as unsettled about what was going on as she felt.

"Okay," she said. It was nice that Noah could handle the bath routine without a second thought from her. It made her uneasy, too. She could get used to that and she wasn't sure that was smart.

Showered and dressed, Mel found Noah and Daniel still in the bathroom, the floor wet, sopping towels here and there. "How's it going?"

"We've got something cool to show you," Noah said. "We did some man training here, didn't we, big guy?" Noah picked up a can of shaving cream.

"Uh, uh, uh." Daniel reached for it.

"Hold on," he said, spraying foam onto his palm. He applied it to Daniel's cheeks, then used the back of his disposable razor to scrape it away. "I put him on the sink while I shaved and he looked interested, so I gave it a try."

Daniel held out his hand for more foam, then slapped it on the tile above the tub and smeared it around.

"Finger paint that cleans the tile," Noah said. "A household hint for you. Plus, it made him less afraid of soap, I think."

"That is very clever," she said. "I'm impressed."

"Me, me." Daniel reached toward Mel with what was left on his hand.

"Looks like he wants to give you a shave."

Mel leaned in so Daniel could clap her cheeks with his soapy hands.

"Allow me," Noah said, carefully scraping the fluff from Mel's face, staring into her eyes the entire time. Daniel crowed and clapped.

Later, in Daniel's room, she read the stories while Noah sat on the chair arm, his arm across her shoulder, his cheek resting on the top of her head, exactly like her fantasy on Daniel's first night home. It was eerily perfect. Mel could hardly breathe.

"I could listen to you read all night," Noah said. "Well, not *all* night. There are other things I'd like to do to you, besides listen.…"

His words sent lust pouring through her, mixing with the tenderness and wonder she was already feeling. Was this really happening? And did it mean more than a lovely moment in time?

She'd barely finished a song before Daniel's eyes began to close.

"Amazing," Noah said. "I must have sung 'Were-wolves of London' a dozen times last night and he was still wide-awake."

"No wonder. That's hardly a lullaby."

"Slower than 'Psycho Killer.' I ran through all the Talking Heads. He seemed to like 'Burning Down the House' a lot."

She laughed. "You are too much." She stood to put Daniel in his crib, tucking Paquito against his cheek. Noah stood beside her, looking down at their child. They looked up at the same time and their gazes locked.

In an instant, she knew for certain that she was in love with Noah.

"We need to talk," he said, low and serious. Did he love her, too? Talk about ripples. It felt more like a flash flood.

Without a word, they left Daniel's room and headed to the living-room sofa, sitting close, knees leaning in. Noah clasped her hands between his. "Here's the deal, Mel. I want to stay in Daniel's life. I want to be his father."

Mel could hardly breathe. She forced herself to think, to stay calm. "How would that work? Your plan is to leave at the end of the year."

"Plans change," he said slowly.

"Seriously? You'll stay? What will you do? For work, I mean?"

"More freelance. I'd keep working for ASU if I can get a flexible schedule. Paul offered me a stipend to mentor his advanced journalism students, too. After that, I'll see what opens up for me."

"I don't know what to say." The idea was thrilling, but hard to believe or trust. "This is so sudden."

"Believe me, I know." He looked a bit confused himself. "The other thing is…I'm in love with you, Mel."

"You are?" She felt filled with warmth and light.

"Yeah. I think about you all the time, I miss you when you're gone. I want to tell you what I'm thinking and hear the same from you. You feel anything close to that for me?"

"Yes," she said. "I do." Her heart seemed about to burst. The man she'd fallen in love with loved her back. And he loved their little boy, too. *Ay, Dios!*

He kissed her fingers. "I know this could be just that stupid fairy tale about love and family that's pounded into our brains—the one that leads to millions of bad marriages every year." He gave a laugh. "But it feels like we could make it work. Take care of each other, love each other and not totally screw it up. I know that's not exactly a ringing endorsement, but I'm new at this." He blew out a breath, smiling sheepishly.

"I feel like you do, I think. The same."

"So you want to give it a try?"

It was her dearest secret dream. "I'd like that," she said softly. "I'd like that very much."

"ARE YOU COMFORTABLE?" Mel asked her mother once they started home late Monday afternoon.

"Very much, yes. And happy to know Noah is again watching Danielito."

"Yes, he is," she said on a sigh. She had to tell her mother what was going on. She took a deep breath. "Things have, um, *changed.* With Noah."

"This, it does not surprise me," her mother said. "Noah needed time for the feelings to show themselves. So you are *novios?*"

"We're trying it out. I don't know what to think or what to do exactly."

"Be in love together. Day by day. Simple."

"You know it's not simple. He says he'll stay here, but he needs a serious reporting job and I don't know if he can get one in Phoenix. I'm afraid this is all a dream."

"When life is good, it is like a dream. And life is very good," her mother said. "I am better and you are in love."

Mel had to smile. She couldn't help but feel the same way. She dared to picture the future—picnics in the park, Christmas Eves with Noah swearing as he assembled a swing set, Daniel rising early to see what surprises lay beneath the tree. She imagined Easter-egg hunts, Halloween costumes, Thanksgiving dinners and birthday piñatas.

It was possible she was in love with the *idea* of a family, that she was having a killer bout of wishful thinking, but for now, for this moment, she would let the ripples swell to waves of happiness that washed right through her into the future.

When she and her mother entered the house, Noah and Daniel were at the kitchen table. Daniel's tray was full of blueberries, as was his mouth, judging by his bulging cheeks

"Mi Danielito," her mother cried, and swooped in to hug him. "And Noah. To see you here, to see my family together, this cures me."

"I think that was the antibiotics and iron supplements, *Mamá,*" Mel said before the moment got ridiculously sappy. Her mother went straight to the shrine, where she lit every single candle.

"Does this mean her wish came true?" Noah said softly to Mel, winking.

"Don't get cocky. The next one might involve a priest and some vows."

"Oh. Right. Good point." He cleared his throat.

"I'm so relieved that she's better," Mel said, smiling at him with moist eyes. "If only the X-rays come out clear. If we have this licked…"

"Maybe we need to light some candles, too." His expression gave her so much comfort, so much hope.

"Maybe so," she said. Somehow, Noah lightened the burden of her mother's condition in her heart. Not that Mel worried less, but that she had someone to share it with, someone on her side, hoping the same hope, fearing the same fears. Noah made the struggle easier.

She smiled, her lip trembling just a little. They would take this day by day. *When life is good, it is like a dream.* Her mother was out of the hospital, Noah was staying. For now, that was enough. For now, that was plenty.

NOAH LIFTED HIS ZOMBIE toward Irena, who beamed at him from across the small supper table. "To your continued good health," he said. It had been a week since she'd been released from the hospital and her oncologist had just declared her cancer in remission. Tonight they were celebrating with Irena's *enchiladas suisas* and some Zombies he'd insisted on making in Mel's honor.

"*Gracias.* I am so happy we are all here together." Irena beamed at him, at Mel, then at Daniel.

"Me, too," Mel said. "Very happy." She lunged forward to hug her mother, her face bright with joy, pink with emotion. She'd been nearly hysterical with relief after she'd heard the results. That had reminded him how strong she'd been all these months, handling her mother's diagnosis, treatment and suffering, the possibility of her death, along with the surprise pregnancy, the loss of her career. Stoic, but hopeful, just as she'd described her mother. She'd been calm and patient and determined, shaping the world to her liking.

He admired them both—their serenity, their grace under pressure, their determination and strength. He clasped Mel's hand and she smiled up at him.

It's like I have her back again, she'd said to him, tears in her eyes, after she'd told him the news. *Like she was lost to me, but found her way home.*

She'd also told him how much comfort he'd been to her, how much help. That meant a lot to him. He hadn't realized how useless he'd felt all these months since Iraq. He'd merely survived. It was time he started living again.

"Tell *Mamá* your news, Noah," Mel said to him.

Caught up in this moment, he'd almost forgotten his own triumph. "The *New York Times* wants my story on Sam Pasamonte."

"This is very good, no?" Irena said.

"Oh, yeah. Very good." He had three weeks to turn it in.

"Plus, they're interested in another idea he has."

"On problems with privately run prisons, yeah. That depends on what my outline looks like. If I get good access." He'd also touched base with Hank Walker at *National Record,* and it sounded as though they would welcome freelance pitches from him, too.

"Things are working out," Mel said to him, her smile so bright it almost hurt.

"Yeah," he said. "They seem to be." He hadn't had a nightmare, flashback or headache in a week, either. He had this new thing with Mel and Daniel, if he could just get past the *what-do you-think-you're-doing* feeling.

He leaned down to kiss her. When the situation seemed like a weird dream, touching her made it seem real and well worth the risk.

"And now, what of your *mamá,* Noah?" Irena's voice broke the spell, her words hitting from out of the blue.

"My mom?"

"You tell her of this news? Of the baby and Mel?"

"Not yet. She's traveling at the moment." He wasn't sure what his mother would think about being a grandmother. "When the time's right, I'll talk to her." He'd planned to take Mel and Daniel to visit his grandmother, too.

"To keep an *abuela* from her *nieto?* You know better than this."

"My mother's not like you, Irena," he said. "She has her own life. She's very independent. We've never been close."

"A *niño* melts away the cold between people," Irena said.

"Noah will handle this in his own way," Mel said. She shot him an apologetic look. Noah squeezed her hand. He didn't mind.

"I'll call her soon. Could you make her one of those photo books?"

"You will invite her to visit?" Irena pushed.

"Mamá!"

Noah laughed. "Sure." Maybe she'd come. Maybe it would change things between the two of them. Daniel had brought out the best in Noah. Why couldn't he do the same for his mother?

CHAPTER THIRTEEN

MEL AWOKE WITH A start to hear Noah shouting at her. "Incoming! Get down! Down! Now!" He lunged at her, shoving her off the bed, landing in a crouch beside her.

"What are you doing?" she mumbled.

He leaned in to grab one of her arms, trying to hike her onto his back, moving clumsily, clearly not awake.

"Noah, stop!" she said, pulling out of his grip. This was horrifying, having to fight the man who'd been sleeping peacefully beside her moments ago.

"I'll get you there. You'll be okay," he said, reaching for her again. His eyes were so blank they frightened her and his face was wet with sweat, as if he'd been running for miles.

Mel was stunned. Was he reliving awful memories of Iraq?

"Noah," she said gently, unable to bear him staring so blindly at her. "Wake up. Please. Noah."

He mumbled, batting at her hand. Then after a few seconds, he shook himself and blinked at her. "Mel? What...?" He sounded dazed.

"You were sleepwalking. You grabbed me and tried to carry me somewhere, like we were being attacked."

"Did I hurt you?" he asked urgently.

"No. I think you were trying to save me." He had to be in so much pain, yet his concern was for her safety. *Oh, Noah.*

"I didn't…realize." He pushed his hair out of his face and took a shaky breath, leaning against the side of the bed. "I've never had anyone with me for one of those."

So he'd had other attacks. The severity of what he'd gone through suddenly seemed more real to her. "Do you remember the dream?"

"It's not a dream. It's a flashback. I know I'm trying to escape. Sometimes I get bruises or my mouth bleeds. I hear myself shout." He'd seemed haunted that first day she'd seen him, now she saw he truly was.

"I haven't had one in weeks. I thought they were over." He was acting calm, but his eyes twitched, as if he sought an escape route. Seeing him this way scared her.

"Do you want to talk it through?" she asked, shaken, but wanting to help however she could.

He shook his head. "No. Let's go to bed."

"Are you sure?" How could he fall asleep after this? She couldn't get the blind look he'd given her out of her mind, his urgency, the way he'd tried to haul her over his shoulder, promised to save her.

"Yes, I'm sure," he snapped. "I'm sorry. I just…my head hurts."

"Let me get you aspirin." She headed for the bathroom and brought water and the pills to where Noah sat on the side of the bed.

"I'm sorry I scared you," he said, taking the glass and tablets.

"It's all right. But I'm concerned about you." He'd told her about the headaches, but never that he had flashbacks. Shouldn't he be treated for this?

"Don't be," he said flatly. "I'm fine. Come to bed." He patted the mattress beside him. Sweat trickled down the side of his face and beaded his upper lip.

She climbed into bed beside him and they both lay staring at the ceiling. Without even touching him, she felt his tension. He was barely breathing. She couldn't forget his eyes, his desperate attempt to rescue her. Who had he tried to save in Iraq? The soldier injured with him?

She shifted onto her side to look at him. "What's going on, Noah?"

"Nothing," he said, then sat up. "I'll be restless the rest of the night. I'll take the sofa so you can sleep." He was gone before she could object, leaving her feeling very, very alone.

He was shutting her out of his troubles. He'd hid them from her since he'd returned. That wasn't good. Couples worked out their problems together, right? Talked things through, agreed on solutions? Noah wanted none of that, she could tell. He was only down the hall, but he seemed half a world away.

NOAH WOKE WITH A JOLT, confused. Where was he? What was he doing? He felt around him and hit the back of the sofa. Oh, yeah. He'd come to the living room to sleep. Damn. He'd had a flashback in front of Mel.

He sat up, his head in his hands. A cold flood of despair washed through him. He wasn't done with flashbacks.

A headache gathered at the back of his skull now, making his scalp crawl and his eyes throb. It would be a bad one, too. Soon, his brain would feel as though it was filled with shattered glass. Again. It was happening *again*.

He could hear voices from the kitchen—Mel and Irena talking, Daniel babbling cheerfully. The smell of coffee and toast turned his stomach sour and he knew he was about to heave. He ran to Daniel's bathroom and threw up bile, shaking and weak.

When he lifted his face from splashing cold water on it, Mel's worried eyes stared at him in the mirror.

"It's a migraine. I'll be okay." His stomach twisted, but he managed to smile.

"Shouldn't you lie down?"

He braced himself at the sink. "I can't. I have work." His vision grayed, then returned.

"Not when you're sick."

"I have to push through this."

"You're allowed sick days. Everyone is."

"Please. Let me be for a minute." He didn't want to be harsh, but the stabbing pain had begun and his vision was going fuzzy. "I'll take a shower and be out in a minute."

She backed away, biting her lip, clearly worried— the last thing he wanted from her.

He turned on the cold water, gritted his teeth and stepped into the icy stream, welcoming the shock to his system. His skin seemed to shrink against it and every muscle clenched, offering welcome counterpoint to the storm brewing in his brain.

You can do this. You can gut this out. He stayed there until he was numb, then patted himself dry. He made his way to Mel's room where he'd thrown a few things in one of her drawers and pulled on clothes, keeping his head level, moving like an invalid.

When he got to the kitchen, Mel sat at the table beside Daniel's high chair. Daniel was splashing oatmeal with his spoon. Irena was gone.

At Noah's place was a plate with toast and a steaming mug, along with aspirin and a glass of water.

"I made you some tea to settle your stomach," she said.

The sunlight was bright, the beams like daggers in his eyeballs. He blinked, squinted and blocked his eyes.

"Oh," she said, jumping up to close the blinds, the clacking sound sawing through his skull. "Is that better?"

He sat down slowly. "I'm not sure I can eat," he said, sipping the tea. This was hell, having Mel hover over him. He should have gone back to the guesthouse, not stayed here at all. "I'll need more aspirin."

She jumped up for the bottle.

Daniel banged his spoon on his tray, the sound a cymbal clash between Noah's ears. Noah stopped Daniel's hand. "Easy on the band practice, pal."

The instant Noah let go, Daniel banged even harder, grinning wildly.

"He thinks you're playing a game," Mel said, handing Noah the pill bottle.

Noah shook out four more pills.

"Those will burn your stomach lining if you don't eat."

He shook his head. "Can't do it."

"I'm so sorry you're suffering, Noah."

"Don't be." He shifted his gaze away from her sympathetic eyes.

"Why not? You endured a terrible experience. You were injured and you're still in pain. You deserve some compassion."

"No, I don't," he snapped, abruptly furious. She had no clue what she was talking about. "The truth is that I deserve every headache, nightmare and shrapnel scar I've got and then some."

"How can you say that? You were doing your job."

Mile-deep fury let him push past the pain in his head to tell her the truth. "I was hunting copy inches, Mel.

I got an officer killed, a soldier injured and I caused a dozen men to risk their lives to save my ass. I forced a career officer out of the Army, and I gave the military justification to limit media access. The last thing I deserve is compassion. Let. It. Go."

She stared at him, blinking, startled by his outburst, but not intimidated. Not Mel. She did not back off. "Those soldiers were trained. You didn't give them the command to fire their weapons."

"I put them in harm's way. I weakened the squad because they gave me a bodyguard. Those men's lives depend on each other. I interfered with that."

He paused for breath, his words echoing in his suffering skull.

"That's not fair, Noah. You didn't ask for a bodyguard."

"That was protocol. Sergeant Fuller got shot ordering Emile Daggett to keep me safe. I saw him drop. His last act was protecting me."

"That's terrible, but that's part of war. Bad things happen when governments keep journalists out. The first casualty of war is the truth, remember? You represented the American people. You had to keep the generals honest, reporting the truth, good and bad. You made the war real for people comfortable in their easy chairs. You were there for all of us."

"I was there for myself. For my career, my reputation, my pride," he snapped. His nerves were raw and each word he said was another stab of pain. He let his anger carry him on. "My mission was to advance myself, not anything lofty as serving truth and justice. Don't you get that?"

She stared at him for a long moment. "I get that you

feel a lot of guilt." She paused. "You need to see some-one. Work through this."

"You mean a shrink? You think poking around in my childhood is going to fix this?"

"There are therapists who specialize in PTSD, Noah, and I'm sure—"

"I don't have PTSD. I'm no special case. I don't have a syndrome or a disorder or a condition. *Please,* just leave it alone, Mel."

Daniel burst into tears and Noah realized he'd been yelling.

"Dammit."

"Shh, Daniel," Mel said, leaning over to hug him in his chair. "It's okay." She looked at Noah. He could tell he'd shaken her. "Tell him it's okay, Noah."

"I'm sorry, Daniel," he said, his jaw tight, his teeth gritted.

Daniel blinked, looking from Mel to him and back, then put his oatmeal-coated fingers in his mouth to soothe himself.

"I didn't mean to scare him," he said, feeling like an ass. "I shouldn't have yelled. I'm sorry, okay?"

Mel just looked at him.

He glanced at his watch. "I should get going. Is his bag set?" He'd told Mel he'd drive Daniel to Bright Blossoms so Mel could run errands.

"I'll take Daniel with me. You're not well enough to drive."

"Why? Because of the headache? I've driven with headaches before." He blinked against the darkness eating at his peripheral vision. "I'd said I'd take him and I'll take him."

"We're fine. I think you should lie down."

"You think I'd endanger him? Is that it? I would never do that."

She didn't speak, only jutted her chin. She wasn't budging.

"Suit yourself," he said, angry again.

"I'm concerned about you, Noah. You need to deal with this. I doubt you'll ever be whole if you don't."

"Maybe I'm not supposed to be whole. What happened changed me. It should have. I can't go back to who I was."

"You can get better. You can heal. If not for yourself, for the people who care about you." Her eyes flashed with anger.

"The people who care about me accept me as I am or leave me the hell alone." He grabbed his keys and stomped out.

A few blocks away, the headache got so bad he knew he had to lie down. He called his boss and told him something had come up and he'd be in by the afternoon. No way was he admitting a headache had dragged him so low.

He pulled into a covered parking spot at an office building and lay across the backseat until his vision cleared enough to drive to Paul's guesthouse, where he loaded an ice bag, closed the drapes and crawled into bed, shaking, pain shrieking in his head, gut clenched against the waves of agony. He forced himself to breathe in slow deep breaths.

He wasn't over Iraq. Mel was right about that. He'd fought with her, raised his voice, made his son cry. What an ass he was.

He remembered his parents screaming at each other over the breakfast table, his father roaring off in whatever muscle car he was working on at the time, leaving his mother sobbing in her room and Noah feeling helpless and afraid. Noah had scared his own son. He was no different than his father.

He groaned, pressing the pillow against the side of his head.

Mel would not leave him alone about this. He knew that absolutely.

All he could do was ride out the pain, wait for the flashbacks to pass.

Except now he'd dragged Mel and Daniel into the mess with him. Even healthy, Noah wasn't much of a bet when it came to being with people. But still hurting, with nightmares and flashbacks still happening? He might be a hazard to them both.

His insides churned with regret and frustration. If he could heal himself by force of will alone, he would have done so by now. What the hell should he do? Bow out of Mel and Daniel's life? Admit his mistake and walk away before he did more harm?

Hell, it had only been two weeks since he'd decided he wanted to stay with them. He'd been in some kind of trance, he guessed, hiding from who he really was and what he really faced. He'd felt so good with Mel and Daniel he'd blocked out his troubles. That was unfair to them both. Somehow, he had to make things right.

THAT NIGHT WHEN MEL got home with Daniel, Noah was sitting on the terrace step. He stood to meet them, wincing slightly. He looked pale and his eyes held shadows.

"You were right. I was too sick to drive." He managed a crooked smile. "I laid down at Paul's for a couple hours, then went to work. I'm better now."

"That's what you keep saying." This was not the Noah who grabbed on with his gaze and wouldn't let go.

This was Noah in distress, struggling, deeply hurt and in denial. "We need to talk about this," she said. "But not until Daniel's in bed." Noah nodded. Her mother was out for dinner and a movie with her support-group friends, so at least they had the house to themselves.

They ate and Noah did the dishes while she bathed Daniel, then he joined them for the bedtime ritual. Outwardly, everything seemed peaceful and lovely and right, but Mel's heart was heavy. She'd done some research on PTSD, its symptoms and treatment options. If Noah refused to address his health problems, they would never last as a couple.

In the living room, they sat on the sofa. "I shouldn't have yelled at you," Noah said right off. "I promise that won't happen again. I won't let my problems affect you or Daniel."

"If it affects you, it affects us, Noah. Why did you hide this from me?"

"I didn't hide it. I'm better. I had a bit of a setback is all."

"But you wear your guilt like a medal, like you deserve to suffer. That's so stupid and macho. It's not like you."

He studied her. "If you want me out of your lives, Mel, I'll go. I wouldn't blame you after that. But I'd like to keep trying."

Her heart froze in her chest and her lungs locked on a breath. "What I want is for you to get help."

He stared at her. "I don't need help. You have no idea how bad I've been. It takes time. That's what I need— more time."

"But with PTSD, flare-ups can go on for years without treatment."

"I had a traumatic brain injury. That's not PTSD.

For example, I had aphasia—that's losing the ability to speak or understand language. I couldn't talk worth a damn for weeks. My thoughts were jumbled for months."

"That must have been hell," she said. "You're a writer. Language is everything to you."

"Yeah. It's only been recently that I was certain I'd be able to write again. So I'm much better."

"You called that *wandering?* You were afraid your brain was permanently injured. That's more than *wandering.* Why didn't you tell me, Noah?"

"What was the point? I was better. It didn't matter."

"It matters to me. Everything that's going on with you matters to me. And you're having flashbacks and migraines. And when the news broke about that reporter in Afghanistan, you had a setback then, too, didn't you?"

"But I'm getting past them," he said, his voice low.

"I've done some reading and one successful treatment involves safely revisiting the trauma, remembering it in detail. It's like desensitization."

"The last thing I want to do is relive what happened, Mel. I don't remember much. Amnesia around the time of the injury comes with brain trauma. When I do remember anything it's in quick flashes that leave me with migraines. Sick, sometimes, for days. So the more I forget, the better off I am."

Mel wasn't so sure about that. "Don't you think that's strange? It seems to me as a reporter you would want to remember exactly what happened. There was serious fallout from that attack and I would think you, of all people, would want to make sure that what got reported was what actually occurred."

He stared at her, emotions warring in his face. Anger

mostly. He wanted her to leave it alone. But it was too important. "You've built your whole career on learning the truth. Maybe the truth is what you need to recover."

He pushed to his feet and walked away, hands at his hips. "I know you mean well, but you don't know what you're talking about." He blew out a breath, turned away from her, then back. "I came here to apologize and to swear I wouldn't let my problems interfere with us. If that's not enough for you, then I don't know what else I can say."

"That's not what I mean—"

"You can't cure me, Mel." He took two rough breaths. "Look, maybe it would be better if I went back to Paul's tonight." His eyes went flat, dead and lost. "Give you time to think. Give both of us time."

"If that's what you want," she said woodenly. She felt sick inside. He was locked in his guilt, determined to suffer. That was no way to live, she knew. And it *would* affect them, no matter what he said.

DAMN IT ALL TO HELL. Noah slammed the heel of his hand against the steering wheel. He'd gone to Mel's to apologize, willing to walk away if that was what she wanted. In return, she'd called him a coward for hiding from the truth he needed to get better. Where did she get off spouting pop psychology like it was God's own treatment plan?

Calm down. She was trying to help.

She'd done research. *Research.* Damn. Like any good reporter. Shit.

He leaned against the headrest, staring out at the moon, pale silver and high in the sky. He rolled down his window and let muggy August air waft into his car.

Mel never held back. That was who she was and he

loved that about her. Until now. This was how it went when someone made a life with you. They dug at you, harassed you, tried to fix you. And Mel was stubborn. She would never let this rest. Worst of all, he couldn't guarantee he wouldn't have another flashback or more nightmares. If she thought he was going to sit in some therapist's office and rehash that horror in living color, she was the one who needed a shrink.

He turned on the engine, then looked at the lit window of Mel's house. He could go in, apologize *again* for losing his temper, tell her he'd think about therapy.

But that was a lie. And his career had been about the truth. She was right about that.

He started the Jeep and drove off. He pulled into a convenience store and went inside to pre-pay for gas. Waiting in line, he picked up the latest copy of *National Record.* He flipped through a few pages, stopping when he saw a photo of the journalist who'd been captured in Afghanistan sitting up in his hospital bed. He'd suffered from dehydration, had a cracked rib. In the photo, he was talking with a corporal from Army Public Affairs who'd come with official get-well wishes from the Army.

They sent a PR guy? Wait a minute. Noah had been visited by a brigadier general. Wade Nelson. Top brass. Not a PR flack.

He remembered the guy getting close, bending down, his tone urgent, his words distinct as he told Noah what he wanted him to remember.

The back of Noah's neck began to tingle.

What had the guy drilled into him? That it had been Noah's fault, that Fuller had violated direct orders, that the squad had initiated an unprovoked attack. *Initiated.*

Hang on. He called up his new memory of the beginning of the attack. The windshield had been cracked, bullets pinging off the grill *before* Chuy fired a single shot from his gunner position. Before that, there had been a close blast from behind. The fight had been started by the Iraqis, not the Americans.

The tingling got stronger and started down his spine. There was something wrong here. Why send a brigadier general with get-well wishes when a PR officer would do fine? Why lie about who started the fight? Why make American soldiers look bad?

"Will that be all?" the clerk asked, nodding at Noah's magazine.

"Put forty bucks on pump three, please," he said, handing over the cash.

He filled his gas tank, then drove straight to Mel's. At the door, he knocked with a fist, fast and hard, burning to talk this through with her.

"Noah?" she said when she opened to him, a flash of pleasure in her face. Mad at him or not, she always lit up when she saw him. That meant a lot to him. Right now, it meant everything.

"It was an ambush," he said, holding out the folded-open magazine.

She took it and waited for him to enter. "Excuse me?"

"The Iraqis fired the first shots, not our guys." He explained to her what he'd remembered after seeing the photo in the magazine. "Nelson told me Sergeant Fuller had acted against *direct* orders from Lieutenant Colonel Reynolds. If there had been orders, Fuller would never have let me talk him into that patrol, no matter how much I offered him. Captain Carver, his commanding officer, was by-the-book, career Army. He would have hammered Fuller."

As he talked, the jigsaw pieces began to fall into

place and he felt as though he'd been blind to a room he'd been living in for a year.

"Why would the Iraqi unit attack the American soldiers training them?" Mel asked.

"That's the question. Insurgents have disguised themselves in Iraqi army uniforms in the past." He paused. "But these guys weren't insurgents..." As he spoke, the memory fluttered into his awareness. "I remember seeing Fariq. In the storeroom where we were jailed. He was talking to another officer, someone over him, I could tell by how he deferred to him. I didn't know enough Arabic to understand a word, but I kept my eyes closed so they would think I was out."

"Why would the Army take the blame for friendly fire that came from Iraqi soldiers? To protect the Iraqi army image?"

"I don't buy that. There was more to it. They exacted a big price for the mistake. There was an investigation. Fuller's legacy trashed. Carver lost his career."

"And they sent a top officer to plant lies in your head."

"Exactly. They were covering something up. What? Carver would know. I've got to talk to him. Maybe he didn't go down without a fight."

Another picture flickered in Noah's brain. *Wooden crates with stenciled letters.* "Something else... There were boxes in the storeroom and...I was trying to take pictures of them. I remember now. It was hard to move because of my leg and I kept passing out or forgetting. Something about that... Damn. Maybe Emile would remember. He had to be awake for some of those hours."

"Can you talk to him?"

"I'm sure as hell going to try." Emile hadn't replied

to his written apology, but months had passed. "I'll talk to anyone I can get to respond."

He was on fire. There was a story here. If the American soldiers had been attacked, that changed everything. It didn't make Noah any less culpable, but it made the men and their sergeant heroes.

"Sounds like a plan," Mel said.

"Thanks for letting me talk it out with you." He held her gaze.

"This is important, Noah."

"It is. You were right. Truth is what counts. I've been ducking it—out of fear of the pain, yeah, but maybe guilt, too. But that's over now. Thanks to you. You called me on my shit, even though I gave you hell. That means a lot."

He felt a rush of gratitude to her. This was how it worked when you loved someone. They held your feet to the fire when it counted. To make you a better person. "I know you're looking out for me, Mel. Even when I blow off your advice, I know you've got my back."

"I do."

"I'm not used to that…to having anyone—" He shook his head, still letting this new reality sink in.

"I know what you mean," she said with a sheepish smile. "I'm not used to having anyone, either. I'm used to being on my own."

"Guess we're both adjusting," he said, not sure where to go from there. He'd planned to sleep at the guesthouse, to give them both some space. Maybe that was best. "It's getting late," he said softly. "I should go."

She shook her head. "Stay," she said. "Please."

And he was glad. That night, he slept like a stone, holding tight to Mel, undisturbed by nightmares or flashbacks or even dreams. The flash of memory—

the crates, wanting to photograph them—didn't leave
him with a headache. He didn't toss or turn. He simply
slept, feeling a peace he hadn't felt in a year. He was
definitely back. This time, he hoped, for good.

CHAPTER FOURTEEN

"COME TO BED, NOAH," Mel said, standing behind him at the kitchen table where he'd been working for the past few days. "It's late."

"Let me finish this last post." He'd found another soldier from the patrol on Facebook and wanted to send him a message.

Mel yawned, leaning over him, arms around his chest, swamping him with her great smell, her sleepy warmth. "Any luck with Carver?"

"Not yet." He'd tracked the guy to Henderson, Nevada, thanks to some fast-talking on a guessed-at internal number at the Army Benefits Office, an old reporter trick, and left numerous messages that Carver had not returned.

"If I don't hear in a week, I'll go there and knock on his damn door."

"Would Sergeant Haverson call him for you?"

"I doubt it. He was freaked that I called in the first place." Carver's assistant had made him even more certain Carver had information Noah needed to get to the bottom of things. Noah had helped Haverson's son get into the *National Record* internship program with a phone call, so he owed Noah a favor.

The man's voice had squeaked from tension and he behaved as if he thought the line was tapped, talking loudly and deliberately. "The captain liked his emails printed *out*. He had so many *files* to *clear out*."

Had to be code for Carver hanging on to email documentation about the cover-up. That meant Carver was a crucial contact. He had to reach the guy.

"You'll work better with some sleep under your belt," Mel said, running her fingers through his hair.

She was right, but it was hard to stop. He felt driven again, like the old days. There were lies to unmask, truths to reveal, an important story to tell. And he was equipped to do it—his brain clear, his instincts firing.

Mel understood. She knew how important this was. She'd left him alone to work, handling Daniel and her mother's needs on her own. He was battling to keep his head in both games—his new family and his new mission—but it wasn't easy.

The *New York Times* deadline for the Sheriff Sam story was snapping at his heels, but he'd become obsessed with Iraq. It turned out to be pure relief now that he'd stopped fighting the memories. He hadn't had a nightmare, panic attack or flashback since Mel confronted him.

"You go on," he said. "I want to do one last check on Fariq."

"Okay." She sighed, sliding her warmth away with obvious reluctance. "I was hoping we could make love. It's been two days."

"I know. I'll be right there." He wouldn't have believed anything could interfere with getting naked with Mel, but he'd underestimated the force of his drive to get at the truth of what had happened.

Mel sighed and left. He felt her absence as though he'd removed a coat in a storm. This push-pull was confusing. He was in uncharted personal territory here, half expecting a grenade to drop and blow away all this magic and rightness.

He turned his attention to the news search engine and keyed in *Sajad Fariq*. Yesterday, on a military watchdog website, he'd uncovered something that set every nerve ending humming. The article talked about concerns over U.S. intelligence support in the interrogation of allegedly corrupt Iraqi military officers. There was a long list of Iraqi officers accused of working with insurgents. Near the bottom was a name that jumped out at him: Sajad Fariq.

If Fariq had been corrupt at the time of the attack, he might have figured Fuller's patrol had come for him and initiated the assault. But if that were true, why not expose it at the time and let the American soldiers be the heroes they'd truly been? Carver would know, Noah was certain.

He'd already contacted Chuy and Bo, who'd confirmed that the Iraqi soldiers had opened fire first. Both men would let him use their names in whatever story he wrote. Chuy, working at a youth center and going to school for a business degree, said, *Long as you cover my ass like I covered yours, homes.*

Emile continued his silence.

Nothing new on Fariq showed up, so Noah shut down his laptop and headed for bed and Mel's warm arms.

THURSDAY EVENING, NOAH hustled into the house, late for supper again. "Sorry," he said. "Got sidetracked." He leaned down to kiss Mel, hoping she understood the pressure he was under.

"There's stew on the stove." Her smile seemed forced. She liked everyone to eat dinner together.

"Hey, little guy," he said, kissing Daniel on the head. He noticed a cartoon-decorated adhesive strip on the boy's thigh and remembered he'd had his check-up today. "How did the shots go?"

"I hate those so much," Mel said. "He always looks so betrayed."

"Better than getting the mumps." He scooped a bowl of stew for himself and sat at the table. He had news Mel wasn't going to like, but he had to tell her.

"I hope it's not cold," she said.

He took a bite. Cold. "Perfect," he said.

"We've both been working hard, so I was thinking on Sunday we should go to the water park," Mel said.

"That sounds fun." Noah took a deep breath. "The only thing is that the Sheriff Sam story is due on Monday. I'm behind, so I'm going to stay at the guesthouse for the next few nights and work straight through. That way, maybe I'll be finished in time for the water park."

"Oh. Okay. You can't work here?"

"It's tough to concentrate. One look at you and I want to get naked." The house was too damn busy with people and activity, if he were being honest. A shut door never stayed that way.

"Do what you have to do," she said, disappointed, but hiding it. She was a class act all the way.

"Thanks, Mel. I appreciate that."

Once he got to the guesthouse, he felt great. It was quiet, he had the place to himself. There would be no sticky Daniel fingers on his keyboard or friendly questions from Irena or Mel. He loved the three of them, but damn, he'd missed his alone time.

It would take time to adjust, he figured. He'd committed to staying with Mel and Daniel in Phoenix, so he would stay. It was the right thing to do.

He started with a quick draft from his outline, pulling in each element as he scrolled out the story, including relevant facts, using fresh language, building the story without overkill or leaps of logic, noting each place he needed to double-check his interview notes.

As he worked, his thoughts slipped now and then to the Iraq project. He'd received an analysis on friendly-fire incidents in Iraq and Afghanistan from *News Watch,* the investigative news foundation, and it made him wonder, with the rates so high, why the Army would falsify another troubling incident.

He worked until after midnight and woke the next morning to his cell phone ringing. He blinked at the display. *F. Andrews* with a D.C. area code. Frank Andrews was the CEO of *News Watch.* Why would he be calling? Noah had gotten all he needed from the senior editor. The organization was solid and dedicated, embodying the best of his profession. Keepers of the flame, not to be too corny about it. He took a deep breath and answered the call.

Ten minutes later, Noah shut his phone, completely stunned. Andrews had called to offer him a job as an investigative writer. If he took it, he would be part of major investigations in collaboration with top newspapers, doing important news work. It was his dream job.

Except it was in D.C.

He had a week to decide.

If he took the job, he would break Mel's heart. What if he tried it for a year, came home for long weekends every month? She would never buy that. In or out, that's what she'd expect. Noah felt ripped apart. He loved being with Mel and Daniel, felt as though he belonged somewhere for the first time in his life. But he'd come alive to his career again. He was back, ready to work and work hard. How could he say no to an opportunity like this?

NOAH JERKED AWAKE AND saw he'd dropped off at the kitchen table in the guesthouse. Someone was banging on the door. It turned out to be Paul, wearing a half-buttoned shirt, holding one tennis shoe. "He's coming!" he said to Noah.

"What time is it?" Noah asked. "And who's coming?"

"The baby. Who else?" Paul lifted a bare foot to put on the shoe he held, hopping for balance. "It's a little past midnight. Would you sleep in the house, then drop Emma at the hospital on your way to work in the morning?"

"Sure. I can do that."

Paul handed him a key. "Cindi's water broke in our bed, so if you don't want the couch, you'll have to change the sheets."

"Couch is fine," he said. "Go have your baby."

"Great. Thanks so much. I'll call you when it happens." He looked happy and anxious at the same time. He turned to run.

"And tie your shoes!" Noah called after him. A face-plant was the last thing he needed with a pregnant wife in the car.

It felt as though Noah had barely drifted off when he opened his eyes to find Emma staring at him. "Where's my mom and dad?" she demanded, hands on her hips.

Noah looked at his watch. Seven a.m. "They're at the hospital. Your mom's having the baby."

"They left me all alone?" She sounded startled and a little afraid.

"Not alone. What am I, chopped liver?"

"I hate liver, Uncle Noah. Why are you so weird?" He was glad to see annoyance had replaced fear in her tone.

"I don't know, Em. It's just how I roll. Go get dressed, we'll eat breakfast and I'll take you to the hospital on my way to work."

She gave him a sly look. "Can I have Pop Tarts?"

"It's a special occasion. Why not?"

"Goody!" She headed off.

Noah's cell phone held a message from Paul:

He's here. William Paul Stockton, 8 pounds, 7 ounces, born at 6:33 a.m. He's got my hair and Cindi's nose.

When Emma came into the kitchen, Noah decided not to comment on her outfit—a pink tank top, a tutu and a pair of bunny slippers. "Your dad called. You've got a baby brother now. They named him William."

She scrunched up her nose. "William? I hate that name."

"So give him a nickname. Willie…Billy…Will?"

"Crybaby," she said glumly. "That's what babies do. Cry, cry, cry. My friend Brianna has one and she has to put cotton in her ears at night." She took a bite of her cinnamon pastry.

"They do more than cry, Em. And pretty soon, you can play with him."

"Uh-*uh*. Babies can't talk or walk in for*ever*. They just cry, drink milk, poop and pee and cry more."

He studied her. She wasn't going to buy any BS. "At first, sure, they're not that much fun. But just wait." That was dumb. She could hardly wait from one Popsicle to the next. How was she going to wait for a baby to grow?

She glared at him.

"You're probably thinking your mom and dad won't have time for you with William needing so much help, but you were here first. You're the big sister. Don't forget that."

She shrugged, but tilted her head, considering his words.

"Plus, they won't want you to feel left out, so I bet they'll do special things for you."

"Like what? Buy me toys?" Her eyes lit up.

"Probably. Plus, they'll say yes more to you, I bet, since you're so grown-up." He felt sorry for the freshly dethroned princess. He'd had his own life turned around, too, and it wasn't easy at any age.

"Really? So I can watch more TV? Stay up late? Wear my swimsuit to school?"

"I wouldn't push my luck, Emma. You'll have to be reasonable."

She frowned. "Pro'ly not the swimsuit." She drank some milk, then dipped the treat into the glass and swished it around.

"The best part is that your brother will adore you. You're the top dog. He'll be your slave. Just be sure to use your powers for good, not evil."

She scrunched up her forehead. "Do you say weird stuff like that to your little boy?"

"I guess I do. Is that bad?"

"It's pro'ly okay. He pro'ly loves you anyway." She bit off the soggy chunk of pastry and smacked her lips.

"I hope you're right," he said. "I really do." But how would Daniel feel about a father who walked out after a month? How *could* he feel?

Sorry, buddy. Got a great job offer. Had to roll out.

IN THE HOSPITAL ROOM, Cindi was holding the baby in bed, with Paul grinning in wonder.

Emma ran to her mother. "You left me all alone, Mommy."

"I'm sorry, sweetie, but look, you have a little brother now."

She studied him. "He's all red and smashed in the face." She sighed, then turned to Noah. "Scrunchy. That's my name for him."

"Scrunchy?" Cindi said to Noah.

"I told her she had nickname rights," Noah said, bending to kiss Cindi on the cheek. "You look great. Scrunchy, too. He's perfect."

"You think so?" she said, completely blissed out. "Thanks for bringing Em."

"Happy to help."

"Can I buy you breakfast, Noah?" Paul asked.

"Coffee, sure." The two men headed down the elevator and followed the cooking smells to the cafeteria. They separated to get food—Paul a big breakfast of pancakes, eggs and bacon and Noah a cup of black coffee—and found a table near the atrium. "Congratulations, man," Noah said. "You've got a son."

"I know. I'll tell you what. The whole thing is amazing. You can't believe it's actually happening to you— well, to your wife—and that you get to keep that little miracle for your very own and watch it grow up."

Noah wished Mel were here with her camera to capture the expression on Paul's face, more tender and powerful than any soft-focused Hallmark card. "I imagine it's pretty wonderful."

"I'm sorry you missed that with Daniel."

"Yeah." He kind of was, too.

"Next time, huh?" Paul said.

"Next time?" He laughed. "No way." Then he stopped. Damn. Mel would likely want a second child one day. He couldn't let that possibility into his head, especially with the job offer upping the ante.

"You'll surprise yourself," Paul said.

"I've surprised myself enough as it is."

"What's with the tone? You and Mel having problems?"

"No. Things are fine." Noah studied his friend. Might as well get Paul's thoughts on his dilemma. "*News Watch* offered me a job as an investigative writer."

"*News Watch?* Wow. That's great. They don't hire many people."

"No, they don't."

"Ah. You'd have to move to D.C. Right." Paul took a bite of eggs, thinking that through. Noah sipped coffee, tension swirling in his chest.

"So are you going to take it?"

"Families require sacrifice, I guess. You gave up *National Record* for Cindi and the baby."

"I gave up *National Record* for a life I wanted more. I knew there were other jobs I could love. And teaching has been great."

"Yeah, but I'm not selfless like you, Paul."

"Hell, I wasn't selfless back then. And, yeah, at first, I missed having nothing to worry about but work, friends and good times." He bit off a hunk of bacon and chewed thoughtfully. "But what I got was more than I ever expected. Every life has its price."

"I get that. I do. Mel and Daniel mean a lot to me. But I'm back on track after more than a year, finally writing, and I'm dying to dig in."

"It's a tough call, Noah. What does Mel say?"

"She doesn't know yet. She'll want me to stay, but

she'll understand if I decide to go. And hate me for it, no doubt."

"She might surprise you. When do you have to decide?"

"I've got a week." He drained his coffee. "I should get to work. Congratulations again on William. Except, too bad he's got your hair."

"What's wrong with my…?" Catching the joke, Paul laughed.

"I should warn you I promised Emma she'd get extra treats out of this baby-brother deal. You might swing by Toys "R" Us for another plastic pony with comb-able hair."

"Jesus, Noah. Thanks a ton."

"I had to cheer her up. Listen, I'll be finished with the story this weekend. Is Sunday soon enough to clear out of the guesthouse for your in-laws?"

"The longer we put them off, the better. Take your time. Good luck with the job decision. You'll do the right thing."

"I'm glad one of us thinks so."

On Sunday, he had to call Mel and tell her he couldn't make the water park, since he was still revising the story. He expected her to be hurt, even angry, but she wasn't. She was quiet for a long moment. Then she said, "You have a deadline, Noah. I understand. There will always be water parks. Come back when you can."

He sat for a long time after that, thinking. She could have accused him of wanting to avoid them, of choosing work over family, even of having second thoughts about being with her, but she hadn't done any of that. She'd been stand-up. She'd been solid and supportive.

She might surprise you.

And then Noah surprised himself.

Monday morning after emailing his completed story to the *Times* editor, he turned down the *News Watch* job, explaining that his family circumstances wouldn't permit a move right then.

Afterward, he fought the sick churn in his gut, the ache in his heart, the sense that he'd done something he'd forever regret.

What was he doing? Noah was a journalist. He was ambitious. He never missed a chance to get more, do more, be more. Yet that very ambition had led to the tragedy in Iraq. Maybe the lesson was that he had to make different choices, curb his obsession, change his priorities. It hurt, it scared him, but he would focus on Mel and Daniel and it would all make sense.

Eventually.

He couldn't wait to see them, so he headed over to catch the tail end of breakfast with them, despite how exhausted he was from a weekend of little sleep and a life-changing sacrifice.

He figured once he saw them, he'd know he'd done the right thing. Mel and Daniel made it all worthwhile. What had Paul said about throwing away the *National Record* job? *I gave it up for a life I wanted more.*

Okay, Noah would go with that, despite his doubts. He couldn't wait to walk in the door and pull Mel into his arms and kiss his son.

Except, when he got to the house, chaos reigned. Daniel was throwing food and the dog was jumping up to grab it. Mel was scurrying around, buttoning her blouse, a half-eaten piece of toast in her mouth.

"Noah, hi!" She brightened at the sight of him, but only fleetingly. "I'm running late and I have to grab dry cleaning on the way in. Would you mind dropping Daniel off at Bright Blossoms?"

"Sure. No problem."

He started to lean in to kiss her, but she took a bite

of toast. "The greatest thing just happened," she said, chewing quickly. "We're getting a family portrait done by Laszlo Moritz. This afternoon!"

"A portrait?" Huh?

She rattled on about how this newly famous art photographer, in town for a couple of days, had squeezed in the sitting as a favor to her. Through his mental fog, Noah got the key points: *Tremendous favor... Charges a thousand dollars for the sitting alone... What a thrill... can't wait... Perfect timing...*

"So, be at his studio at exactly 6:00 p.m.," Mel said, scribbling onto a piece of scrap paper. "Wear a white dress shirt and 501 jeans. Mom and Daniel and I will meet you. Here's the address." She jabbed the paper at him. "Don't be late."

"Okay," he said. He owned a white shirt, but it needed ironing and his 501s were crumpled in his laundry basket at the guesthouse.

"Thanks so much. You're saving me. I've got to fly. Just wipe off his face and he's good to go. Diaper bag's by the door." Then she was gone.

Without a kiss or even a fragrant hug, the pressure of her hips against his, the swell of her breasts, her sigh in his ear. Damn. So much for making him glad he'd done what he'd done.

Oh, grow up. She'd had no way to know what he'd given up for her. Later on, they would talk. He would tell her what he'd sacrificed and she would be glad and he would know he'd done the right thing for her and Daniel, the right thing for himself, too.

Right?

MEL PULLED UP TO Laszlo's studio, so excited she was trembling a little. Everything was working out perfectly, almost like a miracle, almost a sign. Daniel, her mother and Mel looked great in their white shirts and jeans. Even her stubborn hair had cooperated and held its curl all day.

As soon as Noah arrived, Laszlo would photograph them and they'd have museum-quality proof that their lives were working out just right.

She'd had flickers of doubt the past week as Noah became more and more obsessed with his Iraq project and the Sheriff Sam story. He'd seemed almost relieved to escape them for four days at the guesthouse.

Had she asked too much of him? Had Daniel been too cranky? She'd begun to count on Noah and that might not be wise. Noah had said he wanted them to be a family, but did he know what that entailed? Did she?

She was probably being paranoid, expecting the worst when the best had been offered to her with open arms. Noah said he'd stick, so he'd stick. They loved each other and they loved Daniel and the rest would fall into place.

She pushed through the studio door. Her cell phone buzzed, signaling a text. She checked it.

Can't make it. Alumni event in Chandler, 5-7. Reschedule? Noah

Can't make it? Just like that, he blew off the portrait. You didn't reschedule with Laszlo Moritz when he gifted you a sitting. Hadn't she made it clear to him how important this was? Damn, damn, damn.

She started to write him back, to demand he show up, but she realized he was an hour away. Too late. They'd get the family portrait, of course. Of Mel and her mother and Daniel. No Noah. Maybe that was the sign after all.

CHAPTER FIFTEEN

MEL WAS IN BED WHEN she heard Noah's key in the front door. It was nearly 10:00 p.m. He'd clearly been elsewhere after the alumni event without bothering to let her know.

Was this how it would be? Noah disappearing into his job, treating the family like an annoyance he could set aside at will?

She didn't want to be unfair. Of course she respected his devotion to his career. He was making a fresh start. He had to give it everything he had. She understood deadlines and the need to follow leads wherever they took you for as long as they took. Noah had told her that the night they met. That was basic to being successful in his job.

But still. An alumni event? And no phone call?

Do not be cranky. Do not whine. That wasn't Mel, but she felt the simmer of hurt and worry in her stomach.

The bedroom door opened slowly and Noah tiptoed in.

"I'm awake," she said, turning on the lamp. "It's late." She kept her voice level, not accusatory.

"One of the alumni turned out to be with the county prosecutor's office, so we talked about privately run prisons. I took him out for couple beers. Got some great background."

Why didn't you call? She bit back the question. "That's good, I guess."

Noah pulled his shirt over his head and tossed it to the floor. "Did you rebook the portrait?" He started unhooking his belt.

"It was a favor from Lazlo. We took it without you." She sounded sharper than she'd intended.

He stopped at the pants clasp and met her gaze. "So you got a portrait at least. That's good."

"It was supposed to be the family."

"So, we'll book another one," he said irritably. "It won't be the famous Laszlo Whatzit, but it will be good."

"There's no need to sneer. It was a rare opportunity, that's all."

"Alumni cocktail parties won't earn me a Pulitzer, but they put a paycheck in my pocket. If they want me somewhere, I have to go." He sounded bitter, almost braced for a fight.

"I realize that, Noah. I'm just disappointed."

"Sorry," he said, but he didn't sound it. "It's late and I'm beat. Can we fight in the morning?" He was clearly trying to joke, but it came out harshly.

She bristled. "Is that want you want? To fight?"

"No." He sighed and sat on the bed beside her.

"Can we start over?" she said. "We haven't seen each other in days—"

"Because I had a deadline. You know that. You said you understood."

"I do. Stop it. I mean we haven't talked much, okay? Why are you so angry?"

"I'm not. It's just that I came over this morning to see you for a few minutes before work and all you did was order me around and dump Daniel on me."

"*Dump* Daniel on you? Is that how you see it?"

"Come on. You know what I mean. Look, I'm doing what you want. I'm here, aren't I?"

"What *I* want? What about you? Don't you want to be here?" Her chest was so tight she could hardly draw a breath.

"Of course I do." But reluctance flickered in his eyes.

She felt sick to her stomach. "You told me you wanted to be with us. Now it sounds like some heavy obligation to you."

"That's not true. You're reading things into it. I want to be here."

"Really? Because you sound angry to me."

"You don't believe me now? You want proof?" His tone was sharp. "Okay. How's this? I gave up a job to stay with you."

"You what? What job?"

"*News Watch* asked me to be an investigative reporter."

"The journalism foundation? That's great. How did that...happen?"

"I contacted them about friendly-fire casualties in Iraq and the CEO called to offer me the job."

"And you said no?" Her mind couldn't seem to grasp what this signified, but she knew it wasn't good. It wasn't good at all.

"I had to. It's in D.C." He looked as though he was trying to be brave about a terminal diagnosis.

"No wonder you sound bitter," she said, the truth thundering through her. "That's the job you wanted."

"There will be others. The point is I'm staying, like I said I would. So stop second-guessing me. I'm doing the best I can with all this." The lamplight caught the scars on his shoulders, injuries he'd sustained pursuing the career that meant everything to him.

"I know you are, Noah." Her throat tightened. "We both are." She wanted to accept his words, tell him he was right to give up the job, to stay with them. Family mattered more than a career, didn't it? It did to her. She'd given up her dream job for Daniel. Why shouldn't Noah do the same?

It was only fair, wasn't it? It was the right thing to do.

"I love you, Mel. And I love Daniel. More than I thought possible." She looked into his eyes and saw that he meant this. But she also saw the pain he felt and the confusion. And she knew she had to do the right thing, no matter how much it hurt.

"But that doesn't change who you are," she said dully, the truth forcing its way out of her mouth. "Your work is everything to you. I knew that from the day we met. I respected that about you. I still do."

Oh, how she wanted to keep him here. It would only take time and he would forget. The family dream would be real. There were other jobs he could get, right?

But he'd been *wandering* since Iraq and now he was back and she knew how much that meant. She knew it to her soul. "We can't be the reason you turn down your dream job," she said, her voice wobbling at the end.

"There will be others." The muscle in his jaw ticked quickly, showing her how tense he was.

"And in the meantime, you'll resent us." She felt the truth of her own words sink through her like lead weight. "You'll stay because you keep your word, but bedtime stories and walks in the park won't make up for this sacrifice. Your job at ASU is boring. Freelance is far from a sure thing. You're an investigative reporter. That's your calling. That's where you shine."

"Mel—"

"No. I mean it. I can't live with doing that to you."

"It's done," he said. "It's over."

"You say there are other jobs, but where? New York? Surely *National Record* will want you. Chicago? L.A., maybe? Not Phoenix, not with news departments cut to the bone here. Even if they could hire you, you'd take a huge pay cut."

"I won't walk away like my dad did...or yours."

"You didn't want a family in the first place."

"But I have one," he said stubbornly. "I want this to work."

"You love Daniel and me, but that doesn't mean you want to live this life with us." She blinked back tears.

"You want me to leave, just walk away?"

For a moment, resentment spiked. Noah was free to chase his passion, pursue his dream, while she'd had to postpone hers to raise their son. It was so damned unfair.

Get over it. It was reality. And Mel was too practical to fight reality.

Her better self broke through. *Think what Noah has already suffered. Think about how good he is, how much he has to offer.*

She couldn't hold him back. Not for herself, not even for Daniel. She loved him too much to do that. And she loved herself and Daniel too much to keep him here when he'd rather be gone.

"You've come to life, Noah. And your life is your work. We're only holding you back."

She watched the truth of her words register in his face. He looked away, considering, the muscle in his jaw working so hard it seemed ready to pop from his cheek. When his gaze returned to hers, he said, "I'm willing to stay, Mel."

"Willing?" She managed a sad smile. "You mean, you'll serve your time? That's not how family works. Not the family I want for Daniel and me."

"So, what? You're ending this? Breaking us up?"

"What else can we do? This argument we're having now? It would happen over and over. And I don't want to go through that. I'd rather make a clean break, not drag it out until we hurt each other too much." She heard herself speak as though in a dream. She was saying the right things, but her heart was miles behind, screaming at her to *stop, stop, stop.*

"Take some time to think about this."

"I have thought about it. I want this over with," she snapped, angry now. Angry at herself for being such a dreamer and at Noah for not having more sense than to fall for her fantasy.

He frowned. "I'm still Daniel's father. I want to keep seeing him."

"For now, sure. But after you leave?"

"I'll be there for him, no matter what, no matter where I am."

She blew out a breath, giving up. "I don't have the strength to fight you. Visit when you can and call when you can't. We'll leave it there for now."

"What will you tell him about me? Later on, when he asks?" he said, his eyes dark with emotion. His throat worked over a swallow.

"I'll tell him what I planned from before. That you and I were together, but our lives went in different directions."

"And that we loved each other. Don't leave that out."

She nodded. "I'll say that you wanted to stay with us, but that you had important work that meant you had to leave and that I agreed that it was the right decision." Her voice shook so hard she couldn't hide it.

"Mel," he said, reaching for her.

"No," she said, refusing his comfort. "I'm all right. You want a big life, Noah. Ours is too small for you."

"It doesn't have to be. Don't sell yourself short. You have a gift. Don't waste it. You can still take photos that can change the world. I know you can."

The possibility seemed so far away now. She shook her head. Two tears had slipped down her cheeks. She brushed them away, not wanting to show more weakness than she'd already revealed.

"I want the best for you and for Daniel," Noah said, his voice rough.

She nodded. "I was wrong to try to keep you away from him in the beginning," she said. "I thought I could keep us from getting hurt, but I think hurt was part of the package." She tried to smile over the pain, but she was sure it looked more like a grimace.

"You never duck the truth, do you, Mel?" Noah's chest burned with regret.

"I don't see the point."

"I loved that about you from the day we met." Her eyes shone with tears she was holding back. Tears he'd put there and would give anything to erase.

"I'm sorry to hurt you, Mel." If he stayed, would he resent her and Daniel as she predicted? Very possibly.

When he'd snapped at her about the portrait, he'd recognized his father's voice when his mother complained about him being too busy to spend time with her. Despite all his good intentions, Noah was like his father, after all.

He remembered how it had been with Pat, his reporter girlfriend. No matter how much time he gave her, it had never been enough. The truth was that his work mattered more to him than she did and they both knew it.

Why had he thought he could be different now?

Because of the rush of early love. The magic of Daniel. The surprising satisfaction of having a place in the world and people who loved him, who he loved in return. Could he be forgiven for falling for that? He doubted it.

"We should have known better," Mel said. "We were dreaming, you and I. We don't really know each other. Not really."

"You made me see what I had to do about Iraq, Mel. In some ways, you saved me. I'll always be grateful to you."

"I'm glad I helped you," she said.

"And you're wrong about one thing. I do know you, *Melodía.* I know that every night, you evaluate the day in order to improve the next one. I know that you're not religious, but the *Virgen de Guadalupe* gives you comfort and you light your mother's candles when they go out.

"I know that you are magic behind a camera, that every step you take in the world, you're composing the snapshot you would take of it.

"I know that you chew each bite five times because you read that improves your digestion, that when you feel sexy, you wear those gold hoop earrings. I know that you're proud to be *mestizo* and you have a singing voice like an angel.

"I know that you bite the left side of your bottom lip when you're uncertain and the right side as you climax.

"I know that you're smart and funny and strong, whether your name is a song or not, and that I won't meet another woman like you in my life. I will never get over you."

"Oh, Noah," she said, her lips trembling.

He kissed her. He had to. She tasted sweet and sad and salty from her tears. He wanted so much to stay. But she was right. If he was going, he had to go. He broke off the kiss, grabbed his shirt from the floor and pulled it on.

"I'll sleep at Paul's tonight. I can get my things in the morning. I want to see Daniel—every morning, actually. Unless evenings are better?"

She swallowed hard. "Get your stuff now, okay? Visit Daniel at Bright Blossoms at first. Here…it hurts too much. I need a little space."

"Sure. We both do," he said, his heart thudding heavily in his chest. The reality hadn't yet sunk in. He was leaving their lives. He'd be another divorced dad negotiating summer trips and holiday visits with his ex. It made him feel ill, but there was nothing to be done about it now.

"Good night, Mel," he said. She looked so sad and pretty in the golden light from the lamp.

Before he left, he looked in on Daniel, who slept sprawled out, Paquito under one arm. He looked so small in the big crib, so vulnerable. Noah missed him already. "I'll always be your father," he whispered. "Count on that." And he sang a line from "Duermete, Niño Lindo." He'd memorized it after all.

"MELODÍA, WHY DO YOU not forgive?" Mel's mother said to her. "This I do not understand. I teach you different. You give chances to those you love."

A week had passed since the breakup and her mother would not let up on the recriminations. As if Mel's heartbreak weren't enough to deal with.

"It can't work, *Mamá.* Noah's career is his life. We don't fit. We tried, but it's impossible. Put St. Jude in the alcove. Isn't he the patron of lost causes?"

"You're not lost. You are…*difícil.* Stubborn. Where did this need for the perfect come?"

"I don't want perfect. I want reasonable. I want do-able."

"Noah loves Daniel. Every day, he comes to Bright Blossoms to see him. Twice each day. You don't permit him in our house."

"It's too hard, *Mamá,* don't you see? The phone calls are bad enough." Her voice cracked. It was wrong to limit Noah to brief visits at day care, she knew. She hoped that when he returned from his trip to talk to Captain Carver and Emile Daggett, she'd be able to handle seeing him. As it was, he called twice a day to see how she was doing and what was new with Daniel.

"I think again you give the brush-off to him."

"*Please.* Maybe one day I'll find a man whose life will fit with ours. One who can build Daniel a fort in the backyard, take him trick-or-treating, coach his Little League team, show up to clap when he's a lowly mush-room in the preschool play." She was breathing hard, her voice sharp.

"He'll be around for all of it—the tedious, the silly, the sad, the magnificent. Noah can't do that. It's not the life he wants."

Her mother shook her head. "This is my fault. Because I never marry, you have the picture of perfect fa-ther, perfect family. Melodía, my way is not your way. My way is not best."

Daniel wrapped his arms around Mel's leg. She looked down and he held up a hand for a high-five. He was trying to cheer her up.

She bent to lift him into her arms and hug him. She didn't want her sadness to affect Daniel, but it was tough to act cheerful. During the nighttime stories and songs, she would remember Noah lying on the floor or sitting on the arm of the chair with her, singing along, and miss him so sharply she nearly cried out in breathless pain. She felt as though someone had cut out her heart and filled her chest with sawdust. *It's for the best,* she kept telling herself. But it felt like the absolute worst.

NOAH KEPT MOVING. Moving saved him. At the moment he was on a flight to Las Vegas, planning to drop in on Gerald Carver.

He hadn't felt so low since Iraq, which was ridiculous, since the breakup was for the best. He'd known it even then.

Each day when he checked in with Mel, he heard the pain in her voice. He'd offered to stop calling, but she told him it was okay, that he needed to know what Daniel was up to. She promised that when he got back from his trip, he could start coming to the house to see Daniel there.

He hoped that would feel better than his visits at Bright Blossoms. Daniel was so preoccupied with the children, he never wanted to sit on Noah's lap for more than a minute or two. Noah had the terrible feeling that Daniel wanted what Mel had said: *If you're going to go, just go.*

What had Mel told him about her father? *It would have been better if he never knew about me.* Now and then, he wondered if she weren't right.

Sick at heart, his jaw locked against the sadness that rode his throat all day long and kept him awake all hours of the night, he missed what he'd had for such a short time: games of blueberry fetch, story time, walks with Daniel on his shoulders, Paco yanking the leash, that baby smell Daniel had and always Mel. He missed Mel like a part of him was gone.

He missed her smile, her no-nonsense gaze, her mouth, her body, her welcoming arms and her generous heart.

So he kept moving. Working on the Iraq story and looking for a job. He'd called *News Watch,* feeling like a fool for changing his mind so quickly, but the job had been filled the day after he'd turned it down. *Openings come up,* the CEO told him, *so keep in touch.* He would, no question.

In the meantime, he would get on where he could as soon as he could. He'd sacrificed Daniel and Mel for his career. He'd damn well better make it work.

Landing in Las Vegas, Noah rented a car and headed for nearby Henderson to surprise Carver. Three days before, he'd lucked out when Carver's wife picked up the phone to yell at him for leaving so many messages. *Stop calling here! Every time you do, he eats his liver for days. I'm sick of buying Mylanta for the man.*

Noah had kept her on the line long enough to convince her that letting Noah talk with her husband might actually help him. She'd given him the address of the Carver's auto shop. *Tell him you found it in the phone book,* she told him. *He'd never forgive me for sending you.*

Her final words haunted him: *Just get me my Gerry back. What happened in Iraq broke him.* Noah promised he'd do his best.

And he would.

If his meeting with Carver went well, he'd next fly to Detroit, then drive north to Emile's house to tell him the truth about what had happened and apologize again in person for what he'd done to the man.

The last leg of his trip would be to New York, where he'd stop at *National Record* to talk to Hank about possible jobs and pitch the Iraq story, assuming he had enough to run with. He owed his old employer first crack at what he hoped would be a significant piece.

GPS took him to Carver's shop and he pulled into a parking slot. The vehicles waiting for service were all vintage muscle cars. Hmm. Noah could work with that, considering his father had had similar tastes.

He stepped into the service bay, where Carver leaned into the engine of a late-'60s red Camaro. Hearing movement, the man raised his head, wiped his hands on a rag, then turned to Noah.

Carver's eyes flickered with surprise, but all he said was, "I've got nothing to say to you," before returning to the engine.

"Hear me out, then decide."

"Not going to happen." The man's profile hardened to steel, but his breathing was uneven, angry.

Noah noticed a photo on the wall to his left—an old and faded shot of an officer in a dress uniform in front of a new Mustang. The towheaded kid standing proudly beside him had to be Gerald Carver.

"My pop had a Mustang about that age," he said, though it had been a Charger. Close enough.

Carver stopped working for a second, then rolled his shoulder, as if to brush off a fly, before resuming.

"The carburetor gave him hell."

"Sometimes. Yeah." The man slowed his wrench work.

"My dad was career Army. He was killed in a Jeep accident on the base. That's no way for a soldier to clock out."

Carver said nothing. Noah let the silence ride for a minute or two.

"The men had a lot of respect for you," he said finally. "They all talked about the time you fixed that Humvee so they didn't have to wait all day for the mechanic."

He paused, took a long breath, then went for it. "I don't get why you got busted out. Fuller would never have defied direct orders from the lieutenant colonel. He didn't even bother to get your okay on the patrol."

"He was under my command," Carver gritted out the words. "My responsibility."

"It wasn't right, what they did to you."

"Lot of wrongs happen in war."

"Doesn't mean they can't be fixed. I know I put the squad in danger and I apologize for that, but—"

Carver jerked his head out of the engine and turned on Noah, a sarcastic smile on his face. "You don't know what the hell you're talking about."

"Then set me straight."

"What's done is done."

Noah waited for a minute before he said, "I understand you keep good records."

Carver froze, then set his wrench on the wheel well. "You talk to Haverson?"

He left that alone. "Here's what I know. Fuller's

squad did not initiate that firefight. But a brigadier general came to the hospital while my brains were still scrambled to convince me they had. Now I find out that the Iraqi captain I went to meet that day is being tried for treason in Iraq. There's a puzzle here and I know you can put the pieces together for me."

"Why are you doing this? To write some article?" He sneered. "Nobody gives a shit about Iraq anymore. And they sure don't care about being fair to some re-tired Army captain."

"The men who were there care. The men under your command. And, if I write a solid story, a lot of Ameri-cans who read it will care, too."

Carver stared at him, breathing hard, eyes red and narrowed in anger. It was fifty-fifty whether or not he would come across that engine block and clock Noah in the jaw. Seconds ticked by.

The smell of motor oil began to get to him, he no-ticed, feeling queasy. His heart surged. The storeroom had reeked of motor oil and shit and blood.

With a jolt, a memory hit him. He'd shoved tarps out of the way to see hidden crates and metal contain-ers labeled in English with item IDs he recognized as U.S. Army issue. "Wait. I remember," he said out loud. "They had stockpiled weapons where they held me. Ordnance. Marked U.S. Army." A stab of pain made him wince. "I tried to take pictures, but my camera jammed or…something. I remember being frustrated." He shook his head, trying to call up more detail.

An unmistakable look of triumph crossed Carver's face. Triumph and relief, as if he'd been dying for some-one to figure this out.

"I tried writing down the codes." He remembered pinching the pencil nub, the dirt-streaked pages of his pad. Then the door had flown open. "But they caught me." Noah had rolled on top of the paper to hide it, but the guard had seen. Then the butt of a rifle came at his head and he was out.

Carver rubbed his hands with a rag so hard he might be taking off skin. A storm raged in his eyes. Wanting Noah to remember didn't mean he wanted to talk about it with him.

"You know more, don't you? Help me sort it out. For the sake of the men." While everything in Noah wanted to push, demand, shame the man, hell, beg him to talk, his reporter instincts told him to hold his tongue, to wait, to be patient, allow Carver to sift through his thoughts and options.

The silence went on and on. Carver fisted and released his hands over and over, glared at Noah, then looked out in the blank distance. Finally, he seemed to focus on the yellowed photograph of his father and that Mustang and his features settled in. He'd made a decision.

His head snapped toward Noah with military precision. "Pete's Tavern. Two blocks south. The back booth. Give me a half hour."

Noah nodded and left, as cool and easy as he could manage when he wanted to shout in triumph. Carver was in. Skittish, but in. Noah trusted his own abilities to keep him there.

Thirty minutes later, Carver walked into the bar with a fat manila envelope under his arm. He strode straight to Noah, head high, sat erectly in the booth and placed the envelope squarely in front of himself with a terse nod.

Noah didn't speak, allowing Carver to run with the ball. When the waitress came, Carver kept his eyes on

Noah while he ordered whiskey with a beer back. Noah made it two.

After she left, Carver said, "You were correct that there were no orders from Lieutenant Colonel Reynolds to avoid that sector. The man *did* have intelligence, however, indicating that Fariq was corrupt and working with insurgents." Carver's ice-blue eyes flared with outrage. Otherwise, his face remained utterly still.

"Lieutenant Colonel Reynolds withheld that intel from myself and my fellow officers, putting Fuller's squad in harm's way. Fariq's men initiated the attack."

"You say he *withheld* the intel?"

"Evidently, a crucial military budget vote was pending in Congress. To acknowledge that the U.S. Army had been training Iraqi traitors, not soldiers, would have embarrassed the Army and possibly threatened the budget."

"So, when we rolled up on Fariq, he thought he'd been caught?"

Carver nodded. "Those crates you saw contained stolen weaponry. Fariq believed Fuller's mission was to recover those weapons."

"How do you know what he believed?"

"We heard him say as much to his superior officer." Half of Carver's mouth lifted into a swift smile.

"How?" Noah asked. "You planted listening devices?"

"We didn't need to. We had a reporter on the scene." Carver's eyes actually twinkled when he continued. "Not only did you take a few photos of the stolen weapons before your camera jammed, but you managed to activate your tape recorder while Fariq and his superior were discussing the attack."

"My recorder? I didn't realize that." Noah blinked.

"My memory's been blocked until recently. I recognized Fariq's voice. I do remember that."

"The recorder and media card were on your person when you were rescued."

"So the Army got the information?"

"Yes. The recording also included comments about a planned assault on Iraqi army HQ in Balad. Further investigation led to the thwarting of that attack."

"Damn." He leaned back against the bench. At least he'd done his job. At least what he'd done had resulted in some good.

"Why wasn't it made public? Why did they cover it up? If you knew, why didn't you report it?"

"I'm a soldier, Mr. Stone. I follow orders. I trusted my superiors to act in the best interests of the Army, our troops in Iraq, the Iraqi military and the American people."

"But that wasn't what happened. Not even close."

Again, Carver gave a half sneer. "As the details came clear, I became angry on behalf of Fuller and his men. And myself, of course."

"But you let them force you out."

"I'm a soldier, as I said." He cleared his throat, then tapped the worn envelope. "Your materials are here, along with a translated transcript. Use them however you see fit. Included are emails and transcripts of phone conversations—to which I was privy—about the cover-up. Also proof that Fariq's corruption was known long before his recent arrest."

"Thank you very much," Noah said, taking the envelope.

"I doubt your story will change much, but those men deserve better."

"So do you, Captain. If it's in my power to get it for you, I will."

His smile was sad. "Shit rolls downhill in the Army, Mr. Stone, and I was standing at the bottom. I've moved on." But he'd been chewing up his stomach, according to his wife. Noah would do what he could to clear the captain's name if only in the eyes of the Americans who read his story.

"Another round?" Noah asked.

"Make it a double and you're on."

CHAPTER SIXTEEN

As SOON AS NOAH returned to his hotel room from his meeting with Carver, he hit speed dial for Mel. More than anyone else, she would know what this triumph meant to him.

"H'lo," Mel murmured.

"Did I wake you?" he said.

"Not quite." He heard the smile in her voice. "What's up? Did you talk to him?"

"Oh, yeah. He gave me what I needed and a hell of a lot more." He told her the story as it had happened, making notes on his laptop as he talked it through.

"That's unbelievable. They maligned you and the squad to cover their screwup."

"And left Fariq in place all those months, doing God knows what harm to the Iraqi military."

"This story will be explosive, Noah."

"I hope so. It not only shows the cowardice of top brass in the face of politics, it also illustrates how difficult it is to separate friend from foe in Iraq."

"Good came from what happened," she said. "And you should feel vindicated. You proved how vital it is to have reporters on the frontlines."

"I still regret what I did, but at least I did my job." He'd felt so terrible for so long it was a relief to hear her say what he desperately hoped was true. "Thanks for listening. I know I'm keeping you up."

"I'm happy it went so well."

"Without you, I might not have taken this step."

"Sure you would have. But I'm glad I helped."

They breathed at each other for a few comfortable moments. He set his laptop aside and lay back on the pillow. "So how was Daniel's day?"

"Very good. He said *Nana* for the first time. Mom was beside herself."

"Wish I'd been there," he said. "This is the first day I haven't seen him. I kind of get how that weekend in Tucson was for you. I miss him."

He heard her gulp. "I'm sorry that it has to be this way."

"I miss you, too, Mel." More than he thought possible.

She didn't speak for a few seconds. She seemed to be holding her breath "If I had to lose you," she said finally, "I'm glad it's to work that's so important."

"That means a lot to me." She was making it easy on him, letting him get away with being a selfish jerk, making it sound as though he had a higher purpose. At the moment, he just felt empty.

IF EMILE DAGGETT'S MOTHER hadn't opened the door, Noah was certain he would never have gotten the chance to talk to the soldier. But before Emile could stop her, she'd set them up on the back porch with tall tumblers of lemonade. As soon as she went back inside, Emile poured vodka from a flask into his and muttered, "Say what you got to say."

"First, I am deeply sorry I put you in danger. I know being assigned to watch me took you out of the game with your squad."

Emile looked away, his profile stony.

"And secondly, I want to tell you that you were a hero."

"Bullshit!" The man jerked his body toward Noah, his face fierce. "I was supposed to protect you."

"I would have been dead where I sat if you hadn't dragged me out of that Humvee. I was too stunned to open the damn door. But it's more than that."

Emile shrugged and looked out over the porch, to the house behind them, a muscle in his jaw working.

"The Iraqis who attacked us were insurgents, Emile. The captain thought we were after the stolen-arms cache they had. It's a long story, but that patrol prevented an assault on Iraqi army headquarters. So Fuller didn't die in vain. At least that's what I want to take from that."

"I didn't hear nothin' about all that."

"And that was deliberate. There was a cover-up." Noah explained all he'd learned to Emile, piece by piece.

"Huh," he said when Noah finished.

Noah let the silence hold, while Emile thought it through. He leaned forward, pressing his fingers to the sides of his head, a gesture Noah recognized well.

"Headaches bad?" Noah asked.

Emile looked at him.

"I get them, too. Any flashbacks? Nightmares?"

Emile nodded slowly.

"I used to have one dream over and over. I was carrying a soldier on my back, tripping over bodies, only I finally looked down and saw that I was the one shooting them all down."

Emile drank straight from the flask.

"You get medical care for the symptoms?" Noah asked.

"I'm not whining to the VA like some pussy," he scoffed.

"It's a medical condition. They're trained to treat it."

"Yeah, well, I hear they got a yearlong waiting list."

Noah knew the services were stretched to the limit, so that didn't surprise him. "What helped me was to talk it out," Noah said. "I resisted that for a long time, figuring it would make me feel worse, but I was wrong."

"You think it's that easy," he said, his voice a growl. "Spill my guts and it all goes away? I can't even hold a job for the headaches. Forget the bait shop."

"I can only say it helped me. Bo and Chuy say they reached out, but you never responded."

"Talk does shit." He jumped to his feet and stomped across the porch. After a few seconds of fuming, he stopped in front of Noah. "Here's more truth for you. That dream you had, about carrying someone on your back? Well, it happened. You carried me out of that machine shop on a damn broke leg." He fairly spat the words. "I was supposed to watch you, but you carried me out of that place like a rag doll. Try living with that."

"I was just the guy who came to first, Emile. You know that. And you saved my life. You got me out of the vehicle before it exploded."

"Shit." He turned away.

"What happened over there was hard, I know. I saw Sergeant Fuller get shot ordering you to get me to cover. I have to live with that. And with the fact I got you hurt and got Captain Carver forced out of the Army and all the rest of the harm that came from what I did."

Hands on his hips, Emile fumed, turning side to side, trying to sort his thoughts. Clearly, he wanted to believe what Noah was saying.

"I made mistakes. You think you did, too. I disagree,

but that's beside the point. Regret can sink your soul and what good does that do? You think Sergeant Fuller would want to see you so low?"

Emile dropped his head.

"All we can do is live the best way we know how from here," he said softly. "A friend helped me see that." Mel. Mel had helped him heal, made him look at what he needed to do.

Emile met his gaze, a flicker of hope in his eyes.

"I'm going to tell Chuy to call you. When he does, talk to him."

Emile didn't object and that was the best Noah could expect. Time would have to pass, he knew, and Noah planned to stay in touch, whether Emile wanted that or not.

MEL LAUGHED AT DANIEL in the tub. He'd slathered shaving cream on his face so that all she could see were his bright brown eyes between foam peaks. She grabbed her cell phone from the counter and snapped a photo, then emailed it to Noah, before pretending to shave Daniel's face, the ritual Noah had started that weekend barely a month ago, though it seemed like a lifetime had passed since that happy time.

She kept the phone with her in the bathroom since Noah usually called at bath time. Breakfast time, too. And often in the middle of the day if something interesting had occurred.

She loved hearing his updates on the Iraq story.

His meeting with the soldier who'd been captured with him had gone well, he'd told her, relieving some of the soldier's guilt and some of his own.

At her suggestion, he was going to pursue a story about the lack of medical services for veterans with

PTSD and TBI—Traumatic Brain Injury. One out of five Iraqi vets got PTSD, but less than half of the 400,000 cases got any help at all. When she'd looked into Noah's condition, she'd read that doctors were only now discovering the overlap of physical and psychological symptoms between the two conditions.

She loved that Noah confided in her, that he valued her opinions. From the day they'd met, they'd had this connection. If anything, it was even stronger now that they knew each other better. And loved each other.

Mel knew it wasn't smart to talk so often. They were dragging out the breakup. It would only hurt more when he finally took off for a job in New York or Chicago or Washington, D.C. And that would happen soon.

Today in New York, he'd met with his editor at *National Record* about the Iraq story and possibly getting hired back at the magazine. She expected he would have news when he called tonight. She wished him the best, of course, but she dreaded hearing that he'd been hired away from her.

Her phone buzzed. She looked at the text.

Loved the shot of Danny's face in drifts of snow. See you soon. Lots to talk about.

Uh-oh. He must have gotten the job, she realized, and her heart sank.

She put soap on a cloth and washed Daniel's back, breathing in the nice smells, fighting her reaction. It was what Noah wanted. What he needed, really, to get back to work at an important job.

Oh, Noah. Don't go. She couldn't help feeling that way. She sat back on her heels and took a deep breath, trying to get control of herself.

It wouldn't be too bad, she told herself, grabbing the shampoo. It hadn't been bad so far. Noah called three times a day. And he would visit a lot, too. She could already tell that. He'd missed Daniel the first day they'd been apart.

It was kind of sweet, really.

Noah was always saying how much he missed her, too. He was on his way back to Phoenix right now to see her. He couldn't wait.

Hold it.

She set the shampoo on the edge of the tub. A series of small bubbles burst out of the top. What was going on here?

Noah had left. They'd broken up. But they'd stayed connected. In many ways, they were still together. They talked constantly.

She remembered all the times Noah had told her goodbye, then returned anyway. Noah was not walking away.

With a jolt, she realized he never would. Whether he got a job in New York or Washington, Mel and Daniel were his family and would always be.

She'd been so determined to save Daniel from her own remembered childhood pain she'd forgotten that Noah wasn't Mel's father, or even his own father. Noah was Noah.

And Noah didn't walk away. *I'll wait...I'll stay.* How many times had he said that to her?

He'd stuck around from the moment he met Daniel. Sure, he was obsessed with his career, but he'd only recently returned to it after a terrible year when he feared he'd never write again. How could she expect him to adjust to having a family so quickly? Of course there would be rough patches.

Was her mother right? Had Mel stubbornly been expecting *perfect*?

Nothing in life was perfect.

She certainly hadn't wanted a child when Daniel came along, but she'd made the best of that.

The same way her mother had done with her cancer. She was in remission now, but it might flare again. In the meantime, she would live as fully and happily as she could. *Así es la vida. That's how life goes.*

Of course it wasn't ideal to fall in love with a man who lived thousands of miles away and loved his work more than anything. But that was what she'd done. Her job was to make the best of it.

Instead, from the moment he arrived in her life again, Mel had been giving him *the brush-off,* as her mother had said—chasing him away before he had a chance to hurt her. But he kept coming back for more.

This time, she would welcome him with open arms.

They did have lots to talk about. Her heart began to race. This felt right. She felt sure. Without allowing a moment's doubt to hit her brain, she pushed Noah's speed dial number.

"Mel?" He sounded surprised.

"I don't want to give up on us, Noah."

"You don't? Good. That's good. Because—"

"So what if your job's in New York?" she said, her words tumbling out, her voice spiky with nerves. "What's two thousand miles when people love each other? Nothing's perfect. Life is what it is. Man plans, God laughs."

"Mel, I need to—"

"Before you object, let me finish. You're a good man, Noah. You're not your father and you're not my father. You don't walk away. You stay. I keep shoving you out the door and you keep coming back. I know your ca- reer comes first, and that won't be easy, but—"

"Hang on, Mel. You've got that wrong."

Her heart stopped, and a chill ran through her. He was saying no? Giving up? The door behind her creaked and she turned to see him standing there, his cell phone in his hand, grinning at her.

"Look who taps at our door," her mother said from behind him.

"I'll be of use, Irena, I promise," he said, ending the call.

"Gracias a Dios!" her mother said. "I have no more candles to light."

Noah came into the bathroom and closed the door behind him.

"You're not in New York," Mel said, stupidly confused, staring at her phone, where she'd been talking to him.

"Not anymore. I'm home." Gently, he took her phone and set it on the counter, sitting beside her at the edge of the tub.

With a happy shriek, Daniel lifted a palm for a high-five.

Noah met his small hand with Noah's big one, warming Mel's heart. "I missed you, little dude." He looked at her. "And you. I missed you like life itself, Mel."

"You were saying I was wrong?" Mel said, her heart in her throat.

"About my career coming first, yeah. As far as the rest of what you said, I vote yes."

"You do?" Her heart sang in her chest. She glanced at Daniel, who'd begun to play with the car stickers on the tile wall.

"It turns out my career's not quite enough for me anymore." He touched her cheek, then brushed her hair behind her ear. "See, I'm a family guy. It took a bunch of obnoxious reporters to point that out."

"Really?"

"Yeah. I went for brews with some buddies from *National Record* and they informed me I was whipped. I told them that's impossible, since I don't even have a girlfriend anymore."

"True," she said, grinning so hard her cheeks hurt.

"Then they pointed out that I'd been showing them pictures of you and Daniel and talking about you both nonstop. Also, I have to admit that I sort of forgot we were broken up, since we talk so much on the phone."

"Me, too. I feel the same way."

"And about my father. I might be built like him, but I don't have to live like him. See, I'm not the same guy I was before Iraq. I'm better, I hope. I want more. I think I have more to give, too. And you helped me get there, Mel. I want you to keep helping me."

Her heart was so full she couldn't speak.

Noah leaned across her to hand Daniel a plastic truck that he couldn't quite reach, then put his arm around Mel's shoulder. "I don't want to miss another photo book's worth of my son's life. I want to see him ride that stupid tricycle. I want to be around when he kisses his first girl, or starts to shave for real. I don't want to miss a minute."

"I want that, too. So much," she said, blinking back tears.

"And then there's you. I don't want to miss a minute of you, either. I want you in my life. Every day. I want your steady eye and your no-bullshit opinions. You're my anchor, the song in my head, *Melodía*. Corny, but true as hell."

He leaned in to kiss her softly and it was more than

she'd dreamed. Noah made her life *más rico,* just as her mother had promised.

He broke the kiss and looked at her, adoration in his face. "It's funny, but I realized something else. Those reporters who always seemed to be apologizing to their wives or girlfriends? I realized they *missed* them. They were sorry to be away or late, sad to miss a piano recital or soccer game."

His gaze held hers. Openness, surprise and pleasure lit his eyes. "My career is important, but so are you and Daniel. Even more important."

"I'm so glad," she said. "So glad."

"Now, on that living two thousand miles apart bit. That can wait, I think." A flicker of tension crossed his face.

"Wait. They offered you a job at *National Record,* didn't they?"

He nodded. "But like I said, I can wait."

"You can't turn down another great job for us. That's way too much of a sacrifice. Planes fly both ways. And I think down the line, when Daniel's a little older, New York would be an amazing place to live. For my career, too. I want to get back to taking news photos. I set aside that dream, but not forever." There were so many possibilities she'd shut out because of stubborn fear.

She felt as though the whole world had opened up before them.

"You would move? What about Irena?"

"She'd have to decide whether or not to join us. I know she wants us to be happy. Every candle she lit was about that."

"We'll see how that goes," Noah said, picking up her hand and linking their fingers as he'd done the night they met and so many times since. "Whatever we do, we'll figure it out together. That's the point. We're a family. That's what's important. That's forever."

Her heart was so full she could hardly speak. Together they got Daniel dried and dressed. Together they read books and sang songs, Noah's baritone beneath her soprano, taking the lead on "Burning Down the House" until Mel learned all the lyrics. Together, they put him to bed and left his room, arm in arm.

In the hallway, Noah pulled her close. "I love you, *Melodía.* You're strong and soft like your name. I never thought I had it in me to care so much."

Noah's gaze, always intense, now held so much power it took her breath away. He smelled of cologne and baby shampoo, sexy and tender at once. She lifted her face to him. "I vote you tuck me in," she said softly.

He swept her into his strong arms. "Damn, I love democracy." They laughed all the way to the bedroom, where they had something far more wonderful in mind, no matter how early the next day began.

* * * * *

COMING NEXT MONTH

Available October 11, 2011

#1734 IN THE RANCHER'S FOOTSTEPS
North Star, Montana
Kay Stockham

#1735 THE TEXAN'S BRIDE
The Hardin Boys
Linda Warren

#1736 ALL THAT REMAINS
Count on a Cop
Janice Kay Johnson

#1737 FOR THEIR BABY
9 Months Later
Kathleen O'Brien

#1738 A TOUCH OF SCARLET
Hometown U.S.A.
Liz Talley

#1739 NO GROOM LIKE HIM
More than Friends
Jeanie London

You can find more information on upcoming
Harlequin® titles, free excerpts and more at
www.HarlequinInsideRomance.com.

REQUEST YOUR FREE BOOKS!
2 FREE NOVELS PLUS 2 FREE GIFTS!

Harlequin® Super Romance®

Exciting, emotional, unexpected!

*Harlequin Romantic Suspense presents the latest book
in the scorching new* KELLEY LEGACY *miniseries
from best-loved veteran series author Carla Cassidy*

*Scandal is the name of the game as the Kelley family fights
to preserve their legacy, their hearts…and their lives.*

Read on for an excerpt from the fourth title
RANCHER UNDER COVER

*Available October 2011
from Harlequin Romantic Suspense*

"**W**ould you like a drink?" Caitlin asked as she walked to the minibar in the corner of the room. She felt as if she needed to chug a beer or two for courage.

"No, thanks. I'm not much of a drinking man," he replied.

She raised an eyebrow and looked at him curiously as she poured herself a glass of wine. "A ranch hand who doesn't enjoy a drink? I think maybe that's a first."

He smiled easily. "There was a six-month period in my life when I drank too much. I pulled myself out of the bottom of a bottle a little over seven years ago and I've never looked back."

"That's admirable, to know you have a problem and then fix it."

Those broad shoulders of his moved up and down in an easy shrug. "I don't know how admirable it was, all I knew at the time was that I had a choice to make between living and dying and I decided living was definitely more appealing."

She wanted to ask him what had happened preceding that six-month period that had plunged him into the bottom of the bottle, but she didn't want to know too much about him. Personal information might produce a false sense of intimacy that she didn't need, didn't want in her life.

"Please, sit down," she said, and gestured him to the table. She had never felt so on edge, so awkward in her life.

"After you," he replied.

She was aware of his gaze intensely focused on her as she rounded the table and sat in the chair, and she wanted to tell him to stop looking at her as if she were a delectable dessert he intended to savor later.

Watch Caitlin and Rhett's sensual saga unfold amidst the shocking, ripped-from-the-headlines drama of the Kelley Legacy miniseries in

RANCHER UNDER COVER

Available October 2011 only from Harlequin Romantic Suspense, wherever books are sold.

USA TODAY **Bestselling Author**

RaeAnne Thayne

**On the sun-swept sands of
Cannon Beach, Oregon, two couples
with guarded hearts search for
a second chance at love.**

Discover two classic stories of love and family
from the Women of Brambleberry House miniseries
in one incredible volume.

BRAMBLEBERRY SHORES

Available September 27, 2011.

www.Harlequin.com

HSC68836